Moskovsky Station

CATHY WORTHINGTON

This novel is a work of fiction.
Names, characters, places and incidents are either the production
of the author's imagination or are used fictitiously.

Any resemblance to actual persons, living or dead, events or locals is entirely coincidental.

For information: cathy888@sbcglobal.net

In loving memory of my mother

Gwendolyn Walsh Stephens

Another orphan who survived

PROLOGUE

They keep the lights on all night long in Moskovsky Station. You can hardly tell if it's day or night. It's cold on the floor next to the wall where I sleep, and it's hardly ever quiet. You get used to it, though. The trains go in and out all day and all night long. At first it kept me awake. The sound of the train coming—it begins with a far off rumble that gets louder and louder as the train nears the station. It turns into a roar, and there's the whistling and the screeching of brakes.

All day and all night long.

I'm eleven, but there are a lot of homeless kids way younger than me here. Most of them get taken off to orphanages. I've heard that's worse than living in the station.

Sometimes I lie on my back and look up through the window in the ceiling to the sky. That's when I forget about the icy hard floor that makes my butt numb and the smell of pee on the wall and the cold that creeps inside my jacket every time I move. Even in the daytime you can see stars, but I don't make wishes any more. I've pretty much given up on that. Something weird happens to you when you don't eat for a long time. You get to thinking funny things and your mind wanders all over the place. Most of the time I think about what it was like back last June before Mom brought me to St. Petersburg. I play little daydream games to trick myself—like what if that email from my aunt hadn't come.

My dad's St. Christopher hangs on a thin silver chain around my neck. He gave it to me before he left for Iraq. It was supposed to protect me, but I guess they don't always work. I pray to him all the time. My prayer used to be: "Please, Dad, help me get back to America where I belong," but lately it's changed.

"Please, Daddy, let me come home to heaven and live with you."

CHAPTER ONE

Ripples of golden light raced across my bedroom ceiling. Leaf shadows danced along my walls. Here in San Diego we never have sunshine this early in the morning in June. What a great sign. What a great summer it would be.

Beside me on the bed my new best friend Marisa chattered into her cell phone. It was the first sleepover I'd been able to have at my house in a long, long time. We'd hardly slept a wink. There was too much to talk about surf camp in two weeks, a beach party at La Jolla Shores, fireworks on Mission Bay, and this summer maybe boyfriends. That's all Marisa ever talked about. Boys were okay, but I couldn't wait to go surfing.

Marisa clapped her cell phone shut. "Taylor says her Mom can't drive us to the mall after all."

I sat up straight and kicked the covers off. "Maybe my mom can."

Her eyes widened. "But I thought she couldn't drive. Your granny always picks you up at school."

"It doesn't mean Mom *can't* drive. Gracie was just helping out. That's all." I hated it when people talked about Mom like she was weird or not normal or something. From down below my window came the sound of a little kid's voice shouting, "Carwy, Carwy, Caaaarwy."

"Who's that?" Marisa asked.

I giggled. "That's Webster, our next door neighbor." I got up on my knees and looked out the window down to where I could see into the yard next door. Sure enough, there sat Webster on his little trike staring up at me.

I waved.

"Carwy come pway?" he shouted.

I shouted back., "Maybe later, Webster. Bye bye." I waved and flopped back onto the bed. "He's so cute. I wish I had a little brother."

Marisa looked up from her text messaging. "You wouldn't if you had one."

I almost had a baby brother once, but Mom miscarried. Poor thing. I'll never forget how sad it made her. She wouldn't get out of bed for two weeks. My grandmother Gracie had to come and take care of me.

Marisa jumped off the bed, and began fishing around in her backpack until she found her new pink and yellow striped cosmetics case. She pulled out three tubes of Shiny-licious lip gloss, bubble-gum, strawberry and cherry red.

I hopped down off the bed and sat on the floor beside her. In the mirror the two of us almost matched. We both wore our new tank tops, mine light pink with lacey straps, hers the same only in lavender. We were the same height, five foot two and a half, same size, a hundred and five pounds, same hair style, cut just below the ears, only hers was dark brown and mine was ash blond. Neither one of us had boobs yet. That was for sure.

Marisa squeezed some of the strawberry gloss on her lips and rubbed them together. "Ohmygod," she squealed. "It looks so cool." She spent all her allowance on makeup. "You want to try some?" she asked.

I squeezed some of the light pink gloss across my upper and lower lips. It smelled like bubble gum, and made my lips look wet and puffy.

Marisa stared at me in the mirror. "You look just like your mom." Everyone always said that. We had the same heart-shaped face, the same straight nose, and the same eyes that dipped down in the corners a little, except Mom's were gray and mine are light blue. I wished I looked more like my dad. I have a T-shirt of his hidden in my bottom drawer. Whenever I hug, it I can smell his aftershave, and I feel like he's here.

I stepped out into the hall and picked up a laundry basket full of towels and dirty clothes. Balancing it on my hip, I stuck my head back into the bedroom. "I'll be back in a sec."

"Where're you going?" Marisa asked.

"To start the laundry." If I didn't, I wouldn't have a clean top to wear today.

She wrinkled her nose. "*You* do the laundry?"

I raised my left palm. "It's no biggie. I just do it sometimes to help out."

When I got back upstairs, Marisa suggested we play Ouija with our school yearbook. We sat cross-legged on my bed, our annual open between us. Marisa closed her eyes and leaned back, swaying a little. "I'm searching for my summer love," she chanted in a low, far-off voice. Her finger with the chipped pink polish slowly traced figure-eights across the page of our class photos.

"I feel him. He's coming closer." Her voice sped up. "I see him. He's right—"

Her eyes flipped open. She examined the photo where her finger'd come to rest. A boy with glasses and teeth too big for his face grinned up at her.

"Forey Jacobs?" She slammed the album shut. "He's such a dork!"

The two of us tipped over sideways into the puffy pink cloud of my comforter, kicking our feet, screaming with laughter until we ran out of breath. For a moment the only sound was of our panting and the mockingbird singing from a tree branch outside. Bursts of happiness bubbled up inside of me. It was going to be the best summer ever.

"*Nyet! Nyet!*" The cry came from down the hall.

She never spoke in Russian.

I sat up straight and stiff. Our school annual slipped off the bed and dropped with a thump to the floor.

Marisa stared at me, her eyes big as soccer balls. "What's *nyet?*"

I pushed past her and jumped off the bed. She followed me as I raced down the hall and into Dad's office. Mom sat behind the desk staring at the computer screen. She wore the same silvery night shirt Dad had given her right before he left for Iraq. He said it was because she reminded him of the moon. He used to say poetic things like that.

A strand of ash blonde hair had fallen across the satin skin of Mom's cheek, but the look in her eyes was what really scared me—fixed, staring, but not really seeing me.

Did someone else die?

Oh, God, please, no! Mom wouldn't be able to take another tragedy. She couldn't help it. It's just the way she was.

I caught a whiff of her lemony scent as I brushed past her to get where I could see the screen. She always smelled fresh and good like clean laundry.

"Лара Наша мать умирает" said the subject of the email. Something about the funny characters jogged my memory. *Лара*. Dad once told me that's how you spell Mom's name in Russian characters. It means *Lara*.

Marisa leaned over my shoulder. Her lip gloss smelled like strawberry gum. "How weird. Is it from a terrorist?"

I reached back and poked her in the stomach. "Chill."

Mom's back stiffened. She took a deep breath in and let it out. "It's from Zoya. Mama's in the hospital. I have to go home."

* * *

My grandmother Gracie—she's my dad's mom—lived just fifteen minutes from our house. As we entered her kitchen through the back door, the smell of beef and garlic and onions cooking made me smile. Irish stew. My favorite. Gracie always put cocktail onions and sherry wine in it, and it was so good. She didn't like being called Granny or Nana or names like that. "Just Gracie, that'll be fine," she always said.

She stood at the kitchen sink with her back to us, wearing a soft pink warm-up suit and Nike walking shoes with reflector patches on the heels. In her left hand she held the bunch of late spring roses she'd just brought in from her garden. On her right arm she wore a cast. Her bones break easy. That's from the bone cancer, but it's not going to get Gracie down. *No way!* That's what *she* says, and I believe her. She had chemo, and she's been in remission for two years now.

She dropped the roses and turned. "Well, look who's here." She spread her arms wide, and I rushed into them.

She always smelled fresh like her roses. She put an arm around Mom's shoulders and gave her a squeeze. "How're you doing, Lara?"

"Just fine, Grace," Mom said in her soft voice.

Gracie turned back to the sink and her roses. "Just let me get these into water, and we can sit down."

Out her kitchen window you could just see a thin strip of bright blue from San Diego Bay, the same bright blue as Gracie's eyes. She's Irish and so was Dad, but Mom's Russian so they named me Catherine because it goes with both, only no one calls me that. It's been Carly since forever.

"So, guess what, Gracie," I said to her back. "We're going to Russia."

"Russia! She jerked up straight, dropping the vase she'd been holding with a clatter into the sink. She turned and gave Mom and me an embarrassed half-smile. "Just a bit of a surprise. That's all."

"Her mom's sick, Gracie," I said.

Gracie looked at Mom, "I'm so sorry to hear that, Lara. Is it serious?"

Mom hugged her purse. "I'm not sure. I think so." She looked away for a second like she might be about to cry. It must be horrible to have your mom sick and so far away. I moved over beside her and put my arm around her waist. She gave me a quick squeeze back.

Gracie stuck the flowers in the vase and handed them to me. "Here, put these on the table for me, that's a girl." She limped just a little as she moved across the kitchen and settled into a chair. Mom and I followed and sat down opposite her. Gracie patted Mom's arm and said in a soft voice. "Thought you said you'd never go back to Russia, Lara."

Mom pinched the furrow between her brows. "Well I didn't want to, but now—"

I jumped in. "Her mom's sick, Gracie. She's gotta go."

Gracie nodded. "Of course she must, darling. Of course she must." Her gaze traveled across the room and out the window. "Russia. It just seems so far away."

I jumped in again. "But, Gracie, that's where Mom's family lives."

"Yes, I know, honey. I know." She picked up a yellow rose petal that had fallen on the table and studied it with a frown. I knew what she was thinking—Mom might get depressed again like she did after Dad died.

Gracie looked at Mom. "Wouldn't it be best if Carly stayed with me?"

Surf camp. Marisa. The beach. I wouldn't have to miss any of it.

Mom's eye lowered. She must have read my mind. Gracie and I looked at each other. We both worried when Mom got sad.

Mom took in a deep breath. Still staring at the table, she said, "I kind of thought maybe Carly would come with me."

Oh, no! Now I'm stuck.

Gracie jerked forward in her chair. "But do you think it wise, Lara? All that way? Just the two of you, alone?" She was really worried. I could see it in her eyes. All of a sudden I realized I didn't even know my grandparents' names. I wondered why Mom had never talked about them.

Mom shot Gracie an angry look. "Carly has never met her grandmother, Grace. It might be her last chance, and St. Petersburg is a beautiful city." The Russian accent had crept back into her voice. It only happened when she got stressed.

Gracie patted my arm. "What do *you* think about going to Russia, honey?"

I didn't know what to say. I didn't want to hurt Mom's feelings, but still I didn't want to go. I let my eyes drift around the room, buying time, thinking. All about me were the things I knew, the green refrigerator that made the nice purring sound, the pretty lace curtains over the windows, the little pots of herbs on the sill, the nice fresh smell of everything, and Gracie. Russia sounded scary.

I stared down at the table afraid to look at Mom when I said it. "I'd kind of like to stay here."

Mom wouldn't look at me. "*Da,* Carly, if that's what you want..." Her voice trailed off.

She didn't mean it. She was hurt. Behind her on the counter was the picture of my dad taken when he was only five. Beside it sat the photo of him as a grownup in uniform. He's wearing a nice big smile, and there's a sparkle in his eyes that makes you feel happy like sunshine or summertime or swimming in the waves. My eyes returned to the photo of him when he was a little boy. Around his neck was the same St. Christopher medal that I wore now. "Take care of your mother while I'm gone," he'd said when he gave it to me. That was the day he left for Iraq, the last time I ever saw him.

I thought of Mom going all that way to Russia without me, and suddenly my heart felt sick. What if something happened to her? What if she broke down again? "Stick together," Dad used to say.

That was it. Mom needed me. I had to go.

CHAPTER TWO

St. Petersburg, Russia. Halfway around the world, eleven hours away from San Diego. It was scary and exciting at the same time. Instead of a taxi, a dented van with dusty windows and peeling paint drove us from the airport. The first thing the driver did was turn on an air conditioner that blew hot air and lint in my face. Out the window fields of dry yellow grass sped by. "When will we get to see the churches with the onion domes?" I asked Mom. I'd seen pictures of them in the travel book Gracie got me before we left.

Mom stared out at the empty landscape, her voice vague. "Oh, pretty soon." She'd been awfully quiet the whole trip, probably worried about her mom.

At least I now knew my grandparents' first names—Ogi and Olga. They lived in an apartment in St. Petersburg, not a house.

I wondered if Grandma Olga was pretty and sweet like my mom. And what about Grandpa Ogi? I never knew my American grandfather, but Gracie said he liked to tell jokes. The seats in the van were hard and lumpy, and the drive was taking forever. At three in the morning, San Diego time, all I really wanted to do was go to sleep. Finally we began hitting light signals, sidewalks with people on them, tall buildings like you'd see in San Diego, little parks filled with pink and red tulips. We drove over a deep purple river lined with miles and miles of faded yellow buildings, past a canal, and over a bridge with curlicue metal flowers on the railing.

The van jerked to a stop in traffic in the middle of the next bridge. Beside us a pair of ferocious lion creatures perched on the ledge, their golden wings glistening in the sunshine. They looked out over the canal, their gaze focused on a building in the distance, one of those kinds with onion domes like you see in the travel books. Some of the domes were gold and some were swirls of color, like scoops of soft ice cream. As we got closer I could see figures from the Bible covering the red brick walls. The arches over the windows looked like they'd been squeezed from a cake decorator's tube.

The breath whooshed from my lungs. "Wow! What's that?"

Mom opened her eyes and ducked so she could get a view out the window. "That's the Church of the Spilt Blood."

"Will we get to go there?" I asked.

"I'm not sure, honey. There's so much to see in St. Petersburg." She put her arm around my shoulder and squeezed. "I wish I could show you all of it." She sighed. "But it may not be possible. It will all depend on how Mama is."

"Do you know what's wrong with her?" I asked.

"Zoya didn't say."

I wanted to ask why the church was named *spilt blood*, but Mom had closed her eyes again. Her skin looked pale. Her mouth sagged. I decided not to bother her. The van turned onto an empty narrow street full of shadows and tall brick buildings. Some had statues set in the walls. Others had columns in between the windows, all in nice perfect patterns like they'd been drawn with a ruler. They reminded me of pictures I'd seen in a book about medieval times. The driver pulled in next to a tall curb and stopped.

"Are we here?" I asked.

Mom opened her eyes and stared out at the tall buildings. Scowling faces carved into the stone stared back.

We climbed a short set of stairs up from the sidewalk and passed through some thick wooden doors into a large room like a lobby. The tile floors and the crystal chandelier reminded me of a hotel except there was no one around. The sound of our footsteps echoed in the huge empty space above us. We took an elevator made from metal bars like a cage up a dark shaft to the third floor. The rocking motion made me sleepy.

We stepped off the elevator into a dark hall lit only by a few bare light bulbs over some of the doors. It smelled like car deodorizer mixed with stale cigarettes. I noticed stains on the wall and holes in the red carpet. After seeing the outside of the building and the lobby, I'd have expected something much nicer inside.

At the end of the long hall Mom stopped in front of a door with 310 on it. Her hand trembled slightly as she pushed the buzzer. We stood waiting for at least a minute before an old lady opened the door. She wore a thin sweater buttoned up the front and a flower-print apron over that. Everything about her looked old and faded, her clothes, her skin, her hair. Behind her the apartment was dark. A smell like cooking garbage drifted out. There had to be some mistake. This couldn't be the right place. The old lady stared at us, her mouth hanging open, a kitchen spoon clutched in one hand. Her hair was stringy and mostly gray, held back on the sides by two combs. Her eyes were gray too, and watery, but not like she'd been crying. This couldn't be my grandmother. Otherwise she would have hugged Mom, or Mom would have hugged her, or at least they would have looked happy to see each other.

After what seemed like forever, Mom finally said, "Mama?"

That's when I knew. This really *was* my grandmother.

I stared at her socks rolled down over chunky black shoes, the skin on her face, wrinkled and thin like old tissue paper. She looked way older than Gracie. The kitchen spoon made me think she'd been cooking, but she looked too sick for that. I felt sorry for her, but I felt even worse for Mom.

The old lady reached out and did something really strange next. Quick and delicate, like a butterfly's wing touching a flower, her fingertips just barely grazed Mom's cheek. Mom turned pink and dropped her head the way a little girl might.

I didn't know what to do. Finally I took a step forward. "My name's Carly." I waited.

My grandmother's focus turned on me. Her gray eyes softened. "Katerina?" Her voice had the rustle-y sound of dry leaves.

"It's me. I'm your granddaughter." Did she understand English? I didn't think so. I wondered if I should hug her. I opened my arms and stepped forward. She took a hop back, so I dropped my arms. I had the feeling she might be too shy for hugs.

She stepped away from the doorway, and we wheeled our suitcases inside.

Bad smells hit me from all directions, something cooking that smelled rotten like garbage, cigarette smoke. A skinny yellow cat sneaked out of the dark hallway, rubbing itself against the wall as it came. Some of its fur was missing like it might have been chewed off in a fight. It made a quick dash past us, zipped around the corner, and disappeared.

We followed my grandmother into a tiny kitchen, crowded with bottles, old newspapers, and junk. The stove had four small burners, the bad-smelling stuff cooking on one. Everything looked clean enough, just old, like there were chips in the tile countertop, and peeling paint, and holes where some of the drawer knobs should have been.

I noticed signs on the cupboard doors. "What are those for?" I asked Mom.

She didn't answer. Her eyes were focused on the next room, down two stairs from the kitchen where two men sat smoking and drinking and watching TV. In front of them on a glass coffee table sat two liquor bottles. The younger man wore a uniform. The older wore a plaid long-sleeved shirt unbuttoned down the front with his undershirt showing. He had a narrow little moustache and hair the color of gray metal, shaved off on the sides and slicked over smooth on top. He took a big sip of his drink. His head bobbed, his eyes closed, and he was asleep. Smoke from the cigarette still in his hand traveled in a blue haze across the ceiling. I felt like saying something about it giving us cancer, but that would have been impolite.

My grandmother shuffled over to the stove and began stirring the pot. She seemed way too weak to be doing the cooking. I wondered why the men weren't helping out. Mom dropped her shoulder bag on a chair and rushed to my grandmother's side. She took her by the shoulders and made her sit down. It must have been terrible for her to see her own mother so frail.

While Mom stirred the pot, I looked around the little room. "What are those little signs for on the cupboard doors?" I asked Mom.

"It's because everyone has their own cupboard with their own food."

"Oh." I stepped to the side so that I could see what was going on down in the next room.

"Who are those guys?" I whispered.

She stepped over beside me, still stirring the pot. "Your grandfather and—"

My jaw dropped. "That's my grandfather?"

I wanted to ask why she didn't go hug him, why he didn't come hug her, why no one even said hello. I stared at the checkered linoleum squares beneath my feet. What was wrong with everyone here?

My eyes returned to the two men. "Who's the blond guy?" His shiny pink skin was smooth as a baby's.

"The new renter," Mom said.

He rose halfway to his feet, waved and gave me a big smile.

"Is he our relative?" I asked.

Mom shook her head. "No. He just lives here." Her eyes never left the gray-haired man with the moustache, my grandfather. Suddenly his head snapped back and hit the wall. He snorted, rubbed his face, and rose from the couch with his bottle and glass.

Mom drew me close as he approached. I could feel her heart pounding. Halfway across the room, my grandfather's foot caught on the carpet. He tripped, but he didn't fall. Mom stiffened and drew me closer.

He continued across the room and up the two steps into the kitchen, his sharp beady eyes pinning Mom and me. He stopped and rocked back on his heels. Teetering a little, he put his face up close to Mom's. "Lara!" Mom's name came bursting out of him with such force that it almost caused him to lose his balance. He recovered and spread his arms wide, cigarette and empty glass in one hand, bottle in the other.

Mom's arm dropped from my shoulder. She smiled and blushed. It was like she was a little girl again. My grandfather's arms encircled her in half a hug, bottle, glass, cigarette and all. I was scared he might burn the back of her jacket. Just as I was about to say something, he stepped away. The two jabbered in Russian for a minute, then Mom put her hand on my shoulder and said my name, "*Katerina.*"

My grandfather set his bottle down on the countertop and turned to me. Up close I could see webs of red blood vessels all over his cheeks and yellow stains on his lower teeth. "*Vnuchka,*" he shouted.

I had no idea what that meant, but he looked happy enough to see me. He took a step toward me. For a second I thought he was about to hug me. Instead he reached out and pinched my cheek real hard with the hand that had the cigarette in it. It hurt so much my eyes watered. I was afraid he might light my hair on fire. Some of the ashes from his cigarette dribbled off onto my shoulder. The smoke made me want to cough. Finally he let go and stepped back.

I stared at him, my cheek throbbing. It was hard to believe this creepy guy was really Mom's father.

He picked up the empty bottle and tilted it over his glass. Nothing came out. My grandmother had slipped from her chair and returned to the stove. She hovered over it with her back to us, stirring the pot. Every so often a fit of coughing seized her.

Grandpa Ogi held the bottle close to his face, squinting at the last few drops. His eyebrows drew together into one angry frown. He stuck out his jaw and chewed his moustache with his lower teeth. "*Zhena,*" he bellowed.

My grandmother froze. Grandpa Ogi tapped her on the shoulder. She turned. He raised the empty liquor bottle and shook it over her head. A few drops dribbled out and trickled down her forehead. He grinned at everyone like it was some big joke.

I didn't think it was a joke. I thought it was mean.

When he saw that no one was smiling, his grin disappeared. He waved the empty bottle in my grandmother's face.

She let out a long sigh. "Oh, Ogi." She turned and opened one of the cupboard doors that had a sign on it, took out a full bottle like the first one, and handed it to my grandfather. The grin returned to his face.

Mom turned to me, shrugged, and tried to smile. She didn't fool me. Her face was bright red. She was embarrassed. Embarrassed of her own parents. I felt awful for her.

She gave me a quick squeeze. "It's okay, Carly. Everything's fine."

It wasn't fine at all.

Grandpa Ogi stumbled back into the living room, holding his drink out straight in front of him, not spilling a drop.

Mom made Grandma Olga and me sit down. She ladled some of the stuff that had been cooking into bowls and handed them to us along with a loaf of bread. The soup had cabbage in it and little pieces of something red floating around. My stomach was empty and angry and growling, so I ate a lot of the bread. Thank goodness I had some little packages of pretzels off the plane still in my backpack.

The renter rose to his feet, crossed the living room, and climbed up the two steps into the kitchen. "*Dobriy vyechyeer*," he said with a big smile. At least someone around here was friendly.

He extended his hand to Mom. "*Meenya zavoot Vlad.*" His fine blond hair was shaved short around the sides, his eyebrows so light you could barely tell he had any.

Mom shook his hand and said something that sounded like she was introducing herself. They spoke in Russian for a minute, and then he turned to me.

"My name Vlad," he said.

"You speak English?" It would be great to find someone I could finally talk to.

He put two fingers almost together. "Leetle bit."

Mom reached over and hugged my shoulders. "This is Carly."

"Actually, Katerina in Russian," I said.

"Katerina." Vlad smiled and winked. "Is preety name for preety gil."

Pretty? No one since Dad had ever called me that. I couldn't wait to tell Marisa.

I looked at Mom.

She laughed then smiled at Vlad. He had baby-smooth skin with dimples in his cheeks. He turned, opened one of the cupboard doors with the signs on it, and retrieved a small metal can. It was flat with a pull top lid and made a *poof* sound when he pulled back the top. Fish smells, stronger even than tuna, filled the air. He picked up a handful of toothpicks and offered me one of the little silver things in the can.

I stared at them. "Uhm, no thank you."

He grinned. "You are sure? Is herring. Special Russian treat." He was actually pretty cool-looking except for the puffy eyelids. I'd noticed a few other Russian men had the same thing.

He offered Mom some of the fish, but she also said *no*. My grandfather was sipping his vodka when Vlad returned to sit next to him on the couch. The two of them shared the fish, stabbing chunks of them with the toothpicks and popping them into their mouths.

During dinner I kept my eye on the next room. Vlad continued to watch TV. My grandfather's chin dropped to his chest, and his eyes closed. The scrawny yellow cat appeared over the top of the couch. Slowly, carefully, it climbed down onto my grandfather's lap. He didn't even wake up. First the cat sniffed his face. Then it began licking his moustache. He still didn't wake up. Lick. Lick. Lick. I let out a giggle and covered my mouth. Mom rolled her eyes.

My grandfather sat up straight and let out a fart as loud as the blast of a car horn.

Vlad rose halfway off the couch and fanned the air with a magazine. The cat yowled and dug its claws into my grandfather's undershirt. He grabbed it, ripped it from his chest, and hurled it across the room. It landed on all fours, shot up the stairs to the kitchen, and disappeared down the long, dark hall.

Vlad moved to the other end of the couch and sat there laughing his head off. I couldn't stop giggling. Mom laughed too. The edges of Grandma Olga's mouth turned up but just for a second. If you'd blinked you'd have missed it.

Grandpa Ogi grunted, picked up his glass, and rose to his feet. With a mean glare in his eye, he headed our way. The room turned silent. He shuffled over to Mom's chair and stuck his empty glass in her face.

Mom blinked and leaned away like a little kid about to be slapped.

I jumped to my feet. "Leave her alone."

I gave him a shove, not that hard. His body felt brittle, like a twig about to break. He tripped backwards. Barely in time, his hand grabbed the countertop, and he recovered his balance.

His eyes turned icy dark. He stepped toward me and raised his hand. I scrunched my eyes closed, waiting for the slap. It didn't come.

Instead, "Henk, henk, henk." It came out through his nose like a snorting pig. He reached down and pinched my cheek again. Hard.

CHAPTER THREE

"How can you stand him?" I asked.

Mom shook her head. "I don't know, Carly. I just don't know."

I sat on the edge of her bed, chewing on my dry toothbrush, watching her ruffle through stacks of clothes, wondering how my aunt and my cousin when they came tomorrow, and Mom and me were all going to fit in this little room. Furniture cramped the space, a low glass coffee table in the middle, a boxy brown sofa bed for my cousin and me behind that, an old fashioned oak closet against one wall, and the queen-sized bed for Mom and my aunt just inches from that. The closet was already stuffed so full of clothes that there wasn't any room for ours. Everything was so close together there was barely space to move.

Mom stopped and stared at her half-empty suitcase. "Gracie was right, Carly. I never should have brought you. I'm so sorry." Her shoulders slumped. Her head hung down.

"Oh, Mom." I put my arms around her. "Don't worry. It's okay."

Slowly her eyes rose to meet mine. "Things weren't this bad last time."

I wondered what it had been like growing up with a father like Grandpa Ogi. My dad had been so great—always hugging me, always loving me, always telling me I was the best. He was the only one who could put the sunshine in Mom's eyes. No wonder she loved him so much. I swallowed hard and willed myself not to cry. I needed to be strong for Mom.

* * *

I looked at my watch. Two a.m. Russian time, and still I couldn't sleep. Outside the window cats yowled, a ton of them, screaming all at once. It sounded like babies crying. Even with the curtains drawn, you could tell it was still light out. On the plane I'd read something about the white nights of St. Petersburg and how it stays light all night long in June and July.

On the other side of the room, Mom lay on her back in bed, one arm thrown over her head, breathing evenly. With a soft whish the door to the hall slid open, only a couple of inches, then a couple of inches more. "Mom," I whispered, "someone's trying to come in."

Silence. She must not have heard me.

"Who is it?" I called out.

The door closed with barely a sound.

Mom coughed and cleared her throat. "What's wrong?"

"Someone was trying to come into our room," I whispered.

Mom rose slightly and looked around. "Are you sure?"

"Yeah." I realized now how hard my heart was pounding.

Mom flopped back down again and said in a sleepy voice. "Probably just a mistake, honey. Try to go to sleep."

I turned onto my side. The sofa-bed was the most uncomfortable thing I'd ever slept on, bumpy and uneven, with a mattress so thin you could feel all the metal springs poking through. I tried not to think about how much I wished I were home in my own bed. Even the sheets here smelled different. There was only one bathroom, and we all had to share it, the other renter, my grandparents, everyone. It was scrubbed clean, but the toilet seat was cracked, and there were permanent brown stains in the bathtub. The worst part was that you had to go down a long dark hall to get there, and twice when I was in there, someone knocked on the door. I wished like everything we could go stay in a hotel, but I didn't say anything because I didn't want to make Mom feel bad.

I wondered who had peeked into our room—creepy to think that someone might have been spying on us. I rolled onto my stomach and buried my face in the pillow. "Our Father who art in heaven…" At home it always used to put me to sleep. Not here. Finally I gave up.

Please God, make this trip go by fast.

* * *

At seven a.m. the morning sun slanted down from the high windows in the living room making a path of light across the worn-out carpet. Up the steps in the kitchen Grandma Olga sat, sipping something hot from a pink plastic teacup. The smell of dirty ashtrays and gas from the stove met me as I entered the room.

"*Preevyet,*" I said to my grandmother. It meant *hi,* but I wasn't sure I'd pronounced it right.

A smile sparkled in my grandmother's gray eyes. "*Dobraye ootra.*" Her voice crackled like the static on

Gracie's old record player. Every breath she took made a raspy sound. She placed her hands on the table and with a groan pushed herself up. Limping slightly, she moved toward the cupboards. On the bottom shelf of the one where she'd gotten the vodka last night sat a box of cereal with a blue Smurf on the front. She pointed and questioned me with a raise of her eyebrows.

"Okay," I said. "*Da.*" After last night's dinner, I was so hungry I'd try anything.

She put the cereal box on the table then got a bowl and spoon and a carton of what looked like milk. As she sat back down again, her elbow hit her cup and knocked it over. Tea spilled all over the place.

"Oh, oh." She put her hands on the table and started to get up again.

I stopped her. "*Nyet, nyet.*"

I found a dish towel and used it to mop up. After that, I got matches and lit one of the burners on the stove the way I'd seen Mom do the night before. When the kettle whistled, I poured my grandmother a fresh cup of tea. She smiled as I sat down opposite her. The cereal she'd set out for me had no flavor. The milk tasted thick and heavy. I added a ton of sugar and ate it anyway.

Mom, in her silvery robe and white slippers, appeared out of the long dark hall, moving slowly toward us. When she entered the kitchen and saw Grandma Olga with me, the happiest smile lit her face. She bent and kissed the top of my head. "Getting to know your grandmother?"

"Yeah, she's real nice."

Mom leaned over and put her cheek up next to Grandma Olga's. "*Dobraye ootra*, Mama."

"*Dobraye ootra.*" Grandma Olga didn't smile, but you could see something happy in her eyes.

Mom made herself some tea. While she and Grandma Olga talked quietly in the kitchen, I wandered into the living room. All the ceilings were high with molded decorations along the edges. Mom said the building used to be owned by a rich Russian family. There was a big hole in the ceiling where maybe a chandelier once hung. No one had even bothered to stick the loose wires back in. I wondered what the room looked like when the rich people owned it. I'll bet it didn't have the weird wallpaper with the zigzag patterns on it or the shaggy green carpet or the plaid couch with the cigarette burns in the upholstery. Nothing went together.

I walked over by the window and looked out. The buildings across the street were so close you could almost touch them. My grandparents' cat appeared from out of nowhere, jumped up on the couch, and from there onto the bookshelf. It licked its paw and followed me with its yellow eyes.

I reached out to pet it. "Nice kitty." Just as my fingers were about to touch its fur, it hissed and batted at me with its paw. I jumped back. It leapt off the bookshelf and skittered across the carpet toward the kitchen. I wondered how it got to be so mean. I'd noticed where it had made snags in the carpet and where it had clawed some of the wallpaper off.

I ran my finger along the top of the dusty bookshelf. On the second shelf, amid a bunch of Russian books with Cyrillic titles, I found a photo album. I blew off the dust and opened to the first page. A faded color photo of two little girls stared back at me, one blond, the taller brunette, standing in front of a bed of red tulips.

"Mom!" I raced with the album into the kitchen and laid it on the table. "Is this you and Aunt Zoya?"

Mom let out a soft sigh. "*Da.* I remember. It was Zoya's birthday. I think she was turning seven."

I leaned in to get a closer look. "How old were you?"

Mom smiled. "I would have been five."

Down the hall a door opened, and the renter named Vlad stepped out. He marched toward us wearing his policeman's uniform and carrying his hat. As he entered the kitchen, he brought with him a cloud of cologne, something thick and strong, not like anything Dad ever wore. "Good morning," he said with a thick Russian accent. On his face was the same friendly smile he'd worn last night.

"You sleep nice?" he asked Mom.

She turned pink and gave him a shy smile. "So. So."

He fixed himself a cup of tea then stood, leaning against the counter in the crowded little kitchen, watching as we thumbed through the photo album. Mom turned to a picture of a palace that stretched out like a giant layer cake across a long green lawn. The colors made me think of a fairy princess's gown, pretty sky blue with gold and white frills.

"Wow, what's that?" I asked.

Vlad pointed at the photo and touched my shoulder. "Is same name like you. Katerina."

Mom laughed. "It's the palace of Catherine the Great, Carly. She was empress of Russia."

Vlad touched Mom's shoulder. "You like, I get tickets for you to see."

I looked up at him. "Really could you?"

Mom smiled. "That's very kind. Are you sure?"

He nodded. "*Da, Da.* Sure. Is okay. Just tell me day you want go." He picked up his hat and headed for the front door. "*Au revoir.* See you ladies tonight."

I turned to Mom. "Wow, he's really nice."

Mom turned the page to another scene of the red tulips in front of the blue lake. She and Aunt Zoya were in the photo. Only this time there were two more people standing with them, a blond woman who held the hands of the two little girls and a man in a uniform with dark hair. He had his arm around the blond woman and was gazing down at the two little girls with the softest expression on his face.

I pointed at the man. "Is that Grandpa Ogi?"

Mom smiled, her hand warm on my shoulder. "It sure is."

"But he looks so nice there."

"He *was—*" she sighed. "—once."

My eyes were drawn to his uniform. "Was he in the military?"

Mom shook her head. "The police force."

"You mean like that guy, Vlad?"

"That's right."

As if he'd known we were talking about him, I looked up, and there stood Grandpa Ogi in the doorway. He wore the same thing he had on last night, even the same undershirt with the claw marks. He rubbed the gray stubble on his chin and gave everyone a confused look. "*Dobraye ootra.*" His voice sounded quieter, less gruff than last night. He took a step into the room and squinted hard at Mom. "Lara?" His breath smelled like nail polish remover.

Mom nodded at him, but didn't smile.

He opened his arms. Slowly, as if she wasn't sure what to expect, Mom rose to her feet and went to him. It was different this time when he hugged her, more like he meant it. He stepped back, gave me a puzzled frown, and asked Mom something in Russian.

I stared at the table. If he pinched me again, I was going to sock him in the nose.

Mom put her hand on my shoulder. *"Eta* Katerina," she said to my grandfather. "Say *hi* to your grandfather, Carly," she said to me.

"But we met last night."

"He doesn't remember," Mom whispered.

"Hi." I fluttered a wave at him and went back to looking at the photos. The blond woman in the one we'd been looking at looked just like Mom, same heart-shaped face, same eyes, just like my face too. I moved the album so Grandma Olga could see and pointed. "Is that you?"

She leaned in close then drew back, nodding her head rapidly, dabbing at her eyes with a little piece of white cloth she kept tucked in the sleeve of her sweater.

Grandpa Ogi had moved over behind Grandma Olga and was looking at the picture too. He put a hand on my grandmother's shoulder and pointed at her in the photo. *"Kraseeviya,"* he said.

Grandma Olga shook her head, wheezing, smiling, thumping her chest. *"Kraseeviya? Nyet. Nyet."*

I looked up at Mom. "What're they saying?"

Mom giggled. "He told Mama she was pretty."

"He did?"

He pointed at the photo again and began talking excitedly. I was able to pick out Mom's name, Lara, and Aunt Zoya's name in his words. He began making laughing sounds, but when I looked, I realized he wasn't laughing at all. Tears poured down his face. His nose ran. The sobbing grew louder and louder.

I didn't know where to look.

CHAPTER FOUR

At nine in the morning the narrow street along side my grandparents' building still lay in darkness. High above the sky was blue, the sun was shining, but none of that made it down to where we were. Mom stopped me on the steps just outside and reached into her travel pouch. "I'm giving you two hundred and fifty rubles so you'll have some Russian money, Carly. That's worth about ten dollars. Be careful with it."

I unzipped the pocket on my backpack.

Mom's hand on my arm stopped me. "No, honey. You've got to put it in your travel pouch. Remember, we talked about pickpockets."

"But we have pickpockets in San Diego and we don't have to—"

She shook her head. "This is Russia, Carly. Just do as I say."

We walked single file along a dark narrow sidewalk. Halfway down the block we skirted around an old lady selling silvery fish which she displayed in rows on a small card table. Further ahead a group of teenage boys stood on the corner smoking and laughing. They wore levis with holes in the knees, one had chains, and they all had piercings. They didn't move, so we had to step out into the street to get by. One of them grinned at me as I passed.

Mom's hand gripped my arm. "Don't make eye contact, Carly."

What was the big deal? She never acted this jittery at home.

The internet café was about a fifteen minute walk, up the street and around the corner where a beautiful blue and white cathedral peeked out from behind some flickering elm trees.

The café turned out to be just a room full of desks with computers on them, no food. A kid wearing a lot of metal stood behind the desk near the door. He gave us a little piece of paper with the time written on it.

Mom sat down first and emailed Gracie to tell her we'd made it safely. Next I got a turn to check my emails.

I leaned in and shaded my eyes. It was hard to see through the fingerprints on the screen. The keyboard felt sticky like someone might have spilled Coke on it. A bunch of spam came up first, then this from Marisa:

From: mar999@abcmail.net
Subject: *ttly cool party*
hey carly wuz up? heatherz beach party was last night.
like sooooo ttly cool. ull never believe who was there as
in JOSH YOU KNOW WHO. jenny thinks hez ttly hot.
me & her been hangin. missya pos gtg mar999

I wanted to kick. I wanted to scream. I wanted to throw a brick at the computer. My whole life was going on back in San Diego without me. We'd been gone only two days, but it felt like two years. No, more like two lifetimes. I hated Russia. It felt like I'd been rocketed off into outer space and ended up on some weird planet in some weird universe where everyone was mean and ate rotten food and drank vodka all the time. If only we could just go home. Marisa's email stared back at me in that funny squiggly pink font she uses. All that stuff about Jenny. Marisa always said she hated Jenny and now they were best buds. Would I have any friends left when I got home?

I clicked on *Reply*.

To: <u>mar999@abcmail.net</u>
Subject: *Re: ttly cool party*
like russiaz ttly cool. therz all these palaces and gold and my grandparents r real nice and therz this guy vlad. like hez so hot. like ull never believe this – he said im pretty.

There. I clicked *Send* and felt a lot better.

* * *

When we got back to the apartment, I was hungry again. Grandpa Ogi came back into the kitchen just as I was sitting down with another bowl of corn pops. The smile I was about to give him dissolved when I saw the hard glint in his eyes. I held my breath and concentrated on the round golden puffs waiting for him to pass by. He grabbed his bottle of vodka out of the cupboard and headed for the living room. With a grunt he settled down onto the sofa and lit a cigarette.

A soft rumble sounded in the hall outside the apartment, getting closer. Next came voices, and the doorbell buzzed. Down in the living room Grandpa Ogi sat like a mean old troll drinking his vodka. I'd noticed a permanent dent in the sofa cushion where he always sat. If he'd heard the doorbell, he didn't look like he was going to do anything about it.

No one else was around, so I answered it.

In the doorway stood a woman with short dark hair, about Mom's age. She wore tight Levis and a skinny black top. Beside her suitcase was a girl with blond hair who looked about my age.

"Katerina!" The dark-haired woman burst through the doorway, her arms spread wide. She grabbed me and kissed me on both cheeks then held me at arms' length. Her perfume smelled like incense.

"Aunt Zoya?" Who *else* could it be? Mom hadn't told me very much about her, except that she was a single mom and that she and my cousin lived a thousand miles away in a city named *Novorisk* or something like that.

She laughed a deep sort of chuckle, her blue eyes sparkling. "*Da, da.* I am Zoya." She cupped my chin in her hand. "Ah, such beautiful face."

The girl standing behind her in the hall flashed me a shy smile. I figured she must be my cousin Natalia. Her blue capris were just like a pair I had at home, same stitching on the pockets, same color, same everything. Aunt Zoya pulled her inside and turned us to face the mirror by the front door. "Tweens!" Her face shone bright behind our two faces in the dusty, scratched-up glass. Silvery green eye shadow glistened on her eyelids. Thick mascara caked her lashes.

I stared at my cousin. She stared at me. Except for the blond hair we didn't look that much alike at all. Maybe the mouths were the same and the shape of the eyes, but her hair was much finer than mine, so fine you could see her ears sticking through.

She laid her arm over my shoulder and waved in the mirror.

I laid my arm over her shoulder and waved back.

Behind us Aunt Zoya beamed. She wasn't pretty like Mom, but she had a great smile. "Cousins be good friends," she said. "You shall see."

Maybe she was right.

A little ways away down the hall stood Mom. She'd changed into a pair of capris and a T-shirt.

Aunt Zoya wheeled her luggage inside and stopped when she saw Mom. "Lara?"

Mom didn't smile or move. The two of them stared at each other. Just when I was wondering if anyone was ever going to do anything, Aunt Zoya stretched out her arms and gave Mom a stiff hug. After that everyone smiled and acted happy to see each other.

Aunt Zoya turned in the direction of the kitchen where Grandpa Ogi stood in the doorway. I hadn't seen him get up. His eyes met Aunt Zoya's, and everyone stopped talking. I hadn't realized until now how much they looked alike. It was the narrow jaw, the small, bright blue eyes set close together, the long straight nose.

"*Zdrastvooyi*, Papa," she said. I figured she must be saying *hello*, but there was no smile in her voice.

My grandfather nodded and took a deep drag off his cigarette.

Grandma Olga appeared in the hall, moving slowly toward us.

Aunt Zoya ran to meet her. "Mama?" She held her mother by the shoulders and studied her face. She stepped back and turned to Mom. "She look bad."

Mom moved over beside Grandma Olga and slipped an arm around her waist. "Well, at least she's up and around." Aunt Zoya slapped the air. "She is very weak. She went to hospital. Almost died." She shook her head. "You not know. You not here. You never here."

Mom dropped her arm. "But, Zoya, we got here as quick as we could."

"Oh, sure." The way Aunt Zoya said it with her Russian accent, I couldn't tell if she was being sarcastic or not. She seemed nice enough. Still, I wondered if she and Mom liked each other.

"What do the doctors say about Mama?" Mom asked.

Aunt Zoya touched her chest. "They say problem is here. They say is emphysema."

Mom took a deep breath. "Emphysema!"

Aunt Zoya glared at my grandfather and the cigarette hanging from his lips. She made a spitting sound. "Is him. He have his cigarettes. He is why she gets so sick."

"What are the doctors doing for her?" Mom asked.

"They give her special treatments, but they say is not much hope."

Mom closed her eyes, and shook her head. I wondered how she'd handle it if her mother died. Would it be as bad as after Dad died?

Grandma Olga looked from face to face, her watery gray eyes wide, hopeful, a little confused. Maybe she hoped they were saying in English that she didn't have emphysema, that she wasn't going to die.

Aunt Zoya's nose twitched. "Smell is bad here." Leaving Natalia and the luggage by the door she rushed up the hall to the kitchen. Dishes clattered. Pans banged. When Mom and I reached the kitchen, we found Aunt Zoya at the kitchen sink. She directed a pointed glare at Mom. "Is no one ever do dishes in this place?"

Mom shrugged and looked around. "I was just about to do them, Zoya."

Aunt Zoya batted the air, sprinkling tiny drops of sudsy water everywhere. "I know. I know." She pinched my cheek gently. "Is nothing to worry, Katerina. Cousin Natalia and I are here." She swept her arm in a half circle. "Is family reunion. We make the best. We have good time. See St. Petersburg. Is beauuutiful city."

I wiped the dampness off my cheek. Make the best of it? I wondered how we could if Grandma Olga died.

CHAPTER FIVE

After going out once already this morning, Mom didn't want to leave Grandma Olga again, but Aunt Zoya insisted. "Is only bad food in this place. We need go to market. Cousins will see St. Petersburg." She pinched my cheek. "Is good idea, *da*, Katerina?"

In spite of everything, I grinned. It was hard not to.

We set off in the opposite direction from the internet café. Once the sidewalk widened, Natalia moved up beside me and hooked her arm in mine. I wasn't sure I liked her doing that, but then I noticed two other girls our age doing the same thing. Maybe it was safer that way.

I blinked as we stepped out of the dark street and into the bright sunlight. A canal ran in front of us with a line of faded yellow and gold buildings all along the edge on the other side.

We stopped and Aunt Zoya pointed. "You know why buildings in St. Petersburg color yellow?"

I shook my head.

Her bright blue eyes sparkled. "Is because yellow is *happy* color." She made the word sound like a burst of sunshine. "Is color of St. Petersburg."

Yellow was my favorite color too, only not this faded, dirty color. What I liked was the bright, clean yellow, like daffodils or sunlight or the paint on my bedroom walls at home.

We crossed over a metal bridge that had iron leaves chasing each other in circles between the posts. On the next street we turned into an open mall. An old woman with a caved-in mouth sat on the ground just inside and shook her cup at us. Further down two men in gypsy costumes played guitars. The stores weren't at all like at home. The cosmetics store had only five lipsticks in the glass display plus a compact, a tube of something, and a bar of soap. The people behind the counter looked mad. I wondered if it was because they had so little to sell.

Behind the cold glass of a supermarket display, a real pig head stared back at me. It sat right next to the steaks and the hamburger meat and beside that a bunch of dead chickens with the heads and feet still on. A big blob of something red and slimy lay all by itself on a white tray. I put my nose to the glass to get a closer look, then jumped back when I realized was it was a giant tongue. Gross! How could anybody eat that?

I moved on to the next set of displays, picked up a box of cereal, and examined the Smurf on the front.

"*Nyet. Nyet.*" A woman with a scarf on her head ran out from behind the display and snatched the box away. She muttered something about "*Americanka,*" and gave me a dirty look.

I looked at Mom. "What'd she think? I was stealing it?"

She patted my arm. "It's okay, honey. Here you're not supposed to touch."

"I don't think they like Americans."

"It's not that, Carly." A hint of sadness clouded her eyes. "It's just that well... It's just Russia."

Aunt Zoya caught up to us carrying a package wrapped in white butcher paper under her arm. "We have special treat tonight in honor of family together."

My mouth watered. Would it be those big red steaks I'd seen her looking at? I sure hoped so.

We left the supermarket and turned onto a street lined with old stone buildings. I noticed signs like "Coke" and "CitiBank," even McDonald's only it was spelled out in those funny Russian characters. You could tell what it was by the golden arches and the red umbrellas in front.

Mom and Aunt Zoya paused in front of a bookstore. Natalia kept going and stopped in beside a store window with a sign that said "SEX SHOP," spelled out in plain English. Natalia caught my eye and motioned frantically for me to come look. When I reached her side, she gave me a sly grin and pointed in the window. Just on the other side of the glass was this thing that looked like a giant purple gummy worm. It sat on a little pedestal and had a cord attached. Beside it were some black leather panties and a leather bra. Natalia kept nudging me and pointing at the worm.

I stared and stared, but I couldn't tell what was so funny. Finally I said, "I don't get it."

She pointed at her crotch and rolled her eyes. "Is boy."

I gasped and covered my mouth.

Natalia giggled. Then I couldn't help it, I giggled too. It turned into a laughing frenzy, Natalia, hysterical, rocking back and forth, me barely able to breathe.

The faces of two men in business suits appeared in the reflection. I knew I should stop laughing, but I couldn't. It was like when someone passes you a joke at school, and the teacher's standing there glaring down your neck. One of the men said something in a low voice, all in Russian, but I heard the word *fuck* mixed in.

Natalia froze. My laughter dissolved. The men smiled at us in the glass, evil smiles that meant something dirty. My heart began to pound. Natalia sidled closer and locked her arm in mine. We stared at each other in the mirror, mouths open, eyes wide.

One of the men said something that sounded like a question.

"What should we do?" I whispered to Natalia.

Before she had time to answer, Mom's and Aunt Zoya's faces appeared in the reflection. The two men's faces vanished. When I looked over my shoulder, they were strolling casually away down the sidewalk, heads turned inward, talking in low voices.

Aunt Zoya grabbed Natalia by the arm, jerked her away from the window, and scolded her in Russian.

Mom put her face up close to mine, her eyes gray and stormy. She gave me a little shake. "What were you thinking, Carly?"

"But how was I supposed to know?

We continued on our way in silence, this time Mom and me arm-in-arm followed by Aunt Zoya and Natalia doing the same.

After about ten minutes of walking, we turned a corner and there it was, the Church of the Spilt Blood, the same church I'd noticed on our ride from the airport. Up close it looked even more awesome than before. Aunt Zoya informed me that it got its name because of the bloody battle fought there back in 1881 when Tsar Alexander II got stabbed. She waited outside with our groceries while Mom, Natalia and I went inside.

Crowds of tourists bumped and pushed us as we entered. Once inside they scattered in all directions, following the waving flags of their guides. I stopped and took a deep breath. There was gold everywhere, on the ceilings, on the walls, in the tiny bits of dust that floated down through the sunlight. Not one spot wasn't decorated with something—like fleur-de-lis, and pretty colored shapes, Bible stories, and angels, all made out of mosaic tiles, everything in patterns. In the darker corners of the church, candles flickered. Incense floated in the air.

Natalia nudged me and pointed at a boy our age. I ignored her.

Slowly I turned and looked up. The kaleidoscope of shapes and colors spinning high above me made me dizzy. On the inside of the dome, a man's face stared down. I wondered if he was supposed to be God. His face was so serious, almost angry, and he had his fingers crossed. I wondered what it meant. There was so much to see it wouldn't fit inside my brain. I could have stood there forever just looking up.

Mom's voice was like waking from a dream. "Time to go, Carly."

Just as we were going down the steps outside the church, a scream like an ambulance siren split the air. Across the street a white-haired man lay on the ground beside one of the tour buses. Three kids held him down while another yanked on the travel pouch around his neck. The kids didn't look much older than me, but there was a whole bunch of them, kicking and hitting and screaming all at once.

Another white haired man, one of the tourists, tried to stop them, but in the scuffle the kids knocked him down too. The Russian tour guide dropped his sign and ran off down the sidewalk yelling, "*Meeleetsia! Meeleetsia!*" I figured he was calling for the police.

"Stop! Stop!" An American lady—she must have been the man's wife—with hair the same silver color as Gracie's—pulled at one of the kid's jackets and beat him with her bag. She lost her balance and landed on the curb.

Mom, Natalia and I crossed the walkway to the curb where Aunt Zoya waited.

A crowd had gathered and stood staring at what was happening across the street.

A blade flashed in the sunshine. Someone had to do something. I broke free from Mom.

Horns honked, and cars screeched around me as I raced across the street.

"Carly, stop," Mom called after me.

Just as I reached the spot where it was all happening, the kid with the knife cut through the strap on the man's travel pouch. The kid jumped up, grinned, and waved it at the others. He pushed me out of the way and took off.

The old man had stopped struggling. His face had turned gray. He gasped for air.

"Howard! Howard!" His wife kneeled over him and held his head.

I turned and looked at the people around me. Why had they all just stood there like stupid statues? "What's wrong with you?" I screamed.

A few looked down and shuffled their feet. The rest just stared at me, their faces blank masks.

Mom caught up to me and grabbed my arm. "Listen, Carly, when I say stop, you stop. You almost got run over back there."

I jerked my arm away. "I don't care. Someone had to do something." I looked at the old man on the ground, and my eyes filled with tears. "Poor ol' guy."

She shook my shoulders. "You can't just go running off like that. You hear me?"

I swallowed back my tears. "It's what Dad would have done."

She let out a big sigh and pulled me gently into her arms. "I know."

Natalia and Aunt Zoya, carrying the groceries in two cloth bags, caught up to us. Aunt Zoya scanned the scene, her face pinched with worry. "Street kids," she muttered. "They all over Russia." She looked at Mom. "Is dangerous situation. We need go."

Just as we were leaving, an ambulance pulled up. Halfway down the block, I stopped and looked back. The man was on a stretcher with a sheet laid over him. It covered his face. That meant he was dead.

What if it had been Gracie lying in the street? What if it had been Mom or me?

CHAPTER SIX

Cow tongue with turnips and cabbage for supper—no salad or potatoes or anything else. I stared at the gray slice of meat on my plate and wondered if I could live on Power Bars for the rest of my trip. Grandma Olga and Grandpa Ogi had already had their supper. While Mom, Aunt Zoya, Natalia and I ate dinner in the kitchen, she and Grandpa Ogi sat in the living room watching T.V.

Aunt Zoya's eyes were on me as I tried a tiny bite of the meat. It was tough and had no flavor except for the onion.

"You like?" she asked, her face cheerful as sunshine.

"Yeah, it's real good," I lied.

When dinner was over, she frowned at the food I'd barely touched. She put a hand on my forehead. "Katerina sick?"

"I guess it's just jet lag." I didn't want to tell her that the smell of the tongue made me want to throw up. But it wasn't just that. I kept seeing the mugging, the old man lying there on the sidewalk, the crazy, howling kids, the poor old lady's face as she gazed down at her dying husband.

Mom carved slices out of a dark brown layer cake. At least we were having *one* good thing for dinner. The minute she set my plate in front of me I dove in. The taste was sugary sweet, but not a bit like chocolate. Tiny bits of something gritty felt dry and fluffy on my tongue. I turned to Mom and made a face.

She laughed. "It's poppy seed cake. Very popular Russian treat."

"Ohhh." A few of the seeds blew out of my mouth. After struggling to swallow what was left, I took a big gulp of water and laid down my fork.

A yellow flash caught my eye as my grandparents' cat hopped in from the fire escape through an open window. Something gray and furry dangled from its mouth. I got up from my chair and moved closer to the stairs to get a better look. From there I could see that the tiny gray bundle was a baby kitten.

"Ohhhh." I wanted to hold it and pet it and tell it how cute it was.

The cat trotted across the carpet to Grandma Olga and dropped her baby at my grandmother's feet. I stepped down into the living room and moved closer. The kitten's leg wiggled just a fraction, but it didn't make a sound.

Grandma Olga leaned over to have a look. She raised her eyes to mine and shook her head.

I sunk down onto my heels. "Poor little kitty." I could see it was barely alive. Natalia, still chewing a mouthful of cake, sunk down beside me.

The mama cat stared up at Grandma Olga and cried, "Meowww. Meowww."

Natalia pointed at the kitten. "Baby is sick."

Before I could take another breath, Grandpa Ogi was on his feet and across the room. He clapped his hands at the yellow cat and kicked at it with his foot. The cat yowled and took off for the open window. My grandfather lowered himself over the baby kitten, bending slowly as if every bone in his body hurt.

Just as I was reaching out to stroke the baby cat's fur, he snatched it away. Dangling the poor little thing by its tail, muttering under his breath, he lurched across the room to the kitchen and tossed it in the trash.

Natalia and I raced back up to the kitchen almost bumping into my grandfather as he came shuffling back down the stairs. I was in too much of a hurry to even bother to give him a dirty look. Natalia and I bumped heads as we leaned over the trash. The gray kitten lay still on top of a mound of dirty napkins, its body so light that it barely made a dent. Slowly I lowered my hands into the trash and cupped them around the baby cat. It felt like it weighed nothing at all as I lifted it out. Its eyes weren't even open.

I looked at Natalia and Aunt Zoya and Mom's faces. "I can't tell if it's alive."

Aunt Zoya turned back to scraping the dishes. "Is better for cat baby to die."

My voice rose to a squeak. "I can't believe you actually said that."

My aunt turned and looked me full in the face. "Is no food, Katerina. In Russia is better for these cats not live."

The kitten let out a tiny mew. I hugged its fury body to my chest and stifled a sob. The yellow cat appeared from out of nowhere and scampered up the stairs into the kitchen. There it stopped at my feet and began to cry.

Mom put her arm on my shoulder. "I think the mommy cat wants her baby back."

I crouched down and held out the kitten. The yellow cat picked it up by the back of its neck and scampered off, disappearing through the open window onto the fire escape.

* * *

Mom and Aunt Zoya left Natalia and me in the kitchen to clean up while they helped Grandma Olga back to her bedroom.

I loaded plates into the sink, poured in some soap, and turned on the water. It made me feel good to be doing something, more like being at home. "Here," I handed Natalia a dish towel. "I'll wash. You dry."

Instead of drying the plates Natalia stepped on a foot stool and stuck them on a rack above the sink where, if I leaned forward, they dribbled on my head.

Grandpa Ogi rose to his feet and stumbled toward the kitchen. Natalia and I faced the sink and shared glances as he passed behind us. Without a word, he dropped his empty vodka bottle into the trash and headed off toward the bathroom.

Natalia got down off the stool with an angry stamp of her foot. "He is bad grandfather for be mean to small cat."

"He sure is," I agreed. "You should have seen how mean he was to Grandma Olga last night. What's wrong with him?"

Natalia gave me a look that suddenly made her seem much older. "Is vodka."

I nodded.

"Hey!" I grinned. "That gives me an idea." I wiped my wet hands on my pants, then tiptoed over to the trashcan and retrieved the empty vodka bottle. Back at the sink I filled it with water and dumped in half of the salt from the shaker on the table.

Natalia tried to hold back a giggle that ended up coming out her nose. "Oh, Carly. You bad girl."

"Shhh." I screwed the lid back on the bottle.

Natalia's eyes suddenly grew large. "But Grandfather Ogi be very angry."

"So what?" I whispered. "He deserves it." I opened my grandparents' cupboard and pulled out the two big new bottles of vodka sitting there. Natalia helped me bury them in the trash, replacing them on the shelf with the bottle of salt water.

Mom and Aunt Zoya returned, and we all went down into the living room.

Aunt Zoya clapped her hands. "I know. We play game. Have good time."

The game turned out to be Russian Monopoly. Everything on the board looked the same except that the words were spelled out in Cyrillic. If you already knew the game, you could kind of figure out what some of them meant. It was fun, but we had to sit on the floor to play, and the carpet smelled like cat pee. I was sure I was sitting right on it.

Just as we were starting the game, the renter Vlad arrived home from work. He smiled at everyone all nice and friendly, then got some vodka out of his own cupboard and settled down on the couch. Every time he moved even the slightest, I got a whiff of his cologne. I didn't so much like the smell of it, but at least it drowned out the cat pee. After a few minutes he took off his uniform shirt. Underneath he wore a thin white T-shirt, sleeveless and low in the front. It showed the rose tattoo on his chest surrounded by a few straggly blond hairs. The muscles along his shoulders looked like he'd been lifting weights. My dad had strong muscles too, only his weren't bulgy and big like these.

Natalia nudged me, flashed her eyes at him and gave me her impish grin. I wondered what she'd think if I told her he'd called me pretty.

He caught me looking and winked. My face flushed, and I looked away.

Just as we were getting the money counted out, Grandpa Ogi appeared in the kitchen. Sure enough, he went straight to his cupboard for the vodka. He left with the bottle filled with salt water and headed back down the hall toward his bedroom. Natalia slid me a sly grin. I nodded and grinned back.

Aunt Zoya rolled the dice first and landed on one of the railroads. Then Mom took her turn and landed on Community Chest. I was just counting out my move when the roar of my grandfather's voice came thundering down the hall.

Natalia sat up stiff and straight.

Adrenaline raced up my spine. All of a sudden I wasn't so sure our little joke had been such a good idea.

Mom cast a worried look in the direction of my grandparents' bedroom.

Aunt Zoya let out a big sigh. "What is happen now?"

Within seconds Grandpa Ogi appeared in the kitchen, vodka bottle in hand. He stormed down into the living room ranting in Russian, fuming with rage. He wore a shabby flannel bathrobe hanging open in front, the tie dragging behind him like a tail. He stopped right on top of where I'd just made neat little stacks of Monopoly money and waved the bottle at us. The veins on his cheeks had turned dark purple. He looked like he was about to explode.

Vlad laughed and put a hand on his shoulder. "Okay, Ogi. Okay."

Grandpa Ogi wasn't listening. His bloodshot eyes traveled from face to face and stopped on mine.

I was scared, but I wanted to laugh at the same time.

"He say someone spoil his vodka," Aunt Zoya said.

"It wasn't you," Mom whispered, "was it?"

I looked back at my grandfather, at his socks with the red and black diamond pattern, one longer than the other, at his skinny bare legs, his saggy, torn undershirt. He stuck out his chin to try and chew on his moustache, but there weren't any lower teeth in his mouth to chew with. He must have taken them out before he went to bed. I tried to think of anything that would keep me from laughing, but the edges of my mouth kept twitching.

Natalia let out a snort followed by an explosion of giggles. That did it. I couldn't hold back any longer. I started laughing too.

My grandfather took a step toward me. In his socks he was barely taller than me. He raised his hand.

I cringed and stepped back.

"*Nyet*, Papa, *nyet*," Mom cried out.

If it hadn't been for Vlad grabbing Grandpa Ogi's arm just in time, I think for sure my grandfather would have slapped me.

I gave Vlad a grateful look. He nodded and smiled. I'll bet he would have done something if he'd been at the mugging this afternoon.

Aunt Zoya turned to Natalia and me. "Okay, what is happen to Papa's vodka?"

She made us get it out of the trash and give it back. Then she made him go back to bed. I don't think she was as afraid of him as Mom.

After that we settled down in the living room and went back to our game.

Vlad reached a glass from the ledge behind him, and held it out to Aunt Zoya.

She nodded her head. "*Da.* Okay."

He poured it full and gave it back to her. She took a sip, closed her eyes, and let out a deep sigh.

He reached down another glass, poured vodka into it, and offered it to Mom. She stared at the clear liquid. I didn't think she'd take it. She never drank at home. Whenever Dad had a beer, she always had a Coke.

Aunt Zoya watched Mom, her mouth partly open like she might be about to say something but wasn't sure if she should. Suddenly, Mom's hand shot out and took the glass. With a jerk of her wrist she downed half of the clear liquid in a single gulp. Choking, her eyes watering, she smiled at everyone.

Icy drops of dread ran up and down my spine. I didn't like what vodka does to people, especially after seeing what it did to Grandpa Ogi.

Vlad raised his glass. "*Na zdarovye!*"

Mom grinned and raised hers back. "*Na zdarovye!*"

Aunt Zoya frowned and shook her head.

I whispered to Mom, "I thought you didn't drink."

"In Russia I do," she answered.

Mom and Aunt Zoya invited Vlad to join the game. It got all loud and crazy after that, everyone laughing and jabbering away in Russian and pretending the money was real. Every time I passed *GO*, Vlad gave me high five. Whenever I landed on a good spot, he raised his glass to me. If he even gave Natalia the slightest glance, she got all pink and giggly.

I tried to laugh and pretend I was having fun, but it was hard to. I was getting more scared by the minute watching

Mom drink. Her hair kept falling over her eyes, and she kept clawing it out of her face. Her words had become soft and mushy. Aunt Zoya had turned into a motor-mouth, her eyes dancing, her cheeks dark red. The smile never left Vlad's face.

"You're having another drink?" I asked Mom as Vlad handed her, her fourth.

Mom gave me a look. "You're not my mother."

It felt as if I'd been slapped. I jumped up and left the game. I wanted Gracie. I wanted to go home. If only Grandma Olga weren't dying. If only we *could* go home.

Mom caught me halfway down the hall. "I'm really sorry, Carly. I shouldn't have said that." Her words sounded slurry, and the Russian accent was back. I let her hug me, and felt a little better, but not much.

* * *

About eleven the Monopoly game broke up, and everyone decided to finish off the poppy seed cake. I couldn't stand how stupid and drunk they were acting, so I disappeared down the hall to our room. A minute later Natalia joined me. I wanted to ask if everyone in Russia always got drunk like that, but I wasn't sure how she would take it. Aunt Zoya hadn't really been that bad. Mom was the worst.

Natalia sat cross-legged on the sofa-bed in just her underpants, cotton ones with ladybugs and flowers all over them like the little kids wear. She pooched out her lips and examined her face in a pocket mirror. She lowered the mirror and watched me as I flipped through my CD case. "So Carly, you have iPOD?" she asked, her brown eyes hopeful.

I shook my head and held up my cheapo Sony walkman. Her face fell. "But *all* Americans have iPOD, yes?"

"No way. They cost almost three hundred dollars, you know." Did she think we were rich or something?

Her eyes turned bright. "I have this." She pulled a little pink stuffed pig out of her backpack. "Name is *Miss Pig*."

"It's real cute." Beanie babies weren't popular in the United States anymore, but it wouldn't have been nice to tell Natalia that.

Vlad stuck his head through the open door. "Night night, gils." He smiled and waved.

With a shriek Natalia tried to cover her bare chest. Vlad laughed and disappeared. I ran and closed the bedroom door.

Natalia gasped. "He see my boobs."

She cracked me up. Like where'd she learn the word, *boobs*? And what boobs, anyway? She was flat as the mattress we were sitting on.

We were still laughing when Aunt Zoya burst in. Her eyes zoomed straight to Natalia's bare chest. She glanced at the bedroom door where Vlad had just been and frowned. A flood of angry words followed. I didn't need to understand Russian to know that Natalia was getting another scolding.

Mom came through the door, bumped into Natalia's suitcase, and nearly fell. She straightened and laughed. "Lil' crowded around here, isn't it?"

Aunt Zoya sighed. "We are accustomed."

She and Mom stumbled around for a while, rearranging, picking up clothes, trying to get ready for bed in the crowded little space. By the time they turned out the lights, it was nearly midnight and Mom seemed to have sobered up. Natalia had fallen asleep right in the middle of our bed. I curled up on what was left of my side and wondered how I'd ever get to sleep.

Across the room Mom lay on her back beside Aunt Zoya. "Are you sure there's nothing they can do for Mama?" she asked in a quiet voice. "They have all kinds of cures for things these days."

Aunt Zoya let out a disgusted poof of air. "We are not rich Americans like you, Lara. This is Russia."

Were we rich? I guess maybe we were in comparison to people in Russia.

Mom's voice was small. "But, maybe if we got on the internet—"

Aunt Zoya turned over onto her back. "What? You think I not take care of Mama?"

"Oh, no, Zoya. Of course you do. But maybe there's something you, I mean we, haven't thought of."

Aunt Zoya's voice rose. "Listen to you, Lara. You leave Russia, your family, everything jus for big American Marine with all his money."

Mom sat up in bed. "How can you say that, Zoya?" Her voice cracked. "You don't know what it's been—"

"Leave her alone." I could barely finish the sentence my voice was so choked with tears.

"Carly!" There was scuffle of sheets as both Mom and Aunt Zoya turned to face me. Mom jumped out of bed and practically tripped over the coffee table as she hurried to my side. "Oh honey—" She sat down beside me. "—I'm so sorry you heard all that. I thought you were asleep." She stroked my forehead. "I loved your dad. I still do."

Suddenly Aunt Zoya was there trying to hug me. "Very sorry, Katerina." She straightened and turned. "Is vodka. Is late. Is worry. We go to bed."

1:15 A.M. The sound of light footsteps brushing past jarred me from my sleep. My heart pounded. Had someone come into our room again like last night? The silvery shape near the door transformed into Mom. I relaxed as I watched her tiptoe out into the hall. She was probably just going to the bathroom. As quick as the thought came to ask her to bring me back some water, I fell asleep.

2:45 A.M. The crash of something falling woke me up. In the dim light I realized the shape sprawled on the floor by the door was Mom

I slipped out of bed and hurried to her side. "Are you all right?" I whispered. I tried to take one of her arms and lift her up.

"Iz okay. Iz okay," she muttered. She raised herself on one knee, placed a hand on the coffee table, the other on the edge of the couch and managed to push herself up. Lurching forward, she landed on her face on the bed. Aunt Zoya turned over and grumbled something, then went back to snoring. There was no mistaking the smell on Mom's breath. Vodka. She'd left us to go drink. She was drunk.

CHAPTER SEVEN

Careful not to spill a single drop, I carried Grandma Olga's pink teacup down the hall to her bedroom. The door stood part way open, but I knocked anyway. Grandma Olga, already dressed in a pair of thick wool pants and the same knit cardigan sweater she always wore, sat in a cushioned chair over by the window, beside her a tiny table with a white lace hanky on top. A tiny smile crossed her face when she saw me. Just a flash, then it was gone.

Smoke hung in a thin haze across the high ceiling of the bedroom, drifting toward the oxygen tank that stood near the door. Grandpa Ogi, wearing an undershirt and a pair of saggy brown pants held up with suspenders, sat on the bed reading his newspaper. A cigarette dangled from his lips. When I entered, he lowered his paper and nodded. He seemed to have gotten over that we spoiled his vodka—if he even remembered.

I slipped across the room, stepped over a heap of clothes, and set the teacup down on the little table beside Grandma Olga.

"*Spaseeba*." My grandmother's voice sounded small, like there was barely enough air inside of her to push it out. I leaned down and kissed her wrinkled cheek. She didn't smile, but her eyes brightened. She gave my grandfather a quick glance then motioned for me to take the chair opposite her.

As I sank deep into its dusty cushions, the smell of mold filled the air. I stared at my grandparents. It was going to be hard having a conversation when no one spoke English but me. Out the window there wasn't much to see, just another gray building like ours, a few pigeons—that's all. I pulled my English/Russian translator out of my pocket. "*Loochshe*? Better?" I asked my grandmother. I enunciated it slowly, not sure if I was pronouncing it right.

"*Da. Da.*" She smiled and patted my arm, nodding her head excitedly. The effort started her coughing. Her body rocked back and forth, jostling the tiny table, causing the tea to slop over into the saucer. She clutched at her chest and gasped for breath. The sound was loud and raspy like air being sucked through gravel.

I didn't know what to do. "Mom," I shouted. "Come quick."

My grandfather stubbed out his cigarette, slipped his legs over the side of the bed, and hobbled over to the oxygen tank. He began fiddling with the transparent plastic tubes, but his thick fingers were trembling so bad he couldn't get them untangled. Finally I helped him. We got the strap over Grandma Olga's head and the little clamp under her nose. My grandfather turned on the oxygen, and together we stood watching.

Grandma Olga's eyes closed. The skin around her mouth turned blue. You could tell from her squeaky gasps for air that the oxygen wasn't helping. I wanted to scream, *do something!* Grandpa Ogi leaned down and fiddled with the tubes, frowning, rubbing his forehead. "Olga?" he whispered.

Her eyes fluttered open, and she looked at him, then closed again as she struggled for breath.

I looked at my grandfather. "Isn't there something we can do?" His eyes searched mine, as if he were begging me for help.

"Mom," I screamed, "hurry."

By the time she and Aunt Zoya came into the room, Grandma Olga was slumped sideways in her chair, her mouth wide open, her chest working up and down. From the sound you could tell she wasn't getting any air in or out.

Aunt Zoya pulled out her cell phone, punched in some numbers, and spoke to a person on the other end.

Mom sunk to her knees beside Grandma Olga's chair. Grandpa Ogi put out a trembling hand to the dangling oxygen tube and gave it a little shake. Aunt Zoya finished her phone call and clapped shut her cell. Natalia peeked into the room. Her eyes grew huge, and she disappeared.

"We've got to do something," I said. No one paid any attention.

The movement of Grandma Olga's chest was slowing down now, as if maybe she was too tired or just giving up. Mom stroked her mother's arm, whimpering, "Mama, mama." Aunt Zoya stood watching, her jaw clenched, her lips in a straight line.

"Can't we try CPR?" I asked. They'd taught us that at Junior Lifeguards the summer before.

No one said anything.

"But she'll die," I screamed. No one reacted. It was as if they hadn't even heard me.

The minutes ticked by. The room was silent. I hugged myself and watched my grandmother, counting the rises and falls of her breath.

By the time the sirens sounded her chest had stopped moving. I ran to the window and looked down, wishing there was some way I could break the glass and scream at the guys getting out of the ambulance to hurry up.

When I turned back, my grandmother had completely changed. She'd turned yellow, and her eyes had flipped open. It didn't even look like her anymore.

No one needed to tell me. She was dead.

I wanted to go dig a hole somewhere and crawl in. The yellow cat yowled and leaped out of my way as I raced down the hall to our bedroom. I ran inside and slammed the door, nearly tripping over a pile of clothes. I hated death. I hated Russia. I hated everything.

Flat on my back, I stared up at the cracks in the ceiling. It wasn't fair. Why did she have to die? It didn't matter that she couldn't speak English, and I couldn't speak Russian. I could still tell she loved me. I kept picturing how confused she'd looked when everyone was talking about her sickness in a language she didn't understand.

As I turned to reach for a Kleenex, I saw Mom. She lay across the room on the bed curled up in a ball like a little kid, her face to the wall. She hadn't said a thing when I came in. I hadn't even realized she was there.

My mind flipped back to the day two years ago when the two marines came to our house to tell us about Dad— Marine Lieutenant Colonel Ian McOwen, killed in combat in Iraq. I'd just finished fourth grade. Mom ran and locked herself in the bedroom. The marines waited until I called Gracie. Then they left, and I threw up.

I felt like throwing up now, but I couldn't. I had to be strong for Mom. This time there was no Gracie to call. The next morning Mom didn't get out of bed at all. I ended up spending the whole day with Aunt Zoya and Natalia. Aunt Zoya said Mom was just acting this way to get attention. "She same way when leettle girl," Aunt Zoya informed me.

"But her mother just died." I said.

Aunt Zoya shoved her face in mine. "And is not my mama which die also?" The angry sparkle in her blue eyes, the straight set of her thin lips—it could have been Grandpa Ogi's face glaring at me.

I leaned away. "Well, yes, but Mom lost her husband too."

Aunt Zoya batted the air. "Does not matter, Katerina. Your mama is not leetle girl. She is adult. She have responsibilities—" She touched my face and her voice softened. "—like you."

Another day passed and still Mom wouldn't leave the bedroom. When I went in to bring her tea, I found her crying over the Russian family album. When Dad died, she didn't get out of bed for almost a month.

* * *

At three in the afternoon Mom still wasn't out of bed. I sat by myself at the kitchen table staring at my open book. I hadn't read a word. Down in the living room Aunt Zoya and Natalia watched a movie in Russian on TV. Grandma Olga's burial would be Friday. After that Mom and I would go home. The day couldn't come fast enough.

Vlad came into the kitchen, wearing a regular pair of khaki pants and a golf shirt. He was having a day off. "Hallo preety gill." His eyes widened. "What sad face." He looked around. "Where is Mama?"

I stared at my open book. "Still in bed."

He sat down across from me. "Ahhh. Is feeling badly, Lara?"

I nodded.

He raised his shoulders, lifted his palms. "But is understandable, no? Is her mama just die."

"Yeah, but I just wish she'd get up."

He placed his hands on the table and rose to his feet. "Perhaps I talk to her? See if make happy, *da*?"

I felt my spirits rise. "Oh, would you?"

"No is problem." He disappeared down the hall and called out Mom's name.

It was like magic. About ten minutes later Mom was up and dressed. She'd even put on a little lipstick. Vlad guided her into the kitchen. "I take Mama out for leetle while. Is good, *da*, Katerina?"

Mom's face looked awfully pale, her eyes a little frightened. "Are you okay?" I asked her.

She took a nervous glance over her shoulder then managed a weak smile. "Yeah, I think so."

Vlad took her shoulders and pointed her toward the front door. He glanced back at me and winked. "We go."

* * *

The sun moved from behind a billowy gray thunderhead and shone down hot on my shoulders. I moved a few inches to stand under the shade of a tree, closer to the pyramid of brown earth that rose beside the hole where Grandma Olga would be buried. The Russian cemetery with its dirt and weeds and iron fence was nothing like Fort Rosecrans where Dad was buried. His grave was on a grassy hillside with a beautiful view of San Diego bay.

I slipped a hand out and ran my fingers along the rough edge of Grandma Olga's casket, feeling the splinters, smelling its piney scent. It was hard to believe she was really inside. I remembered thinking the same thing about Dad. His casket was made of smooth, shiny mahogany, and an American flag was draped over it. I'd wanted so badly for someone to open it up so I could see him one last time.

Near where I stood was the tombstone of my Russian family, already etched with the names of past relatives, mostly "Казнэтсов," Cyrillic for "Kuznetsov," Grandpa Ogi's last name. I noticed flowers on some of the other graves, plastic flowers, not like the real kind they put on the graves at home.

The Russian Orthodox priest wore a tall black hat that draped down over the back of his neck. Sweat dripped from his chin. I felt sorry for him in that heavy black robe standing there in the sun. He droned on and on, every so often making the sign of the cross. I didn't understand the words, but it sounded like he was saying the same thing over and over again. Beside him stood three other men, strangers with long beards all dressed in black. Every so often they echoed what the priest was saying in the same flat monotone. There were some other people there too. I wondered if they were from my grandparents' building. It didn't matter. I was just glad that Grandma Olga'd had friends.

Grandpa Ogi had dressed up in a shiny black suit and a white shirt with a narrow black tie. He stood in the sun, his eyes fixed on the hole where his wife would be going. He lifted a yellowed handkerchief to his gray forehead and wiped off the sweat. Near him Aunt Zoya, wearing a long black dress, stood with her eyes lowered. Sunlight glistened off her shiny green eye shadow. I couldn't tell from her face if she was sad or mad or what. Mom stood next to her. She wore the same black suit she'd worn for Dad's funeral, only now it fitted her like a sack. The black scarf over her head practically covered her entire face. Every so often she raised a trembling hand to her eyes and dabbed at them with a piece of shredded Kleenex. Her hands trembled so badly this morning she broke a dish in the kitchen sink. Right before we left to come to the cemetery, I caught her alone in the kitchen drinking vodka. When she saw my shocked face, she said, "Mama died." I wanted to get mad, tell her that it was no excuse, but there was such sadness in her gray eyes I couldn't make myself do it.

Vlad in his uniform stood half way between the men in black and Mom. His eyes were on her the whole time. Two nights in a row now they'd been out together, and each time she'd come back drunk. Mom whimpered softly. Vlad slipped over beside her and snuck an arm around her shoulder. Thunder rumbled in the distance. The Russian priest chanted on and on.

Beside me Natalia yawned and rolled her eyes. She and I both wore our denim capris. Neither one of us had brought a dress or a skirt. She nudged me, nodded at Mom and Vlad, and gave me a sly grin. What was she trying to say? That there was something going on between them? That was crazy. Mom still loved my dad.

The priest droned on and on. Would he never stop? We'd already been through two hours of this at the church.

Some sweaty men in T-shirts and jeans appeared. They slipped ropes under Grandma Olga's casket and edged it closer to the hole. This was when the two Marines had taken the flag off Dad's casket, folded it carefully end over end, and placed it in Mom's lap. She'd hugged it to her chest, rocking back and forth with it, crying softly. Sitting beside her, I remember wondering if it was all a bad dream. I couldn't imagine anything real hurting so bad.

Mom's shoulders shook with sobs.

"Olga, Olga." Grandpa Ogi cried openly.

Slowly, the two men lowered Grandma Olga's casket into her grave. I watched, but it wasn't her I was seeing, it was Dad.

When it was all over and I'd dried my tears, Vlad put an arm around me. He led me to stand by Mom. One arm on her shoulder, one arm on mine, he made the announcement:

"We go for eat and drink at Restaurant Alexander. Have good time, celebrate life of Olga. Is, how-you-say, drinks on me."

* * *

I blinked as I stepped from the bright sunlight into the cigarette smoke filled darkness of the restaurant. Candles flickered on each of the tables and light came from behind salmon-colored shades on the walls. Now that we were here the smell of onions frying made me realize how hungry I was. Images of steaks, French fries and onion rings floated through my head.

A waiter waved us forward.

Mom stepped back, her palms against the door. "This was a bad idea," she muttered. "I never should have let myself be talked into coming." After the burial she'd begged to just go back to the apartment, but somehow Vlad talked her out of it. He'd gone on ahead of us to the restaurant to make sure everything was set up. Aunt Zoya said something in Russian to Mom and tried to take her arm. Mom pressed herself against the door, her eyes darting from here to there like a frightened bird. Right after Dad died she was afraid to leave the house.

Suddenly Vlad was beside us. "Welcome," he said in his thick Russian accent. His shiny pink face beamed. "Come." He put an arm around Mom's shoulder. She lowered her head and let herself be guided toward the back of the restaurant. Aunt Zoya, Natalia and I followed, Grandpa Ogi staggering along behind.

Vlad led us past a bar full of men talking loudly, then past tables of people eating plates of fried food with some pale leafy vegetable on the side. When we got to the back, a long table covered in a white cloth had been set up just for us. Some of the people from the funeral were already there, already drinking vodka from tiny glasses. Vlad sat at the end of the table with Mom and Grandpa Ogi on one side of him, and Aunt Zoya, Natalia and me on the other. A waiter handed out menus, then left and returned with another bottle of vodka and four baby-sized glasses. I cringed, remembering the night we'd played Monopoly.

Vlad poured the little glasses full, handed one to Aunt Zoya, one to Grandpa Ogi, and one to Mom. He raised his glass high. "To Olga." With a jerk of his wrist, down went the vodka.

Mom raised her glass, hesitated for a second, then… "To Mama."

Aunt Zoya raised hers. "To Mama."

Grandpa Ogi's hands were trembling so bad he couldn't get his glass to his mouth. Finally he just grabbed the bottle and took a big swig from that.

By the time the waiter brought our food, they'd toasted Grandma Olga four more times. Grandpa Ogi couldn't stop crying. Mom was beginning to smile. Vlad egged her on, talking to her in Russian, telling jokes, winking, putting his arm around her shoulder. I didn't like it the way his lips kept touching her hair when he whispered in her ear.

Natalia nudged me, nodded at the two of them, and rolled her eyes. "Your mama is hot for him," she whispered. It felt like I'd just been stuck by a fiery poker. "She is *not*." I stared at my plate and bit my tongue. I wasn't about to let Natalia think she'd gotten to me with that stupid comment.

She whispered in my ear. "They suck face. I see it."

The words sent waves of nausea through my stomach— Mom and Vlad, lips pressed together, tongues roaming each other's mouths.

I leaned away from Natalia. "No way."

She whispered again. "Is true. Was last night. I think they do…" She rubbed her palms together.

Oh, God, was she right? Mom never came to bed last night. I grabbed Natalia's arm and shook her. "Shut up, Natalia," I hissed. "Just shut up!"

My chicken had a white pasty sauce all over it. I scraped a little off and found a piece of fried meat underneath that was so tough I could barely cut it. I couldn't get rid of the sauce flavor either, musty tasting, like some kind of herbs. It didn't matter. My appetite was gone.

A hunk of hair kept falling across Mom's eyes. When she tried to cut her meat, it slithered off her plate. She giggled, stabbed it with her fork, and put it back. I looked around to see if anyone else had noticed. She began speaking louder in Russian, gesturing with her knife and fork. She was usually so shy. I'd never seen her act like this.

Natalia nudged me, grinned, and pointed at Mom. "Is *pyaniy*."

I gave her what I hoped was a threatening look. "*Pyaniy?* What's that?"

"Is when…" She fell limp against me, crossed her eyes, and stuck out her tongue.

"Very funny." I didn't smile.

Vlad leaned across Mom and filled Grandpa Ogi's glass. Grandpa Ogi's eyes kept falling shut. He swayed like he was about to fall off his chair.

Vlad poured Mom more vodka.

I whispered to her, "Don't you think you've had enough?"

I don't think she even heard me. Her eyes were stuck on Vlad.

Aunt Zoya's eyelids were sinking lower, showing more and more of her sparkly green shadow. "So, Lara—" She wobbled her head toward Mom, her words slurring slightly. "—is good thing for you now Mama is dead, *da*? You go back to your big United States of America. Be happy."

I sat up straight. "That's not fair, Aunt Zoya. Mom loved Grandma Olga just as much as you did."

She brushed the air. "Oh, sure."

Mom's eyes suddenly teared up. She reached over and put a hand on her sister's arm. "We'll keep in touch, Zoya," she slurred. Her face brightened and she sat back. "Maybe you come visit us in San Diego, *da*?"

Natalia bounced with excitement.

Aunt Zoya raised her eyes to Mom's. For just a brief second I thought she was going to say *yes*, but then she shook her head and looked away. "No is money."

Natalia let go of my arm and slumped back into her chair.

Vlad put his arm around Mom and raised his glass high. "To Olga."

CHAPTER EIGHT

I watched my cousin put her comic books and her toothbrush into her suitcase. She and Aunt Zoya were leaving in the morning. She handed me her beanie baby. "For you."

"Miss Pig? For me?" I'd seen her sleep with the little pink and white pig every night. I couldn't believe she'd actually give it up. Suddenly I felt really guilty for all the mean thoughts I'd been having about her lately. After all she *was* my cousin.

Natalia leaned back. "So, Carly. Maybe Aunt Lara marry Vlad, maybe you come back live in Russia?"

"Mom marry Vlad?" I screeched. "What are you talking about?"

Why did she always have to say things like that? It's like she knew just how to freak me out. All I'd been thinking about for the last two days was Mom and Vlad. They were together most of the time, and Mom was acting so weird. Again last night she didn't come to bed. I didn't want to think where she might have spent the night.

I ran my finger along the arm of the sofa where the cat had clawed the fabric thin. "So, how about your mom? Doesn't she have a boyfriend?"

Natalia brushed the air. "Russian boyfriend? No way. She gonna marry American like your mama did." A glint appeared in her eyes, followed by an evil grin. She was about to say something I didn't want to hear. I could just tell.

I jumped to my feet. "I've gotta go."

She smiled sweetly. "I know secret about Vlad and your mom."

I put my fists on my hips. "Look, no more secrets about Mom and Vlad, okay? I think you're making a lot of this up, anyway."

She pressed one nostril and pretended to be sniffing something off the bedspread. "You know what is this?"

"You mean snorting drugs?"

She nodded, her eyes wide. "I see your mom and Vlad do."

"No way." I shouted. "Absolutely not. My mom would *never* do that."

Natalia shook her head. "Is true."

"I don't believe you."

Natalia's head bobbed up and down. "Uh, huh. Was yesterday. Vlad's door is open like…" She put her fingers just an inch apart. "I see in room. I see them do it."

I turned away so she couldn't see my face. What if it *was* true? I hated that Vlad. I just hated him. The way he could get Mom to do anything he wanted, the way they were always getting drunk together, his smile, the way he called me *preetty gill*. Why had I ever liked him? He was nothing but a jerk!

* * *

Finally. The day I'd been waiting for the whole trip. I couldn't believe it had finally come.

I turned off the alarm on my watch, lay back against my pillow, and stared at the ceiling. In just twenty-four hours we'd be back in San Diego, one stop in Frankfurt, another in London, then L.A., then home.

My clothes hung over the chair where I'd left them last night waiting for me to put them on. Quietly I dressed, loaded the rest of my little stuff into my backpack and was ready to go.

No sound from Mom yet. I tiptoed across the room and shook her shoulder. "Mom. Time to wake up."

She moaned and turned over onto her face, a cloud of vodka fumes rising above her. I shook her shoulder again. "Mom, come on. Get up. We've got to get to the airport."

When finally she got out of bed, she wasn't even packed. I had to do most of it for her. Her hands trembled worse than ever. It was okay. We were going home. Safe back in the United States. Things would be better there.

Thanks to me we made it to the airport in time, just barely, only an hour before the plane was to take off.

The lady behind the desk held out her hand. "Passports?" She wore a uniform and no makeup, and her hair was pulled back so tight it made her skin look stretched.

Mom drew her travel pouch out from inside her shirt and fumbled around for the passports. Her face turned bright red. She gave the lady a stupid smile. "I know they're here somewhere." She ran a finger through the inside of a pocket. A few coins spilled out.

The airport lady frowned at Mom's trembling hands.

"I'm sorry," Mom mumbled. "If you'll just give me a minute."

"Here." I reached for Mom's pouch. "Let me look." I felt through all the little secret places in her travel pouch. Her ATM, a few rubles, but no passports.

Tiny furrows appeared between the lady's eyes. The overhead lights glared off her forehead. "If you would please move aside so the next in line can come." She pointed to a little area on the other side of the rope.

"Will we lose our place?" I asked her. It was getting late. The line we'd been in snaked all the way out the door. I was scared we'd miss our flight.

"You come back here—" She stabbed the counter with her finger. "—when you have your passports."

I turned to Mom, breathless. "Where are they?"

She didn't answer. She was too busy trying to turn her suitcase around and get it out of the way. My heart beat so hard it was about to burst right through my ribs. "Mom, does it mean we can't go?"

"Shush, Carly. Just come over here."

We moved to the spot outside the ropes and plopped down onto the floor. First we searched Mom's backpack, then her suitcase, then my backpack and my suitcase. Spread around us were piles of sweaters, Mom's hair dryer, a box of Tampax, a stack of undies, a plastic bagful of dirty clothes, my set of Russian nesting dolls, but no passports. A janitor in a stained green jumpsuit swept the floor around us, every so often shooting us a mean scowl like he wished we'd get out of his way.

"I thought you always kept our passports in your travel pouch," I said to Mom.

"I did," she replied.

"I can't believe it. How could you just lose them?"

She pinched her forehead. "You're not helping, Carly."
She began putting things back in her bags.

Mostly the people in line ignored us. A few smiled sympathetically. A girl about my age stood next to her parents and stared at me. I wished she'd quit.

One by one the groups of travelers moved up to the desk. The uniformed lady looked at their passports, tore off their visas, and allowed them through.

I couldn't stand it. They were getting to go, and we weren't.

The janitor reached his broom up next to my foot to catch some slips of trash. Mom closed her suitcase and stood up. "C'mon, Carly."

We stepped back in front of the passport desk. The people who were in line waiting to go next grumbled and gave us dirty looks.

Mom raised her trembling fingertips and placed them on the edge of the counter.

I held my breath.

"It seems we've left our passports back at the apartment."

The lady official shook her head. "Sorry. If you don't have your passports, you can't go."

"But—" Mom wiped her forehead with the back of her hand.

"Do you have your birth certificates?" the lady asked.

Mom frowned. "Birth certificates?" She glanced at her pouch. "Not with us."

The lady straightened her arms against the counter. "We need proof of citizenship. If you don't have passports and you don't have birth certificates..." She shrugged her shoulders. "I'm sorry, but you can't go."

I tried to tell myself this wasn't happening. "But, what are we supposed to do?"

The lady looked over Mom's shoulder and motioned for the next in line.

"You mean we really can't go?" My voice had begun to shake. "Please, my mom and I need to get home to San Diego."

The lady just shook her head. "Sorry. Please move aside."

The janitor clapped down the lid of his dustbin and walked away

On the subway on the way back I broke down and cried. Mom covered her face. "I'm sorry, Carly. I just don't know what could have happened."

Nothing she could say mattered. We were still in Russia.

* * *

When we got back from the airport, we searched the entire apartment. No passports.

"Do you think someone stole them?" I asked.

Mom put her face in her hands and shook her head. "I don't know. I just don't know."

She said the American Embassy would be able to issue us new passports, but since it was Sunday, they were closed. She was tired. She went to bed.

Later, when I went out to the kitchen to fix myself something to eat, Vlad was home, sitting in the living room with Grandpa Ogi, watching TV. A half empty vodka bottle sat on the coffee table in front of them.

Vlad called to me from across the living room, "Katerina."

I walked over and stood on the first step.

"You not go back to America?" He said it with a laugh in his voice.

I put my hands on my hips. "Our passports are gone. Have you seen them?"

"Passports?" He lifted the cushion beside him and looked underneath. "*Nyet, nyet.*"

Something about the way he was smiling made me wonder.

Grandpa Ogi squinted at me from the couch. I don't think he even knew who I was anymore.

Vlad poured a little glass of vodka and raised it to me. "You like try?"

I stepped back. "No way."

He elbowed Grandpa Ogi. "She no like Russian vodka." They both laughed.

I moved down into the living room. "So, are you sure you haven't seen our passports?"

"Passports. Passports. Why you need passports?"

"To go home with." I almost said, *stupid.* "You can't leave Russia without them, you know."

He shrugged. "Perhaps you stay in Russia." He nudged Grandpa Ogi again. "Is good place for to be, *nyet*?" They both laughed at the look on my face.

I folded my arms and shook my head. "Come on. Have you seen our passports?"

Vlad beckoned me to come closer. "You ask nice, preety gill. Maybe give Vlad a kiss—"

"Jerk!"

He practically rolled off the couch laughing at me as I stomped out of the room.

CHAPTER NINE

At one thirty in the afternoon the next day Mom was still in bed. She lay on her back, her face pale as the sheets. I couldn't get her to wake up.

I crawled into bed beside her. "Please, Mom," I choked. "We've got to go to the American Embassy. Our passports, remember?"

She didn't respond.

"Please, Mom, we've got to figure out how to get home." I put my arms around her and hugged her tight. "I'm so scared, and you're my only mom and you gotta help me."

She put her arms around me and hugged me back. "Love you, Carly," she mumbled.

We stayed wrapped around each other like that for a while. It was what we used to do when I was a little girl.

Mom turned onto her back and began to snore. Her breath smelled like the rubbing alcohol Gracie used to dab on my cuts. I lay thinking. By now we should have arrived in San Diego. Gracie must be worried to death. I needed to call her. She'd tell me what to do. She gave me an international phone card right before we left on our trip. She said it was in case of an emergency. This was an emergency all right.

The thought of going out on the streets of St. Petersburg all by myself made me stiff with fear.

Suddenly Dad was before me, holding me by the shoulders, looking me straight in the eye. "Be brave, Carly." Those were his last words before leaving for Iraq.

I knew what I had to do. I slipped out of bed and put on my sandals. "I'll be back, Mom," I said in a loud voice.

She smiled in her sleep.

* * *

Hugging my travel pouch inside my T-shirt, I hurried up the sidewalk. I remembered what Mom said about eye contact and focused my gaze straight ahead. Across the street was the pretty blue and white cathedral I'd noticed every time we came this way. Its golden domes poked through the treetops, glistening in the afternoon sun. Further on was the internet café and across the street from it, the little park where I'd seen a public phone.

When I got closer to the park, my heart sped up. Where was the phone? A crowd coming toward me on the sidewalk blocked my view. They passed by, and then I saw it, shining bright green in the sunlight.

I slowed and pulled my travel pouch out of my T-shirt. At the very bottom of the back pocket was the phone card Gracie'd given me before we left. Just as I was approaching the phone, a woman stepped in front of me. I backed up to a park bench and sat down.

She inserted her card into the slot, punched in some numbers, and began talking. She talked, and she talked. Ten minutes passed, and she was still talking.

I fiddled with my travel pouch, pulled out my mirror and stared at my mouth, looked at Dad's picture in my wallet.

Finally the lady stopped talking, took back her phone card, and turned to leave. I rose to my feet and was about to go use the phone when suddenly I was surrounded. Three teenage boys. One had greasy hair and a dimple in his chin. The second wore filthy low-riders with chains. The third had the whitest skin I'd ever seen. His ugly grin showed me his missing teeth. Their eyes focused on my travel pouch.

Damn! I should have put it back inside my shirt.

"Uh, excuse me." I started to move toward the sidewalk. The kid with the dimple in his chin stepped in my way. The other two laughed and their voices cracked.

Just then a line of school kids filed past. When they hit the park, they scattered in all directions, whooping, shouting, ready to play. A swarm of them surrounded us. It was just enough of a distraction. Still clutching my travel pouch, I jumped over the patch of grass between the curb and the sidewalk, and, without even looking, raced across the street to the internet café. Cars honked. Brakes screeched, but I made it.

The guy behind the counter peered up at me through bored, half-open eyes, waiting.

I looked around, suddenly feeling panicked. What if he only spoke Russian? I pointed. "Uh, can I use a computer?"

He ran his tongue over the ring in his lower lip and just stared.

"Computer?" I repeated.

He picked up a little piece of paper from a stack and made a big deal of placing it down on the counter. In slow motion he pulled a short pencil from behind his ear. He licked the tip, wrote the time on the chit, and handed it over the counter.

The last empty cubby was next to a Russian Orthodox priest. He leaned forward and peered into his screen, gently stroking the long beard on his chest. It was the prettiest chestnut color. At first glance I thought it was an animal. He looked over at me and smiled. The way his golden brown eyes crinkled around the corners made me think of Dad. I swallowed hard, afraid I might tear up.

Sunlight from the window beside me blurred my screen. I shaded my eyes and leaned forward. Beneath the dust and fingerprints a bunch of spam lay waiting for me. I scrolled down until this message popped up from Gracie:

Subject: *Homecoming*
Carly,
I opened the newspaper this morning, and what do you know? There was a big picture of the Hermitage in the travel section. Did you get there? Can't wait to have you home again, darling. Have arranged to pick you and Mom up at the airport Sunday. Sure have missed you.
Love and hugs,
Your American babooshka.

A tear escaped my eye and made a trail of mud where it landed on the dusty keyboard.

Beside me the priest started to chuckle. It began with a rumble deep inside his chest. He leaned back in his chair, stroked his long beard, and laughed and laughed until his eyes sparkled.

It was impossible for me not to look. I wiped my eyes and leaned his way. He pointed, still choking with laughter, at Scooby Doo doing hip-hop moves across his screen.

I smiled politely and turned back to my emails. Up popped another from Gracie.

Subject: *Where are you?*
Carly,
I'm frantic. I've emailed your mom, but nothing back from her. I expected you yesterday and you didn't arrive. The airline people said you never boarded the plane in St. Petersburg. They wouldn't tell me why. Please darling, let me know what's happened. Is everything okay?
Gracie

I emailed her right back.

Subject: *re: Where are you?*
Gracie,
weve lost our passports. they wouldnt let us on the plane. the lady at the airport said we need to have our birth certificates. could you maybe mail them to us? Ill try and get an address.
Love Carly

By the time I paid and left the internet café it was already three o'clock. A line of three people had formed in front of the little green phone. I didn't have the nerve to go sit and wait so I headed back to the apartment. Just as I turned the corner onto a narrow, empty street, there they were again—the same creeps from before.

I backed against the wall behind me.

They moved closer, so close they practically touched me. There was no way I could escape. I forced all the muscles in my face to relax, so they wouldn't know how scared I was.

One took a puff off his cigarette and exhaled it through the gap in his teeth. The smoke mixed with his sour breath made me feel like gagging.

The guy with the greasy hair slipped a finger under the cord of my travel pouch. I cringed at the feel of his touch. He was so close I could see the oil on his face, the tiny red pimples, the clogged pores on his nose. Something flashed down by his side—a knife. I wondered if he'd noticed how bad my knees were shaking. I couldn't stop thinking about the old man we saw get robbed outside the Church Of The Spilt Blood. What would these guys do when they found out I didn't have any money?

The long shadow of the priest from the internet café fell across the sidewalk. Relief made me weak. He grabbed the greasy-haired kid by the collar, jerked him away from me, and bellowed something angry-sounding in Russian. The other two boys spun around. The pale-skinned kid said something that sounded like he was making up an excuse.

The priest shot them each a fiery glare. He raised his fist and shouted, *"Provalivajte."* Whatever it meant, it worked. The three turned and raced away down the sidewalk.

My legs felt like they were about to crumble right out from underneath me.

The priest put a hand on my shoulder. "Are you all right?" he asked in English.

My throat tightened. I couldn't make the words come out.

"You are American?" he asked.

I nodded.

"I thought so." He patted my shoulder "Come," he said, "I walk with you."

On the way back, he told me his name was Alexander, that he'd studied for a year at Boston University, and that he had a daughter just my age named Alisa. He asked about Mom and Dad and why I was in Russia.

I told him that Dad died in Iraq and that Mom and I were visiting her parents here. He asked why Mom wasn't with me now. "The streets of St. Petersburg are not safe for a young girl such as you."

I didn't want to tell him that Mom had been too drunk to come, so I told him she was sick in bed.

He noticed me looking at the pretty blue and white cathedral. "You like it?" he asked. "Is my church."

"It's beautiful."

He smiled. "I think so." He put out his hand to keep me from stepping off the curb until the light changed. "So, you are American. *Da*? You like the Boston Red Sox?"

"Well, I'm kind of a Padres fan." I pulled off my backpack and dug out my Padres cap. "Dad gave it to me on my last birthday. He used to take me to the games all the time."

Father Alexander's face lit up. "*Da. Da.* Of course. San Diego Padres." The light had changed. He put a hand on my shoulder and escorted me across the street. "You know, Katerina," he said as we walked, "is a big coincidence we meet. Today I return to the United States for summer session at Boston University. I leave this very afternoon."

"Oh, I wish I could go with you." The words burst from my mouth before I could stop them.

He pulled me to the right to avoid a big stone on the sidewalk. "You are homesick?"

I looked up at him. "Well, not exactly. It's just that Mom and I... Well, we can't go home."

He frowned "You can't go home. Why is that?"

"We lost our passports."

He came to an abrupt stop in the middle of the sidewalk. "You lost your passports?" He continued walking again, but more slowly. "Are you sure they are lost? In Russia people pay lots of rubles for stolen passports. Is very common. There is what you call a black market here."

"Ohhhh." Maybe he was right, and all this time I'd been blaming Mom for losing them, thinking it was because she was drunk. I wondered who could have stolen them. I remembered the weird way Vlad had acted when I asked him if he'd seen our passports, almost like he knew where they were and was teasing me about it. I'll bet he took them. I was tempted to mention it to Father Alexander, but then I'd have to say that Vlad was Mom's boyfriend, and the drugs might come up and that might get Mom in trouble.

"You must go to the American Embassy," Father Alexander said. "They will help you get new passports."

I nodded. "We're going there tomorrow." I'd go by myself if I had to.

We'd reached my grandparent's apartment building.

Father Alexander took my hand. "So, Katerina, it is time we say good-bye." He made a small bow. "Perhaps we shall meet again."

I had a sinking feeling as I watched him walk away. He'd seemed so nice. I'll bet he would have helped me and Mom with the passports if only I'd asked. But he was leaving for America the next day, so it was impossible.

I stood in the shadows of my grandparents' apartment building and looked up, praying, hoping Mom had sobered up and was out of bed.

CHAPTER TEN

I had no idea something was wrong until I reached the third floor. People peered out of their doors into the hall, their gazes pointed toward the end, the same direction I was going.

A scream rang out—Mom's.

I flew down the hall. My fingers wouldn't work fast enough to make the key go in the lock. Once inside the apartment I raced down to our bedroom and burst through the door.

Mom cowered on the bed. Vlad, wearing only a pair of pants and his sleeveless undershirt, hovered above her, his arm raised, ready to strike. The whole left side of Mom's face was bright red, her shirt torn. Blood streamed from her nose. Her left eye was swollen shut. The muscles along Vlad's shoulders bulged. I smelled his sweat mixed with his cologne.

Just as his hand came sweeping down towards Mom's face, someone screamed, "No!" It was my voice.

He spun and started toward me.

Mom lurched forward and grabbed his arm to stop him. He slammed her in the chest with his fist. She sailed backwards onto the bed, her head hit the wall, and she slumped over.

I stepped toward him. "You leave her alone."

His mouth contorted into a cruel grin. He grabbed my arm. His breath reeked of vodka.

Go for the eyes. It was a move I'd learned in the self-defense class Mom and I took. You make a *V* with your first two fingers. One quick jab.

My fingers made contact with his eyeballs and slid inward. I didn't have the nerve to poke any deeper.

He roared, let go of my arm, and covered his face.

The next thing our teacher told us to do was run, only I couldn't, because then he might kill Mom.

He staggered toward me, still covering his face.

I put my hands on his chest and shoved as hard as I could. His arms flailed out, and he stumbled backwards, tripping over a pile of clothes on the floor. He came down hard, his head snapping forward as it hit the edge of the glass-topped coffee table behind him. The bottle of vodka tipped over. Glass shattered everywhere. With a grunt he slid to the floor. His eyes closed, his body went limp, and he stopped moving.

I sank onto the bed. He wouldn't be able to hurt Mom any more.

The pool of blood near his left ear spread, turning pale pink where it mixed with the spilled vodka. My head began to reel. I felt light all over. I leaned down and put my head between my knees. Somewhere far off church bells tolled. Up the street a jackhammer pounded.

Slowly the world stopped spinning. I sat up and looked around. On the bed Mom leaned against the headboard, her good eye opened a crack, the other swollen shut.

"Mom, Mom." I crawled over beside her and put my arm around her shoulder. "Oh, God, you're really hurt bad."

She mumbled something in Russian.

"We have to go to a hospital." I said. "Can you get up?"

She slumped back against the headboard.

I shook her shoulder. "C'mon, Mom. Wake up. You can't go to sleep." They'd taught us about concussions in Junior Lifeguard.

She stirred and sat forward. "Carly?" She dragged herself over beside me to the edge of the bed. When she saw Vlad, she let out a soft moan. "Oh God, what happened?"

"I pushed him."

She leaned closer and stared at his motionless body. Slowly she raised her swollen face to mine. "This is going to look bad. Real bad."

I squeezed my hands between my knees to try and keep them from trembling. "Do you think he's dead?"

She covered her face and shook her head. "Oh, God! Oh, God!" was all she'd say.

In the distance sirens squealed.

She sat up straight. "We've got to get you out of here, Carly." She tried to push herself up off the bed, reeled, and sat back down again. "Oh, God, I don't think I can do it."

The sirens were getting closer and closer, my heart racing faster and faster. "What will happen? Will they arrest me?"

Mom closed her eyes and took a deep breath. If only she'd answer me.

"But what if I tell them what happened? Won't they understand?"

She just kept shaking her head.

Sirens filled the room then stopped. I ran and looked out the window. Down on the street two police cars were pulled up to the curb, nose in, their backs sticking out in the street.

Mom clenched her jaw and leaned forward. I put an arm under her shoulder and helped to her feet. She stood for a moment, swayed, then sank back down onto the bed. "I'm just so dizzy."

Footsteps pounded the hall outside the apartment. Deep voices shouted in Russian.

I grasped Mom's hand and pulled. "They're coming, Mom. Please, please, try again." I was so scared I thought I was going to faint.

Her face cleared. She rose to her feet. "Carly. You need to hide." She pointed at the clothes closet over by the wall. "Quick, get in there."

My voice quivered. "But what about you?"

She closed the closet door. "Shhh. No matter what, just don't come out."

* * *

Stuffed inside the closet with all those clothes I could barely breathe. A wool coat scratched my face. The mothball smell was suffocating. Somewhere outside men shouted, their voices rough, faraway-sounding. I gripped Dad's St. Christopher. *Please, please, don't let them find us.* The voices grew louder, clearer. They were inside the apartment now. I held my breath and prayed that Mom had gotten away.

Footsteps came down the hall. Bedroom doors opened and closed. My heart pounded inside my head, waiting. Suddenly the voices grew louder, closer. They were right inside the room. A person gasped, then everyone spoke at once.

A deep voice bellowed something that sounded like an order. Wood squeaked against wood—furniture moving. Men grunted. Feet shuffled. Footsteps left the room.

Were they gone? I parted the clothes in front of me just a fraction without making a sound. All I could see were thin strips of light through the slats in the closet door. A shadow moved across the light. I froze. A deep voice spoke. It was the same man as before, only inches away. My heart beat so loud I was afraid he'd be able to hear it. From across the room Mom's voice answered the man in Russian.

Oh, no. I'd thought she'd hidden herself.

I wanted to come out, but she'd said not to.

The man's shadow disappeared from in front of the closet. He growled a question.

Mom, answered him again, her voice shaking. She was closer now. I'd never heard her sound so scared.

He repeated the question.

"*Nyet, nyet,*" Mom screamed. She'd shifted positions with him. Now she was right in front of the closet. I could see a thin line of lavender from her capris.

The man shouted something that sounded like a swear word. Then came a slap.

Mom screamed and fell back against the closet door.

I couldn't stand it. I had to get out. I pushed, but the door wouldn't open. I tried again. It wouldn't budge.

"No," Mom said it in English this time, strong, like an order.

Then I realized. It was her body leaning against the closet door, keeping me from coming out. She spoke again in Russian, calmer now. Her shadow disappeared. Footsteps left the room.

Again silence.

I waited and waited. Nothing happened. Sirens sounded, moving away this time.

After what seemed like my whole lifetime, I opened the closet door and peeked out.

"Mom?"

* * *

She was gone. Vlad was gone. Everyone was gone. The door to the bedroom stood open with a piece of yellow tape across it.

The smells hit me first, vodka and something rusty that must have been the blood. I had no idea there'd be so much of it. There was a red pool where Vlad's head had been and little spatters of it everywhere. Someone had moved the coffee table away so you could really see it now.

As I stepped down out of the closet, my eyes roamed the room. Where had they taken Mom? Were they going to blame her? Would they put her in jail?

The sound of a man's voice startled me so bad I almost screamed. It sounded like he was just outside in the hall. It had to be one of the policemen. I whipped around and crawled back into the closet. The sound of Grandpa Ogi's voice reached my ears, just blahs and slurs like he was too drunk to talk. Then I heard the other man's voice again. Then silence. I waited and waited.

It seemed like at least an hour passed, but probably not more than about ten minutes. I didn't hear a sound. Had the policemen left? It didn't matter. They'd be back. They'd search the room. They'd find me. I had to leave.

Quietly, I opened the closet door and slipped out, my eyes focused on the open doorway with the yellow tape across. I stepped down and my foot slid. The blood mixed with vodka had made the floor slick as oil. I fell forward and landed on my hands and knees in a pool of it. Little pieces of glass bit into my hands. Larger pieces poked through the legs of my capris, cutting my knees and shins. The vodka stung like lemon juice on a cut.

Right in front of me at eye level was the coffee table, with a big piece of broken shard still in place. Near a book that hadn't fallen off was a piece of foil with white powder in it. I hadn't noticed either before. Had Mom and Vlad been doing drugs? On the floor were a couple of credit cards. It didn't matter. Nothing mattered. I just had to get out of there.

I used one of the cushioned chairs to pull myself up leaving bloody handprints behind on the upholstery. My fall hadn't made much of a sound. Still, I was scared someone might have heard me.

I tiptoed to the doorway and peeked out. The hall was empty and silent. The only light came from the kitchen at the other end. I ducked under the yellow tape, crept out of the bedroom, and started toward the front door. As I passed my grandparents' bedroom, I caught sight of Grandpa Ogi passed out on the bed, snoring. From the kitchen I heard another sound—a man clearing his throat.

I froze, terrified. Should I run back to the bedroom and hide? I had only a few feet to go to get to the front door. Cigarette smoke drifted from the kitchen, through the open doorway and down the hall toward me. The man moved to where I could see him. It was a policeman. He stood on the other side of the kitchen table, his back to me. He put a cell phone to his ear and began talking.

I crept forward. Just one more step to the front door. My hand shook as I turned the knob. Quietly I slid the door open, praying it wouldn't squeak. The only sound was the whisper it made across the carpet as I inched it open.

"Meow." I hadn't noticed the yellow cat sneak up behind me. At the sound all the air escaped my lungs. The policeman turned and saw me. His eyes widened. He snapped closed his phone and jolted forward, but the kitchen table blocked him.

I flew through the front door. Behind me came the sound of the wooden legs of the kitchen table scraping against the linoleum. Chairs fell. Dishes hit the floor. I made it halfway down the hall before the shout rang out. Footsteps chased me. When I rounded the corner, I could hear the elevator coming. I didn't dare stop. I raced to the very end of the hall and burst through the door into the stairwell. My sandals made a hollow clapping sound as I started down the stairs.

Men's voices echoed in the stairwell. Footsteps clattered on the metal steps. I peered over the railing and saw the dark police caps. They were coming up. Had the guy in the apartment called them? I turned and ran back up the other way. I didn't dare get out on the third floor, so I climbed to the next landing.

When I exited the stairwell on the fourth floor, the long hall was empty. I stopped just on the other side of the door to catch my breath, listening for voices, footsteps, anything. Had they followed me? I didn't think so. I tiptoed down the hall looking for a place to hide. A large plastic palm tree in a terracotta pot sat in a corner beyond the elevator. I crouched behind it and hid.

About ten minutes passed, and nothing happened. I decided to give the stairs another try. Two women stood waiting in front of the elevator. I slipped past them and headed back down to the end of the hall. I was halfway there when the door to the stairwell opened and two policemen stepped out. Spikes of fear shot up my spine. I turned and raced back in the other direction. The two women were just getting on the elevator. It was my only chance. The second lady stepped on, pulling her shopping cart behind her. She turned and was about to slide the door closed when I jumped on. The metal grate clanked shut behind me. The elevator dropped with a jerk just as the upper part of the policemen's bodies came into view.

Once Natalia and I had a race to see if I could beat the elevator down by using the stairs. When I arrived in the lobby out of breath, there stood Natalia. The elevator had won by thirty eight seconds.

I prayed it would win this time.

Metal cables slid past. Slowly. *Go faster.*

I backed up against the metal bars of the cage and breathed hard to catch my breath. It was then I noticed the two women's faces. They stood, their backs against the cage, eyes wide, staring at me.

I gazed down at my blood-soaked capris, at the blood running down my legs, at my bloody hands.

Oh, God, I've killed a policeman. Everyone's going to know.

CHAPTER ELEVEN

In my rush to get off the elevator I knocked over the lady's shopping cart. She yelled something angry after me. My sandals slapped the tile floor of the lobby. Just as I was almost to the entrance, the police burst from the stairwell on the other side. The women yelled. The men shouted. I kept going.

Down on the street a small crowd had gathered. I veered around them and took off—stumbling down narrow sidewalks, crashing against sides of buildings, bumping into people as they came my way. I didn't know where I was going. I didn't feel a thing. Sirens came from all directions.

A woman with a stroller blocked my view. I raced around her and ran right into the fish lady's table. "Sorry. Sorry," I mumbled as I pushed myself off her table. The old lady shook her fist and squawked in a dry, raspy voice. I barely heard her. All I wanted was to get away from the sirens.

Two women, arm-in-arm, came toward me. I jumped off the sidewalk into the street to get around them. A car honked. Its brakes squealed. It screeched to a stop and hit me, not that hard, but enough to knock me down.

People screamed.

"It's okay. It's okay." I jumped to my feet. Before anyone could get to me, I was gone.

Gradually the sound of the sirens grew fainter. I slowed to a trot, trying to catch my breath. It felt like someone had kicked the wind out of me. The place on the side of my leg where the car's bumper had hit me began to throb. It didn't matter. Nothing did. All I knew was I had to get away.

Bright sunlight met me as the dark street opened onto the boulevard beside the canal. A row of faded yellow buildings the color of old newspaper reflected back at me off the dark waters. *Keep walking. Stay calm.* That's what Dad would have said to do. If only I were as brave as he was.

I crossed the bridge where the lions with the golden wings crouched guarding the canal. The flash of the sun off their wings nearly blinded me. Through the curly metal grate of the railing I caught sight of the Church of the Spilt Blood.

Blood. It was all over my pants, on my hands, on my arms. People would notice. If only there was a public restroom or even a drinking fountain where I could wash off. I hadn't seen either the whole time we'd been in St. Petersburg.

I headed toward a dark alley. A man crouched down filling plastic water bottles with a hose. Just ahead of him on the main sidewalk was one of the red and white umbrellas where they sell bottled water. As I was about to pass him, the man dropped his hose and hurried up on to the sidewalk to serve some customers. Praying no one would see, I picked up his hose and began washing myself off.

It didn't take long before the man selling water noticed me. "*Provalivai*," he shouted, waving his fists for me to go away.

Halfway up the block I stopped to wring out my pants. They didn't look so bad, but my hands had begun to throb from the glass. I sat on the ground, leaned up against a cement post, and began plucking the slivers from my hands.

Below me on the dark waters of the canal a tourist boat filled with happy passengers chugged past. They waved. I wondered if any of them were Americans. If only I could talk to them, someone would help.

I got up and started walking again. Pieces of advice people had given me floated through my mind: *If you're lost, hug a tree. Don't talk to strangers. Policemen are our friends.* Not here, they weren't. If I were in the United States, I'd have used my cell phone to call Gracie.

Then I remembered. The phone card. Of course!

I fumbled around in my pocket. It was still there. As I felt the smooth plastic, I could almost hear Gracie's voice, calm and reassuring as a warm hug.

I walked for blocks looking for one of the phones that takes cards. As I approached the golden gates of a park, I noticed something shiny and green hidden beneath an overhang of trees. The branches hung down so low you could barely see the phone. I was in luck. No one was using it.

I inserted the phone card. A recording came on asking for my PIN. I punched in the four digit number. "You have five dollars and twenty one cents remaining," said the recording. Next I dialed Gracie's phone number.

"You have—" A truck honked so I couldn't hear the rest.

On the other end of the line Gracie's phone began ringing. I held my breath and counted the rings. One, two, three. A bird chattered on the tree branch above my head. Through the golden bars of the fence, shiny white statues posed half-naked on gray cement pedestals.

Four, five. Would Gracie ever answer? I couldn't wait to hear her voice. Just the sound of it would make everything better. Six, seven. The bird flew away.

I gripped the receiver in my sweaty palm and held on tight to Dad's St. Christopher. *Please, please, God, let Gracie answer.*

"You have reached the McOwen residence…"

My heart thudded to a standstill. It was the recording of my dad's voice on Gracie's answering machine, still there after two years. It had been so long since I'd heard it. I swallowed hard. So much that I loved was at the other end of that phone line—Gracie, memories of my Dad, San Diego, my home. I stared at the phone cord, wishing it would magically suck me up inside, transport me back to San Diego, and drop me onto the floor of Gracie's nice safe kitchen.

Suddenly…

"Hello?" My grandmother's voice on top of the recording sounded crackly, fragile like it might break in two.

"Gracie?" I could barely get out her name before I burst into tears.

"Carly is that you?"

I gasped and swallowed. "Gracie—"

The line went dead, and a recording came on. "We're sorry, your allotted time has expired…"

Oh, God! This is all my own fault. I never should have let Natalia talk me into using the card, but she'd begged me to call Marisa. She'd said she wanted to meet another American girl. We were going home in two days. I figured it was safe enough. Natalia and Marisa must have talked forever.

I beat the phone with my fist. *No, no, God, please, don't let this be happening.* I crumpled up the sticky note with Marisa's phone number on it and flung it into the trash. I tossed the phone card in after that. A lot of good it would do me now.

Halfway into the next block sobs overtook me, the hard dry kind that don't make any noise. I turned and faced the wall. A gray stone goddess wearing long robes stood on a ledge looking down on me, her eyes only empty sockets.

I began walking again, stumbling through a blur of tears.

An old couple strolled along the sidewalk ahead of me. They looked like nice people, hand-in-hand, somebody's grandparents maybe. Gracie was waiting for me to call back. I needed to get to a phone right away. Maybe these old people would help me.

I hurried and caught up and tapped the old man on the back. He turned. When he saw me, the corners of his eyes crinkled. His smile filled me with hope.

"Do you speak English?" I crossed my fingers and prayed.

"*Nyet.* Engleesh." His was high-pitched and squeaky. When he saw the disappointed look on my face, his eyebrows slanted upward.

I yanked off my backpack and fished around for my English/Russian translator. The old man and his wife watched me as I flipped through the pages.

"Pamageetye mnye pazhalsta?" *Can you help me please?* I spoke the Russian phrase out of the guide book slowly, hoping my pronunciation was close. I pretended to hold a phone to my ear. "Telephone?"

"Da, da, telephone." The man nodded his head rapidly. He understood. He took my shoulder, pulled me a few steps to the left, and pointed across the street.

"But I don't have a phone card," I said in English.

"Phone card?" The old man frowned and looked at his wife. She scowled and muttered something in Russian.

I drew a rectangle in the air.

The old man scratched his head.

"Maybe could you give me some rubles?" I asked.

The man's wife tightened her grasp on her purse and stepped back. *"Nyet. Nyet."*

My eyes filled with tears. "Please. My grandmother's waiting for me to call."

The old lady flicked her fingers at me. *"Provalivai."* She took her husband's arm and turned away.

My shoulders slumped. No one was going to help me.

* * *

I wandered into a park full of tall, leafy trees, up a path lined with perfectly shaped hedges, past naked white statues draped in marble robes. A lady with a stroller stopped near a bed of pink and blue flowers and sat down on the bench. I took a seat at the other end. Her toddler stared at me with his huge baby eyes. I fluttered my fingertips at him. He grinned back, showing me his two new baby teeth and a chin glistening with drool. When his mom saw what was happening, she leaped to her feet, grabbed the handle of the stroller, and was off before I could move an inch. I gazed down at the bloody patches on my pants that had now turned brown. Did I look that bad? What did she think—that I was going to steal her baby?

Other moms with babies strolled through the gardens, parents with little kids shouting and laughing, couples holding hands. A mom tossed her little boy's popcorn in the trash. Pangs of hunger attacked me. What a waste. The bag had been almost full. For just a brief second I considered going after it, then the thought of the germs that would be inside the trash bin changed my mind. I searched my backpack—only two Power Bars left. I was hungry enough to have eaten both, but I ate just one. My rubles were gone. I had to conserve.

An hour passed. I took tiny sips from my last bottle of water while I watched some kids play tag. I wondered what was going on back at the apartment. Had the whole thing been on the evening news? I stared at my feet, at the red places on the back of my heels where my sandal straps had rubbed. I didn't know where to go. I didn't know what to do. At least here in the gardens with all the people and babies I felt safe.

7:30 p.m. I rose and began walking again, thinking about Mom. I kept hearing the policeman's gruff voice, the sound his hand made when he slapped her face. Was she in some dirty jail now? Were they torturing her? Would they kill her? Oh, God, if only I could talk to Gracie.

At 8:45 p.m. it was still bright daylight. People began flowing toward the exits. I rose and followed. A bunch of dirty kids sat by the gate, their hands out, begging for money. Two women about Mom's age wearing Adidas and neon pink sports visors were leaving just ahead of me. Bits and pieces of their conversation drifted back my way.

"Are we going to the Hermitage tomorrow?"

"Yes, at eleven—"

It took a minute before what they were saying registered.

English! They were speaking English. They were Americans. Before I could do anything, a bunch of beggar kids swarmed them.

One of the women swatted at the kids. The other yelled, "No. No. Get away." Gradually the kids got the message and backed off. I rushed ahead of the two women and turned, facing them, skipping backwards as I talked. "I'm an American and…"

They stopped. One gave me a cautious look that turned right away into suspicion. The other had soft eyes. Something told me she might help.

"I know this sounds funny," I continued, "but I've lost my mom, and…"

They started walking again. The nice one muttered to the other, "Do you think she's really an American?"

Her friend shook her head. "No way."

"I'm in trouble." The words rushed from my mouth. "Do you think I could have a little money to call my grandmother?"

That did it. They broke eye contact and sped up. The mean one laughed. "Call her grandmother. That's a new one."

I chased after them and grabbed the nice lady by the strap of her purse. "Wait."

She turned, fear sparkling in her eyes. "Let go of me."

I yanked on the strap. "Please, please, let me explain—"

With a powerful jerk the woman broke away from my grasp. "Help, police. Help!" she screamed.

I ran for three blocks. Finally I had to slow down because of the pain in my side. Tears returned to my eyes. No one was going to help me, not even Americans.

CHAPTER TWELVE

Shadows stretched across the six lanes of Nevsky Prospekt, the longest street in St. Petersburg. A lingering band of sunlight turned the domes of the cathedrals into bursts of gold. I must have walked the entire length of the boulevard—past souvenir salesmen packing up their goods, past the water vendors closing their red and white umbrellas, past crowds of people waiting to get on buses to go home—home to warm safe houses and families who loved them. I could hardly bear to watch.

I looked at my watch. 11:15 p.m. On the sidewalk the crowds had begun to thin.The travel guides warned never to be alone on the streets of St. Petersburg after dark. Back when we first got here on July 1st they were having the white nights of summer, and it stayed light all night long. But it was July 27th now. By one in the morning it would be dark. Then what would I do? I couldn't go back to the apartment. Where would I spend the night?

Keep walking.

Maybe I'd walk the whole night long.

The straps of my sandals rubbed the raw places where blisters had formed. I sat down on a bench to rest, but then I noticed a man staring at me. Everything scared me. I felt safer walking.

Footsteps sounded behind me, getting closer. I walked faster. The footsteps sped up. Suddenly I felt something jostle my backpack. Pickpocket! I gripped my straps and ran.

I turned the corner and slowed to catch my breath. From all the walking I was so thirsty I could have died. I stopped and searched my backpack for my bottle of water. Only a few sips were left.

Two men burst out of a bar and staggered toward me. They stopped and pointed at something above my head and began laughing. I glanced over my shoulder. Behind me in the store window a grinning mannequin in black leather panties held a whip. She looked just like the mannequin in the store window of the sex shop that day when Natalia and I got in so much trouble. The drunks advanced toward me. One licked his lips. The other curled his finger at me, beckoning.

I took off running.

Above me the sky was losing its golden glow, barely enough light left to see by. As I passed a dark building, four guys stepped out from the wall—gang members. I could tell by the way they were dressed, all in one color, muted green. One of them said something, but I ignored him and kept walking. The four followed me, whistling and giggling and making weird sounds. One of them raced ahead of me, turned, and started walking backwards. He pulled his elbows back and thrust his hips forward. His friends laughed. I knew they wanted something dirty. It was way scarier than if they'd wanted money. The other guys caught up and formed a circle around me.

Out of the corner of my eye I noticed a group of college-age kids going down the stairs to the metro. Quick, I sidestepped the gang guys and shot across the sidewalk. One of them made a grab for my backpack, but I was able to pull away.

The soles of my sandals made a hard slapping sound as I raced down the stairs into the metro and melted in with the group of students. When we got to the turnstile, I didn't know what to do. One by one people stuck in their pass cards, pushed the metal bar, and passed through. I'd never done anything like this before, but there was no choice. Just as one of the college girls was beginning to push down the bar of the turnstile, I crowded right up behind her and squeezed through with her. She looked over her shoulder and yelled something angry at me in Russian. I didn't care. I just ran.

Crowds of people rode the escalator. "Excuse me. *Izvinite,*" I said as I ran down the moving stairs, weaving my way around the people going down. Posters for Coca Cola and Levis, Shiny-licious lip gloss and American movies flew past me. I had no idea whether or not the creepy guys had followed me. I didn't take the time to look back.

Accordion music drifted up from the tunnel below, happy music like you might hear on a merry-go-round. When I reached the bottom of the escalator, I turned right and wandered toward the sound. There, down near the end of the hall, was a little boy about five or six playing a squeeze box. He wore shorts and red cowboy boots and sat on a small folding stool. He looked way too young to be playing so well.

Out of breath, still panting, my eyes searched the tunnel to see if any of the gang guys had followed me. No sign of them. With a big sigh I leaned up against the wall and closed my eyes.

The accordion music changed to, "It's A Small World."

I couldn't believe it. My favorite song. Whenever I went to Disneyland, it was always the first ride I went on. It would have made me feel happy if I weren't so tired and scared. I watched the dark-haired boy as he swayed back and forth to his music, his face so serious. He never cracked a smile, not even once. His eyes were big and brown with the longest thickest lashes I'd ever seen. Was he homeless? He must have been because his face was dirty, his Mickey Mouse T-shirt had big holes in the front, and his two-sizes-too-big shorts were held up around the waist by a piece of string. His boots were too big also. I wondered how he learned to play the accordion so well.

Some of the people passing by dropped coins into a plastic cup at his feet. When they did, he nodded to let them know he'd noticed, but no smile. Never a smile.

Nearby, a kid who looked like he might be in about seventh grade leaned against the wall fiddling with some silver tape that he was using to patch up a scuffed up boom box. Every time someone dropped something in the little boy's cup, the older kid smiled and gave the thumbs up. I wondered if he was the little boy's older brother.

He caught me watching, jumped to his feet, stuck a second cup on the ground, and pushed the button on his boom box. The CD skipped a beat and made squiggly sounds before blaring out rap music. The boy broke into hip-hop, his arms and legs loose and rubbery, moving in different directions all at once. He tossed his head back to knock the hair out of the way, and I caught a look at his eyes, big and round, gray with little flecks of green in them. He had light brown hair, almost blonde, but real dark eyebrows. His T-shirt had the sleeves cut off, and his Levis had holes in the knees. I might not have guessed that he was homeless except that he was so thin. His skin was pale as skim milk, so pale the veins showed through.

When he was done dancing, he stood there grinning at me. It was the kind of smile where you have to smile back. I almost did, then remembered Mom's warning. *Don't make eye contact.* I lowered my gaze.

He nudged the little cup toward me with his toe. He wanted money.

I took a step back. Was he dangerous? Would he try to rob me? I couldn't give him money. I didn't have any.

He nudged the cup closer.

"*Nyet* rubles." I shook my head. "I don't have any money."

He sprang back on his heels. "*Americanka?*"

I nodded my head rapidly. "*Da, da. Americanka.*" I didn't know what the word meant except that it had *American* in it so it had to be good.

"I am Peter." He bowed.

"I am Katerina," We shook hands.

"I go America," he said, proudly. He rubbed his fingers together. "When get dollars."

"Really?" I was so happy to meet someone who spoke English that I was ready to believe anything.

He strummed an air guitar. "I be big rock star." His mouth turned up at the edges even when he wasn't smiling.

A subway whished out of the tunnel and came to a silent stop. As the people poured out of the cars, Peter did his hip-hop dance. A woman wearing lots of jewelry and expensive looking clothes stopped and watched him for a second. She stooped and placed a paper bill in his cup. Two hundred rubles—eight dollars.

He snatched up the bill, kissed it, and threw her a wave.

He turned to me. "I go America, Katerina. Pretty damn soon."

I gave him the thumbs up.

He grinned and did a few more hip-hop moves, then stopped and peered into my eyes. "You from America. Why you no have money?"

I didn't want to get into a long story so I just shrugged. Out of the corner of my eye I caught movement at the other end of the platform. It was one of the creeps from up on the sidewalk. Panicked, I turned back to Peter.

He was gone. Vanished.

The warning announcement had sounded. The train doors began to close. I caught a glimpse of his back as he jumped onto the car behind the little boy.

"Wait!" I screamed.

You aren't supposed to cross the yellow line of the metro once the warning buzzer sounds, but I did it anyway. With a running dash and a flying leap, I landed, falling forward onto the floor of the subway car.

A hand reached out to me. "*Americanka!*"

I loved hearing him say that word. It was like having a big red, white and blue flag wrapped all around me.

His eyes danced. "Pretty good jump." He settled back into his seat, holding his boom box on his lap. "You go Olympic games, yes?" He smoothed a tip of the silver tape that had come unstuck.

I smiled and felt myself blush. I took a seat opposite him. Beside him the cute little dark-haired kid hugged his squeeze box and stared. The train moved faster, rounding corners, swaying from side to side. The little boy swayed too, but his giant brown eyes stayed glued on me. It reminded me of the way little kids look at you when they're sitting in their mothers' shopping carts at the checkout line.

The train slowed as it reached the next station. Peter rose to his feet. "Later, *Americanka*."

"Wait." I followed them off the train.

Peter turned and stopped near the edge of the platform.

I pulled off my backpack and dragged out my last Power Bar. Would it work? Would he take it?

I held it out. "I-go-with-you?" I pronounced it very slowly hoping he'd understand.

He frowned and stared at the Power Bar

I held my breath.

He stepped closer and studied my face. "Why you want come? Is trouble?"

I made my eyes go wide. "No. No trouble." Would he believe me?

All of a sudden he grinned. "Okey dokey, *Americanka*." He stuck the Power Bar in his pocket and gave me high-five.

I blew a big sigh of relief.

We crossed to another platform and took the red line. The little boy with his short legs and clunky big boots had to skip to keep up. Along the way I asked Peter how he got to be living on the streets. He said his parents died in a car crash and there were no relatives to take him in. He'd had a pretty regular life before that. Sports, school, all that stuff. He learned a little English at school, but mostly from comic books—*Spiderman* was his favorite—and watching American videos.

The little boy kept staring at me. I couldn't tell if it was because he thought I was cool or weird or what. He'd probably never met an American before. His name was

Pasha. Peter found him one day wandering alone in the park carrying his little stool and his accordion. His mother had just walked off and left him. I tried smiling at him, but he wouldn't smile back. Poor kid.

Peter patted the little boy on the head. "Is good boy, Pasha. Make music. People like. Get much rubles."

Peter looked at me. "What do you?"

"I go to school. I'm in sixth grade next year." It sounded so lame.

He frowned. "Why you be in St. Petersburg at night? Where is mama? Where is papa?"

I told him about Dad dying in Iraq and about how we were here visiting my Russian grandparents. "My grandma died. Then Mom got sick…" I raised my palms. "So here I am."

He nodded, so I guess he believed me.

By the time we climbed the stairs from Chernyshevkaya station up to the sidewalk, it was almost midnight and completely dark. I figured we'd be going to some kind of homeless shelter, but I didn't ask where. I didn't care. Anything would be fine as long as I didn't have to spend the night alone on the streets. We crossed a wide boulevard, then turned onto a narrow street that led into a park.

A breeze made the leaves of the trees flutter like silvery butterflies in the moonlight. I hugged my terry jacket tight across my chest. A few people still wandered around—an old guy in a long coat, hunched over, smoking a cigarette. A man and woman with their arms locked weaved in and out of the shadows, their voices blurred like the rustling of the trees. We passed by an empty playground that sat beneath some pines, just a slide, a tiny playhouse, that's all. I wondered where the homeless shelter was.

Peter stopped, looked from side to side, then cut off the path and into the woods.

I followed him.

Twigs snapped under my feet. Branches clawed at my jacket. He stopped again at a spot where the limbs of a tree drooped all the way to the ground. He pushed one away and waved for me to go through.

I found myself in a little cleared away space, all hidden and secret with bushes and trees for walls. Someone had spread a sheet of plastic on the ground, then a blanket over that. Another was draped over a branch for a tent.

I sunk to my knees beside Peter and Pasha and stuck my head inside. It smelled like dirty socks.

Branches snapped. Leaves crackled, and a scrawny dog the size of a small pony broke through the brush. I nearly knocked Pasha over trying to get out of its way. The dog stopped and began barking furiously. Long clumps of brown hair swung from its sides like dreadlocks.

Peter grabbed its collar and commanded, "*Nyet*, Lydya. *Nyet*."

"Put hand," he instructed me.

I did as he said.

Lydya inched forward, licked my fingers, and began to wag her tail. Before I knew it, she was panting fish breath in my face and slobbering all over me.

Pasha crawled into the tent, lay down, and stuck his thumb in his mouth. Lydya lowered her body and slithered in beside him. She licked his face with her long pink tongue then laid her paw on his arm and closed her eyes. Peter went next. He kicked a couple of comic books out of the way, and settled on the other side of the dog. "Warm," he said with a smile as he nestled his head against her scrawny backbone.

In seconds the dog and the two boys were asleep, their chests rising and falling, calm as could be.

I crawled under the blanket and curled up as far away from the dog as I could possibly get. It was cold, and my empty stomach burned, and I was thirsty. Every time I moved I felt the sore place on my leg where the car had hit me. I pressed my eyelids tight shut to try and hold back the sobs. *Mom, Mom, where are you?* I stuck out my tongue to catch the falling tears.

CHAPTER THIRTEEN

"Carly, Carly, Caaarly," All night long Mom called out to me in my dreams.

Morning finally came. Outside the tent the forest was silent except for the song of a bird high in a tree. Inside the tent smelled damp and doggy.

No one else was awake yet. I lay on my back thinking. I had no idea how to even begin looking for Mom. Had the police put her in jail? Were they blaming her for what happened to Vlad? Dad said we should always stick together. I never should have let them take her without taking me too. If only I could go back to the apartment and find out where they took her, but I didn't dare try that now. There'd be police. They'd be looking for me.

A puff of cool air whispered through the trees outside the tent. If only I could remember the name of the place Aunt Zoya lived. If only I could get in touch with her. I know she'd help.

One hairy eyebrow twitched and Lydya's eyes dropped open. When she saw me, she began thumping her tail. Peter sat up. "Good morning, *Americanka*." His smile was as bright as the sunshine peeking into the tent.

I looked away and rubbed my eyes. I hoped he couldn't tell I'd been crying half the night. Pasha, his face pink from sleep, blinked at me. He still wore his cowboy boots.

Peter pulled stuff out of a plastic bag and laid it on a wrinkled napkin, the Power bar I'd given him, three small pieces of dried fruit, a black banana, a little package of crackers and cheese, two oatmeal cookies, one missing a bite, five potato chips... Was the food stolen? Had it come from a trashcan? I didn't want to know.

He broke the Power Bar into three pieces, the same with the banana. Frowning with concentration, carefully he divided everything up. He used a plastic knife, each cut precise, making sure every share was the same. The dog watched, thick threads of drool dangling from its mouth.

When Peter was finished preparing his feast, he sat back on his heels, his gray eyes dancing. "How you say? Bon Appetit."

My piece of cookie had mold on it. When Peter wasn't looking, I fed it to the dog. I patted her bony head. Poor skinny thing.

"Don't you ever feed her?" I asked Peter.

"No is mine dog." Peter pressed his finger on a crumb that had fallen onto the blanket and stuck it on his tongue. "Is man lives in house by park."

I gave him a puzzled frown.

Peter patted the sheet we were sitting on. "Dog sleep here." He shook his head. "No live here."

From somewhere off in the distance came the sound of a sharp whistle. Lydya's ears shot up. Before anyone could move out of her way, she plowed right through us, knocking over Peter's water bottle, mashing Pasha's hand with her paw, flicking me in the face with her dusty tail. Once outside the tent she rose on her spindly legs, stretched, then lumbered off into the woods without looking back.

"Lydya, Lydya," Pasha cried.

Peter patted Pasha's head and said something soothing in Russian.

"What'd you say?" I asked.

"Say Lydya come back when is night." Peter laughed and said in a low voice. "Pasha think is mama, Lydya."

Pasha's round chocolate eyes searched Peter's face and mine.

Poor little guy. He must miss his mom something terrible.

I looked in my backpack and found the pink pig Natalia'd given me. I trotted it across the sheet toward Pasha. He watched it come, his thick dark lashes guarding his eyes—no smile, not even the hint of one. I made the pig do a pretend flip and landed it on his knee. He flinched, but still no smile.

I held it out. "Here, you can play with it."

For a minute he just stared at it. Slowly his hand crept across the sheet. Suddenly his arm shot out, and he snatched it. Softly, round and round, he rubbed it against his cheek. His thick lashes lifted. His eyes rose to meet mine. I'd have missed his smile if I'd blinked.

Peter began picking up our trash and putting it in the bag. I went back to worrying about Mom. Money. Everything kept coming back to that. I dumped out my backpack to see if there were some rubles hidden somewhere. Pasha studied my things as they spilled out onto the blanket: my summer reading paperback, *To Kill A*

Mockingbird, my CD player and some CDs, a pair of shorts, a T-shirt, and some undies. I balled them up real quick and stuck them into my pocket. Mom said to always pack a few clothes in case you got stranded without your luggage. This wasn't stranded. This was worse.

I picked through everything. No money. Pasha trotted the pink pig across the book, over the CD player and back down onto the blanket.

I looked at Peter. "Have you heard of a place called *Norovisk* or something like that? It's somewhere by a sea."

He scratched his chin. "*Norovisk*? *Nyet*. Not heard of it."

"*Notorisk, Novobisk*, something like that?"

Peter shook his head.

I felt like crying. Aunt Zoya would have been so perfect because she was right here in Russia. If only I'd gotten her phone number or email or something.

Peter picked up my Hanna Montana CD and studied the cover. "So if Mama is sick, why you come be with Pasha and me. Why you not be with her?"

I lifted my terry jacket and searched in the pockets. "Well, she's in the hospital, and they wouldn't let me."

"Then why you not be with grandfather?" I wished he'd stop asking so many questions.

I dropped the jacket. "My grandfather drinks vodka and—"

Peter nodded. "Ah, *da*. Comprendo." It sounded weird hearing him use Spanish.

Pasha made the pig do a somersault over his leg.

Peter stared at the CD. "Where live grandfather?"

"In an apartment on the other side of town."

Peter looked at me. "Is food in apartment?"

I shrugged. "Well, sure."

He sprung to his hands and knees. "We go apartment."

"No!"

Pasha looked up.

"I mean, we can't," I said.

Peter put his face up close to mine. "Why can't?"

It was no use. I was going to have to tell him.

I began with the stolen passports and missing our plane. Then I told him about finding Vlad beating up on Mom and how I pushed him. Peter listened, his face without expression. I wondered what he was thinking.

I finished, "...and he didn't move. I think he was dead."

Peter leaned back on his hands. "Ayeee, *Americanka*! Is big trouble."

Ripples of panic washed over me. "So you think they'll put me in jail?"

He shook his head. "Not know. Is very bad."

I wished he'd quit looking at me like that. I lowered my eyes. "He was a policeman."

"*Meeleetsia*?" Peter sprang back on his hands. "They not put in jail. They kill you."

Oh, God! Was he right?

My voice rose to a squeak. "But it was self defense."

Peter frowned. "Self defense?"

"It's when you're protecting yourself from someone who's trying to hurt you. Actually in this case I was protecting my mom."

Peter made a spitting sound. "*Meeleetsia* no care about that."

I covered my face. "Oh, God. What am I going to do?" I raised my eyes, afraid to ask, "So, you think I could hang out with you guys for a while?"

He shook his head. "Not know, *Americanka*. If *meeleetsia* come, is bad for Pasha and me."

I blinked back the tears. "But there's no place I can go, and, and...." Pasha's eyes grew round with worry. Was it my imagination or did Peter's soften?

I swallowed hard. "If only I could talk to my grandmother in the United States."

Peter's face lit up. "You have grandmother in United States?"

I nodded.

"She rich *Americanka*?"

I shrugged. "Well, yeah, sort of. I guess."

"She send dollars?"

I nodded my head excitedly. "Sure. Sure. She'd do that." I didn't even know if she could. "I need to get a phone card so I can try calling her again." And if that didn't work, I'd have to go to the American Embassy. I was saving that as a last resort. They might ask me where my mother was, and then what would I say?

I watched Peter's face.

"No problem, *Americanka*, " he said with a cheerful grin. "I get phone card, but first, we go McDonald's. Have lunch."

Was it possible? A phone card? A Big Mac?

* * *

I'd noticed the golden arches before. They even had red umbrellas out front just like at home. A truck ground past spraying gravel from its tires. We got closer, and the McDonalds smells hit me, a whiff of food frying, the tinge of apple turnovers warming under heat lamps, smells that made me weak. All I'd had to eat for two days now was the Power bar and a few bites of that terrible breakfast back at the tent.

Even from a distance I could see it was crowded inside. For a second I had the panicky thought that they might run out of food before we got there. I had my hand on the door about to pull it open when Peter motioned me away.

I frowned. "What's wrong?"

"No pay rubles." He stooped over a trashcan and peeked inside.

I couldn't believe this was happening. I looked around to see if anyone was watching. A teenage girl sitting at an outside table with her boyfriend noticed Peter. She wrinkled her nose.

A smile crept across Peter's face as he drew first a Happy Meal box, then a soggy ketchup-soaked sack from the bin. He peeked inside the box, and his grin grew even wider. Pasha watched and licked his lips.

My face burned. I couldn't look at anybody. I imagined this happening at Horton Plaza in downtown San Diego, a bum with scraggly hair fishing for his lunch out of a trash bin. No one I knew would ever imagine me doing something as disgusting as this. If my friends at home knew, they'd just die. I wanted to run and hide. I didn't want to have anything to do with Peter and the trash

But my stomach wanted the food.

A hamburger with only a bite missing, a small bag of fries almost full, four and a half onion rings—it smelled so good. I forgot about the germs and all the dirty hands that might have touched it. I even forgot about the little girl at the next table who wouldn't stop staring.

Peter handed me a chunk of meat covered in mustard. I hated mustard, but I ate it anyway. I even ate the slimy part of the onion ring. Cars streamed by. Horns honked. The girl kept staring, but all I thought about was how good the food felt going down.

When we were done, I didn't feel even close to full. I rose and peeked in the trashcan. Smells rose up to meet me, grease, coffee, catsup, the damp dirty smell of garbage cooking in the sun. Some sacks that looked like they might still have something in them lay a few inches away. I stuck in my arm and reached for them. Just inches from my fingers something rustled. Something long and bristly brushed my hand. I jumped back so fast that I nearly knocked the table over. A pair of beady black eyes appeared over the edge of the bin, long whiskers, then a brown body followed by an ugly long tail. It scurried down the side of the trash bin and scampered away into the bushes.

The last bite of hamburger meat I'd eaten rose in my throat. I swallowed hard, forcing it back down again.

* * *

An old man approached the public phone. Peter and Pasha and I sat on a stone bench watching him. He opened his sweater, pulled out a plastic card, and, with trembling hands, put it into the slot.

Peter tapped Pasha's shoulder and whispered something in his ear. Peter then rose and wandered across the sidewalk toward the man and the phone. Pasha stayed with me. Peter stopped just a little ways away from the old man and leaned against a wall.

A garbage truck stopped by the curb and sat there scraping and mashing and sending rotten-food smells into the air.

The old man finished his conversation and with a shaky hand hung up the phone. Pasha jumped to his feet and started across the sidewalk. Just a yard from the old man, he tripped and fell flat on his face.

"Ohmygosh!" I leaped to my feet.

The old man shuffled over to help. Then I realized what was happening. Slowly I sat back down again.

The old man bent down and offered his hand to Pasha, each movement slow and jerky as if every joint hurt. Pasha took the hand and let himself be lifted to his feet.

While all this was happening, Peter had moved around in front the phone booth. Faster than a snake could strike, he'd snatched the man's card out of the slot. In a flash he vanished, down the sidewalk, around the corner, and out of sight. The old man never saw a thing.

Pasha brushed off his knees, smiled, and thanked the stranger. The minute the old man turned his back, Pasha was off, disappearing around the same corner where Peter'd gone.

I stayed where I was, afraid to move.

The old man walked back to the phone and reached for his card. It wasn't there. Slowly he turned, rubbing his chin, scratching his head. He came my way, shuffling across the sidewalk until his scuffed brown shoes were directly in front of my feet. Did he think I'd had something to do with it? Would he call the police?

He asked me a question in Russian, his voice high and scratchy-sounding.

I was too ashamed to even look up. "I don't speak Russian," I mumbled.

He turned and shuffled off, shaking his head, his body bent like a crooked stick.

I found Peter and Pasha leaning against a brick wall just around the corner.

Peter grinned as he handed me the phone card. "Is good trick, yes, *Americanka*?"

I scuffed my sandal along the sidewalk. "Yeah, sure." It was hard to act grateful. I felt bad for the old man.

What would Gracie say? What would Dad have thought? All my life they'd taught me not to lie, not to cheat, not to steal.

The silver numbers on the card winked at me in the sunlight, magic numbers that meant hearing the sound of Gracie's voice again, finding Mom, a way back to the real world.

I stuck the card in my pocket and smiled at Peter. "Thanks."

* * *

I listened as Gracie's phone rang.

Every day for three days now I'd tried to reach her— once early in the morning, once about noon, once late at night. Each time I called, Dad's recording came on. The first time I left a message saying that I didn't know where Mom was and that I was living on the streets. I was about to tell her about Vlad and the police, but the machine cut me off. The second and third time the machine gave me the second beep before I could even get a word in. Gracie's messages must have filled up.

I'd thought about trying Marisa, but I'd thrown away the sticky note with her number on it, and I didn't have it memorized because it was programmed into my cell phone. And my cell phone was at home. *Damn! Damn! Damn!* I never should have thrown her number away. Be prepared. That's what Dad would have said.

I crossed my fingers. Maybe this time would be different.

Seven, eight, nine rings—where was Gracie? What did it mean? I pictured her kitchen, the green refrigerator, the lavender countertop where the phone sat, right near the magnetic photo of me in my soccer uniform. Her phone made a high pitched squeal when it rang, different from the way ours sounded at home.

C'mon, Gracie, answer. Was she outside picking roses? Still she'd have heard the phone. She should have answered by now. Was she gone, maybe on a vacation? No, she'd never do that. She'd be too worried about Mom and me. Oh, God, what if her bone cancer'd come back. What if she'd died?

A woman stood waiting. She shifted from foot to foot and cleared her throat. Where I stood it smelled like old pee. A man walked by, and his dog sniffed the wall.

After twenty rings and no answer, I finally gave up. It felt like I was drowning, sinking down, down, down with nothing around to save me.

CHAPTER FOURTEEN

Peter flipped the rubber flap of sole that had come loose from the bottom of his shoe.

I frowned at my empty travel pouch. I'd just checked it and my backpack for the umptiumth time. Still no rubles. I looked at Peter. "If we can just find my mom, she'll be able help us get some money." It was the same thing I'd said about Gracie. I wasn't sure he'd believe me this time.

Carefully he pressed one end of a strip of masking tape to the toe of his shoe and began wrapping. He raised his eyes "Okay, Katerina, but where *is* mama?"

"That's the thing. I just don't know." I gave him my nicest smile. "Uh, you think you might go back to my grandparents' apartment with me, and maybe you could sort of ask around?"

He examined his shoe, now silver at the toe. "I don't know, *Americanka*."

I fumbled around in my backpack and pulled out my CD player. "I'll give you this plus all my CDs if you'll do it."

His eyes grew wide. He stared at the flat silver CD player on my lap, then at me. "For sure, you do that?"

When no one was looking, we jumped the turnstile into the metro and took the yellow line across town to my grandparents' neighborhood. It was only a five minute walk from the station to their street. I kept my head down just in case someone might recognize me.

Afternoon shadows made the narrow street dark. Pasha and I hid behind a dumpster across from my grandparents' building. Our plan was that Peter would go over there, ring a few doorbells and ask a few people if they knew anything about Mom.

A cool breeze whipped up the street making me shiver. Pasha crouched beside me, his shiny, pink knees sticking out of his shorts. About five minutes passed. A lady with a baby stroller left the building. An old man with a cane came and went. Five more minutes passed.

Finally Peter appeared. I couldn't wait to hear what he'd found out. He raced down the steps and darted across the street, completely ignoring the taxi speeding by.

I was so excited to see him I forgot about hiding and stood up. "Did you find out anything? Did you? Did you?"

"Need go." He was panting so hard he could barely get the words out. Off he raced down the sidewalk. Pasha and I followed him full speed ahead. At the end of the street he turned the corner, veered into a dark alley, stopped, and leaned against the wall to catch his breath.

"What happened?" I asked.

Peter shook his head. "Is bad, Katerina, very bad. Police are look for you."

I gasped. "Oh, God! I was afraid of that. But what about Mom? Where *is* she?"

Peter took a deep breath. "I ask two people. They not know."

"Only two people?"

He rolled his eyes. "What you want I do, *Americanka*?" He pointed at his chest. "People see street kids they call police. Man in building use his phone. I hear him do it. If I stay there—" He drew a finger across his throat. "—is very bad for me."

Way off in the distance sirens sounded. It felt like the police were everywhere. My heart sank. How was I ever going to find Mom?

No one spoke on the way back. The three of us swayed in unison as the subway train rounded a corner. Peter stared out the opposite window at the blank walls speeding by. Pasha wiggled his fingers in his lap and hummed a silent tune. I thought about Mom.

All I had left to try was the American Embassy. I wondered what they'd say when I told them what happened. But they were Americans. Certainly they'd understand, or would they?

* * *

As the revolving door swept Peter, Pasha and me into the Embassy building, I clutched Dad's St. Christopher and said a silent prayer. This was going to work. It just had to.

A guard saw us. "*Provalivajte*," he bellowed, rushing toward us.

Provalivajte. Provalivajte. Why was everyone always telling us to go away?

Peter took one look at the man's badge, gave up, and headed back for the door. Pasha followed him, clopping across the tiles in his red cowboy boots.

The guard gave me a shove in the same direction.

I refused to budge. "I want to go upstairs to the American Embassy."

"*Provalivai,*" he growled, shooing me with his hand.

"But—" Why wouldn't he listen? "I'm an American."

When I said that, he stopped and squinted at my face.

"*Americanka?*"

"Yeah, yeah. I'm American."

He turned and looked at the line of photos on the wall behind him, photos like you see pinned up on the wall at the post office back in the United States, faces of kidnappers, murderers, people wanted by the police. Marisa and I used to check them out to see if we'd seen any of them lurking around the malls.

My eyes traveled the line of photos. When I came to one on the end, I nearly choked. It was a blown-up copy of *me*. My passport photo.

The embassy guard turned and leaned toward me, his dark blue eyes getting wider and wider. He reached for the wall phone and spoke into it, still staring.

I froze. A small group had formed around us. Their eyes moved back and forth between the guard and me. He stepped toward me, his shiny badge flickering in the overhead light.

At last the panic juices made it to my muscles. I stumbled backwards, turned, and ran.

The guard slammed down the receiver.

"Stop!" he yelled after me.

I slid across the floor and skidded into the first open slot in the revolving door. A woman in a business suit was already there. I crashed into her, knocking her against the side. She straightened herself and tried to push me out. It was too late. The door was already moving, swishing us around and out onto the sidewalk.

It felt like everyone was looking at me. I wanted to cover my face. I wanted to hide. Had they all seen my picture? Oh, God, this couldn't be happening. The American Embassy was my last hope.

* * *

Cool jazz music and the smell of coffee floated through the internet café. In the next cubicle over a college-aged kid in a purple and yellow striped sweater leaned back in his chair, eyes half-closed, and swayed to the music. It made me nervous even being there. Someone might recognize me and call the police. But I had to do it. I'd tried calling Gracie twice more with the phone card Peter stole for me, and she didn't answer and then the phone card ran out. Before even checking my emails, I decided to email Marisa. I don't know why I hadn't thought of her before.

To: mar999@abcmail.net
Subject: *help*
im living with some homeless kids in russia. i cant get home. some really bad stuff happened & i dont know where mom is. graciez not answering her phone or her emails. im so scard. plz ask ur parents what to do. i lost your phone num too. send it.
Carly

Next I clicked *Check Mail.*

New emails, mostly spam, splattered across my screen, pages and pages of them. It had been almost a whole month since I'd been able to get online.

Viagra improves erections.
Getting bigger little by little.
Quick approval on your home loan…
I held my breath and paged down.

Come on. Come on. Let there be something from Gracie.

Behind me Peter sighed and shifted from foot to foot. Talking him into letting me do this hadn't been easy. He was boss of the money. I didn't get to keep any for myself.

I deleted a screen full of junk mail.

An email popped up from Marisa. The subject read, "Wait til you hear this." I double clicked and leaned forward, excited. Maybe Marisa had some news.

i was readin som trivia thing and it said its imposible to apply mascara when ur mouth is closed!!! omg like that is sooooooo tru. u gotta try it.
luv mar

Oh, God, why did I ever think she'd be able to help me? I checked the box and clicked *Delete.*

More spam then another email from Marisa.

Subject: *Boy friend TEST*
OMG OMG OMG!!! All you have to do is take this test.
1.   Would u rather go on a date with someone rude & hot or ugly & nice?
2.   ...

Why was she sending me all this stuff? Click. I deleted it.

Peter tapped me on the shoulder and pointed at the clock. I ignored him. I had to keep looking in case there was something from Gracie.

More junk mail. More junk mail. Then this from Marisa:

Subject: *freakin worried*

dude wher r u? everyonz ttly freakin out.
mom just told me your gramma graciez in
the hospital. wher r u???? luv marisa

I took a deep breath and leaned back. No wonder there were no emails from Gracie. No wonder she wasn't answering her phone. I'll bet her cancer came back. My eyes filled with tears. Please, no, not Gracie.

CHAPTER FIFTEEN

I'd heard that if you don't eat, your stomach shrinks and then you're not hungry anymore. It's not true. My stomach burned all the time. Peter had sold my CDs and the CD player for seven hundred and fifty rubles, about thirty dollars, but a week had passed. We didn't even have enough money left to buy bottled water. That meant either drinking from the sinks in the dirty public restrooms or cupping water with our hands from the fountains. I got a bad stomach ache from doing that.

When we left our tent on Saturday morning, people had already begun strolling through the park. We stationed ourselves under the trees along a shady path that led past the playground. Other kids sat around on the ground, their hands out begging. A guard on horseback came by. All the begging stopped. The minute he was gone, out came the hands.

Pasha set up his stool near a gravel path. Peter took his boom box and moved further away. I sat under a tree and watched. People walked by. Some smiled. Others dropped a few rubles in outstretched hands. The rest just looked the other way and hurried on.

Every so often Peter glanced my way. I got the feeling he was expecting me to do something, hold out my hand, stand on my head, perform a magic trick. The problem was if I started begging, someone might recognize me and call the police. I hadn't told Peter about my picture in the embassy building. When he'd asked what happened, I just said that the guard wouldn't let me upstairs. If Peter knew about my picture, he might get scared and tell me to go away.

Little dribbles of money began appearing in Peter and Pasha's plastic cups, a ruble here, two rubles there, not enough to buy much of anything. Peter turned off his rap music and walked over to me. "You want I show you how to take money?"

I got to my feet. "You mean beg?"

"*Nyet*. Like this."

A lady with a stroller came my way. Peter pushed me so hard that I stumbled forward right into the lady's path. She cried out and jerked the stroller out of the way. I ended up on my hands and knees in the gravel. The lady wheeled around me and stomped off.

I got to my feet and brushed off the gravel which had made dents in my skin. I faced Peter and exploded. "Why'd you do that?"

He made a little downward motion with his eyes. Clutched tight in his hand, almost hidden by his pants leg, was a pink wallet.

I took a step back. "I can't believe you did that." By now the lady was way across the park. I'll bet she didn't even realize her backpack was hanging open.

Peter grinned and stuck the wallet inside his jacket. "You try."

"Are you crazy?" I shouted. It was mean. It was wrong. I could never do that.

Peter kicked a flower with his foot. ""Where you think come rubles? From this?" He grabbed the end of a dangling tree branch. "From this? You been with us is six days now, and what money you get?"

Had he forgotten the CD player?

Peter pointed at Pasha. "Is just small boy, but look how much he get money."

I watched the lady with the stroller disappear around a bend. It was all I could do to keep from snatching the wallet from Peter and running after her, but I didn't dare. Peter'd be done with me for sure if I did that. I looked at him. "Just let me try begging first."

He made a spitting sound and walked away.

This was important. I had to show him I could do it. I pulled out my Padres baseball cap and stuffed my blond hair up inside that. Then I put on the sunglasses Mom had bought for me for surf camp. Maybe no one would recognize me now.

The walkways in the park were becoming more and more crowded. I held out my hand. Nothing.

Maybe if I moved further away by myself.

I picked a sunny spot near a bed of bright yellow daisies where a gray stone goddess watched on. A woman carrying a satchel of groceries strolled by. With a big smile I stepped forward and held out my hand. She didn't even look at me. As I watched her walk off, I made a promise to myself. Whenever I got back to the United States and saw a homeless person begging, I'd give them money, lots of money, as much as I could possibly afford.

A nun swept by. I smiled and stuck out my hand. She completely ignored me.

Next came a guy with a red face and droopy cheeks. He smiled at me.

I gave him a huge smile back.

He stuck his hand in his coat pocket, pulled out a little brown sack, and handed it to me. Inside there was some kind of jelly roll. My stomach grumbled just looking at it. Before I realized what was happening, the man had a hand on my arm and was pulling me toward him. He puckered up his blubbery lips for a kiss.

"Get away!" I shouted and pushed him hard.

He stumbled backwards, gave me a hurt look, and shuffled off.

When I pulled the jelly roll out of the bag, I discovered ants all over it. I made a face and stuck it back in the bag. I was just about to toss it in the trash when Peter appeared. He took the sack and looked inside. Shaking his head, he walked with it back to Pasha. The two shared the roll, ants and all, every bit of it. They even licked their fingers when they were done. My stomach growled again. Maybe I should have had some too.

I went back to begging. It was the same story as before. Everyone ignored me.

I tried taking off my sunglasses. Still no luck.

Maybe I just wasn't doing it right. I practiced the look I'd seen other kids do. It's a lot like the way a dog stares at you when it's hungry. No smile. You keep your head down, and raise just your eyes. It makes you feel awful inside, like you're nothing, like you don't even matter. But then all of a sudden it worked. An old man handed me a coin, only five rubles, about twenty-five cents, but still it was something. Next a lady in a brown coat passed by, gave me a quick glance, and dropped a coin worth twenty-five rubles—that's about one American dollar. I caught Peter's eye and flashed the gold coin at him. He grinned and gave me the thumbs up. Five more people passed my way, and three of them gave me money, enough now for a session at the internet café. No one looks at you for very long. Just drop some money in your hand. Look away. That's it. Goodbye. Did they think we had germs?

Women in bright colored skirts set up a little street fair near Peter and Pasha, just a few booths, women wrapped in shawls selling fruit and vegetables, wooden nesting dolls, embroidered tablecloths. A man showed up with a dancing bear cub. He had it on a leash and fed it with a baby bottle. It was the cutest little thing I'd ever seen. I got up and moved over to watch.

"Look, Pasha." I shook his shoulder and pointed at the bear.

He frowned and kicked the dirt. Peter didn't smile either. Then I saw why. All the people passing by had begun to ignore them. All the rubles were being dropped in the bear's cup.

Every muscle in my stomach tightened. I needed that money, every single coin, for emails, for phone cards, for food.

A bunch of kids walked up and sat down on a bench to watch. One had his CD player turned way up loud playing the kind of fifties rock and roll Gracie likes. It gave me an idea. At home Marisa and I used to pretend we were on *Dancing With The Stars*. It was kind of dorky, two girls dancing together like that, but still…

"Want to dance?" I asked Peter. I put on a pretend smile, took his hands, and we began swaying to the music. I never would have had the nerve to do something like this with a boy at home. I added a few kick steps. Peter copied my every move. All of a sudden he caught on and took over, swinging me out, twirling me back, just like you see on TV. His moves got fancier and fancier until I could barely keep up. Every so often he'd jerk his head back to shake the hair from his eyes. It reminded me of the way the guys do on the videos. His gray-green eyes sparkled as he spun me under his arm. He spun me out again, and we both laughed when he almost let me go. He finished with a real cool move where he swept me in and out between his legs.

I stood there gasping for breath and looking around. I snuck a look at Peter. He winked. I'd never danced with a boy before, and he was so cute. Just thinking of what Marisa might say made me smile.

An audience had formed. They applauded. Pasha wore a grin that could have wrapped around his head three times. He nodded at our cup. It was full to the brim.

* * *

The kids with the rock-and-roll music drifted off to the vendor's stalls, and the three of us went back to begging. I hated it. It made me feel like dirt. I'd much rather earn my money dancing. That had been fun. For a while I'd almost forgotten I was living in Russia begging on the streets.

Out of the corner of my eye a figure in the distance caught my attention. She was walking down a path that led out of the park. Her back was to me, but the shape of her body, the blond hair, the haircut—

"Mom!" I broke into a run, veered across a flower bed, trampling red poppies, and sprinted up the path after her. No more begging. No more Russia. Mom and I were going home.

When I caught up to her, I grabbed her by the arm. She stopped and turned to face me. The bright blue eyes, the long sharp nose—it wasn't Mom at all.

I dropped her arm and lowered my head. "Excuse me," I muttered in Russian.

From down the path Peter shouted, "Katerina." He raced toward me, followed by Pasha stumbling along in his great big boots. When they reached me, Peter pulled his jacket open just slightly so I could peek inside.

I don't know what he was all excited about. All I could see was some stupid CD. I swallowed the lump in my throat. If only he and Pasha would just go away and leave me alone.

"You no understand?" Peter's eyes danced. "Is CD for bebop music." He gestured with his thumb over his shoulder. "I take from kids back there."

Pasha tugged my sleeve, pointed at the CD and began hopping from foot to foot like a dancing monkey.

Peter took my hand and twirled me under his arm. "Now we get much rubles. Is fantastic thing, *da*?" He stopped, and both he and Pasha stood there waiting for me to say something.

I looked at their grinning, sparkling faces, and what else could I do but smile. "*Da*. It's fantastic."

CHAPTER SIXTEEN

It had been three weeks since I'd had a bath. I'd never felt so dirty in my whole life, dirtier even than when Dad took us camping. At least then we could swim every day. I knew how bad I looked by how people moved away from me when I passed them on the street. I daydreamed about hot showers with lots of soap and shampoo, gallons of it, Mom's special kind that smells like piña colada, and afterwards plenty of Essence of Peach lotion. How good it would feel to be clean.

I got Peter to show me where there were some public showers down by the river. The women's side was dark, black with mold, and smelled like it hadn't been cleaned in years, big clumps of hair all over the drains, graffiti all over the walls. Right when I was getting naked, a drunk lady staggered in and threw up all over the floor. I gave up on the idea of a bath and left. Ever since I went there, my feet had been itching like mad.

On Sunday the weather cleared and warmed.

"You want go surfing?" Peter asked.

"Surfing?" It had to be a joke. Before I could block them out, images filled my head: hot summer afternoons at the beach in San Diego, surfboards dotting the waves, the smell of suntan lotion and seaweed baking in the sun. It all disappeared as an icy wave of homesickness crashed over me.

Peter pulled the blanket off the tree branch and folded it under his arm. "We go beach."

Did he mean a real beach? I remembered McDonald's and decided I'd better not get my hopes up.

We took the green line and got off near the river. From there we walked across the bridge by the zoo over to the Peter and Paul Fortress where the golden spire on the bell tower rose high into the sky.

The beach was nothing but a narrow strip of dirt running in front of the gray stone walls of the fortress. If you tried hard, you could imagine the ripples splashing the shore were real waves, but the Neva river water didn't look very nice. It was cloudy and brown with little bits of leaves and dirt and stuff floating around. Groups of people that looked like the white-skinned tourists from Arizona that come to San Diego every summer leaned against the wall, sunbathing, older people mostly, the men in tight speedos, a few women in bikinis. Peter led us away from them to an empty spot further down where he spread our blanket over the pebbles.

Even though the day was warm, the breeze off the water felt cool. Just a few people swam, and they didn't stay in for long. I took off my sandals and tiptoed toward the water. Sharp stones stabbed the soft places on the bottoms of my feet. At the shoreline I stuck my toe in the water. It was so icy it stung.

Peter and Pasha dropped their stuff and began taking their clothes off. Pasha stripped down to a pair of worn thin underpants with faded pictures of Bugs Bunny all over them. Peter took everything off but his tattered Levis. The outline of each bone in his ribcage showed. The skin covering it looked like pale blue cellophane.

I dropped onto a corner of the blanket and stared out at the river. A layer of dirty yellow haze hung over it. Near the shore on the other side a big gray ship gave out five loud blasts of its horn. Clouds of black poured from its smokestack as it began moving out into the river.

Peter made a big sweep with his hand and smiled. "You like?"

I nodded. "Oh, yeah, it's great." A cold brown river? A tiny strip of rocks?

He stood up and took Pasha by the hand. The two moved toward the river, stepping gingerly over the sharp rocks. Once in the water, they stood, knee deep, splashing themselves and shivering. Peter rubbed himself all over with a bar of soap, scrubbing his skin hard, lathering his scalp. When he was done, he made Pasha do it too.

"*Adeen, dva, tree,*" Russian for *one, two, three*. At the count they dunked under. No laughing, no clowning around like kids at home would have done.

Pasha rose first, water streaming off his face. He raced for shore and flopped down beside me. His freezing cold skin brushed mine. I jerked away and made a face, pretending I'd been touched by a piece of ice. He didn't smile. His teeth were chattering so bad he couldn't. His thin little body vibrated like a flag in a windstorm.

I pulled my terry jacket out of my backpack and wrapped it around him. "Brrrrr." I hugged him tight, rubbing his arms, his legs.

A rusty metal ship steamed by making a big roar and a wake that crashed against the shore. Peter grabbed a piece of wood floating nearby and used it like a boogie board to surf the waves.

He rose from the water, grinning, and came up on the beach.

"Here, surfer girl." He handed me the soap.

I stared down at my capris with the mud and grass stains all over them. My whole body felt sticky, my hair so oily I could barely stand to touch it. I got up, tiptoed over the sharp stones down to the water, and waded in. The cold made my bones ache. A plastic grocery bag wrapped itself around my leg. "Ick!" I shook and jumped around to shake it off. There were other things in the water that you couldn't have seen from shore, bits of a styrofoam cup, a banana peel, something rubber that looked like a balloon. Finally I worked up the nerve to duck under. I rose gasping for breath. Quickly I soaped what I could, then dunked again, and raced back up onto the beach.

An oily, chemical smell clung to my body. I didn't feel clean at all.

Pasha touched my arm. "Brrrrr." It was a perfect imitation of what I'd just said to him.

Peter lay back on his elbows and gazed up at the sky. He smiled. "How you say this time?"

"You mean daytime?"

He shook his head. "*Nyet. Nyet.* Is when is much sun. Much warm. Much day."

I wrung handfuls of water from my soggy pants legs. "You mean summertime?"

"*Da. Da.* Summertime. Is good time, summertime, *Da*?"

I wondered about winter. Gracie'd told me that St. Petersburg's practically at the Arctic Circle. I imagined blue icebergs, mountains of snow, miles of white. It had been pretty cold last night in the tent, and this was only the first week of August. I couldn't imagine sleeping there with snow on the ground.

"So, what about winter?" I asked Peter. "What do you do then?"

He hugged himself and shuddered. "We go Moskovsky Station."

Something about the way he said it made me shiver.

I rested back on my elbows. The warmth of the sun made my hopes rise. Dad used to say, you can make anything happen if you try hard enough. I needed to keep trying. I needed to see if there was anything back from Marisa on the last email I sent her. If only I knew more about Gracie. It's just that it was scary going to the internet café. I was always afraid someone would recognize me there.

Peter sat up, and his body snapped to attention. Far down the beach a man in uniform strolled our way. I recognized the red band on the cap, a policeman. He broke into a fast walk, almost a jog. Even from a distance he seemed to be looking right at me.

Before Peter could move another inch, I was on my feet. "Let's get out of here."

In a flash we were off the beach, off the island, back on the subway.

Peter shook his head. I knew what he was going to say— *Meeleetsia* bad. Stay away from *meeleetsia*.

He didn't need to say it. I already knew that rule.

CHAPTER SEVENTEEN

First the batteries went dead on Peter's boom box so we couldn't do our dance routine. We didn't have quite enough money to buy new ones, and it was a holiday so the stores wouldn't be open anyway. Then, just as we were reaching out our hands to start begging, along came the dancing bear and stole everyone's attention.

Pasha sat on his small stool, his chin in his hands, his brow furrowed, watching. From the storm clouds in his eyes I could tell he would have liked to kill that bear. Another guy came along with a chimpanzee on a chain. It wore an orange and purple striped sweater and a baseball cap. When it saw Pasha, it peeled back its lips and showed him all its teeth. Pasha scowled. The monkey pulled a wad of chewing gum from its mouth and threw it at Pasha. The crowd looking on laughed. Pasha picked the gum out of the dirt and held it up to inspect it. I knew what he was thinking.

"Nyet, nyet," Pasha. I grabbed the gum and threw it away.

Pasha picked up a handful of dirt and threw it at the monkey. The crowd laughed even harder. The chimp screeched and did a little dance. Clank, jingle, jang went the sound of the coins being dropped in its cup.

Peter made a disgusted face, turned, and walked off without saying where he was going. A family of four settled down on the grass nearby for a picnic. I stared at their happy faces, lit by the golden sun. Mom and Dad and I used to go on picnics all the time, to the beach in the summer, to Balboa Park in the winter. It had been so much fun.

Behind me the man was changing the monkey into a clown suit for its next act. I couldn't take my eyes off the family picnicking. I licked my lips as the little boy popped grapes into his mouth and his sister munched crackers. The dad opened a little tin of something, probably herring, and passed it around. My mouth watered. And to think that just a few weeks back I wouldn't have touched that stuff. I'd eat the whole can right now if I could. For dessert they ate marshmallows raw. We used to roast them over a bonfire at the beach. Sometimes we'd make smores—chocolatey, crunchy, gooey smores. The thought nearly killed me.

The family rose to leave, dropping their sacks in the trash can before they went. I was about to go over and check to see if they'd left anything good when the angry voice of the chimpanzee's owner made me turn. He and Pasha were having a tug-of-war over Pasha's money cup. Pasha ended up on his rear in the dirt. The man emptied out Pasha's rubles into his own cup then tossed Pasha's cup into the flowers. Just then Peter returned. With some patience he got the screaming, crying Pasha to explain. Apparently Pasha had set his cup near the monkey's, and, sure enough, it had begun to fill with money too. Smart little boy!

I retrieved his cup for him and stuck my tongue out at the mean man. The chimp saw me do it and stuck his tongue out too. Then Peter and Pasha did it. Everyone cracked up. The furious owner, his eyes bulging, yelled at us and made us go away.

Just as we were leaving, I remembered the picnickers. When I searched the trash, I discovered their bag of marshmallows with eight left. I opened the bag and sniffed. The sweet smell that flowed back at me made my taste buds go wild. Maybe just one. Peter and Pasha'd gone on ahead. They'd never know. Just then Peter turned and looked back. I clamped the bag shut and waved it at him. "Dinner."

* * *

Above our heads giant pastel curtains danced across the evening sky. Pinks, greens, lavenders, pale yellows. It was the Aurora Borealis. My dad told me about it once, but I never thought I'd see it in real life. The woods around us smelled damp. Our blanket glistened with dew. Every so often a cool breeze whispered through the pines.

In front of us a warm fire crackled. I'd helped Peter clear a spot in the dirt, and we'd made a little fire out of twigs and pine needles. He and Pasha had wanted to eat the marshmallow raw on the way back, but I persuaded them not to. Nothing's as good as roasted marshmallows. Nothing in the whole wide world.

"See, you put them on the end of the stick like this and hold it over the fire."

As it turned out most of them were covered with ants, but it didn't matter. They sparkled and sizzled and dropped off when we held them over the fire.

I popped the first marshmallow into my mouth and closed my eyes. The taste was unbelievable—crunchy and charcoal tasting on the outside and like a hot, sugary cloud on the inside.

After two, I began to feel thirsty. Pasha had already disappeared inside the tent. I crawled in after him to see if I could find some water. I stopped. There lay Pasha, flat on his back, sucking milk from a baby bottle. I wondered if he'd stolen it out of the back of somebody's stroller.

I tried to stifle a laugh, but it came out through my nose.

He gave me a sheepish grin and offered the bottle to me.

I shook my head and called back over my shoulder to Peter. "You gotta see this. Pasha has a baby bottle." I wasn't mad at him for trying to hide it from us. After all, he was just a little boy.

I beckoned to him. "Come on out and show Peter what you got."

Pasha picked up the half-full bottle, slung his other arm through the strap of his backpack and crawled outside.

Peter questioned Pasha in Russian then turned to me laughing so hard he could barely speak. "Pasha say he steal milk bottle of bear."

Pasha pulled another full bottle from his backpack and held it up, smiling. Next he retrieved a striped sweater and slipped it on over his head. When he stood up, it fit fine except that the sleeves dragged on the ground. He did a little dance hopping from one leg to the other and making chimp noises. Peter and I looked at each other and burst out laughing. Pasha'd gotten back at the monkey all right.

After we stomped out the fire, we all crawled inside the tent, lay on our backs, and passed around the bottles of milk. Peter and I kicked our feet in the air and pretended to be babies. Pasha screamed with laughter. Lydia arrived, bringing damp doggy smells. She crawled in beside us and began licking the milk off everyone's face. That made Pasha laugh even harder.

The milk was thick as cream and tasted like vitamins, but, who cared. It was the first time I'd gone to sleep with a full stomach since I'd left the apartment. I lay on my back and stared up through the tent opening at the sky. Behind the pine branches the colors of the Aurora Borealis were shimmering sheets of light. Whoever would have thought that marshmallows, baby bottles, and the sound of a little boy's laughter could make you feel so good?

* * *

Lydya's growl vibrated, deep inside her throat.

I sat up straight. Peter's eyes shot open. Pasha cried out.

Circles of light crisscrossed the roof of our tent. Outside twigs snapped, leaves crunched. Men talked, their words hushed. A figure crouched at the entrance to our tent. Something flickered on his chest—a badge.

Lydya growled again, low like thunder.

A flashlight bright as a car's headlights blinded me. I froze, too scared to move. They'd been looking for me. Now they'd found me.

Lydya lunged. The man at the tent opening cried out and tipped over backwards.

Peter scrambled out of the tent after the dog. I crawled out after him, followed by Pasha.

There were two policemen. Lydya was barking so hard at the one on the ground that I think the guy was afraid to get up. He stared up at the growling dog, his face pale as the moonlight. The other guy yelled something at Peter in Russian. Peter tugged at Lydya's collar, but he couldn't get her to budge. I pulled Pasha out of the way.

The policeman who was standing pulled his gun. A flash exploded from its nozzle, followed by a loud pop.

Lydya let out a shrill yelp, and her rear collapsed sideways. Peter let go of her collar and sprung backwards. Pasha jerked out of my grasp and started toward the dog. Before he could get to her, one of the policemen pushed him away.

Slowly Lydya straightened on her hindquarters. Without a look back she shuffled off into the forest, loping on three legs, whimpering as she went.

"Lydya, Lydya," Pasha shrieked. He started to go after her and tripped in his clumsy big boots. Tears streamed down his face. He got to his feet and ran screaming at the man with the gun. His little body became a small tornado, kicking, hitting, biting, punching.

The man picked Pasha up by the arm and tossed him to the side like a sack of garbage.

Something inside of me exploded. I didn't care if they were policemen. I didn't even care if they recognized me. Head down I went straight for the man who'd thrown Pasha and butted him in the stomach. Kicking, screaming, I pounded him with my fists.

He slammed his elbow into my chest and knocked the wind out of me. I doubled over onto the ground, struggling for air.

The other policeman yanked our tent apart, kicking at piles of our clothes, tossing things onto the ground.

Still gasping, I got to my feet and stood beside Peter and Pasha.

The first policeman advanced toward us waving the back of his hand.

We didn't argue. We left.

The playhouse at the edge of the park became our shelter for the rest of the night.

"Lydya, Lydya," Pasha sobbed.

I wanted to cry too, but I needed to be strong for Pasha. I tried to hug him, but it did no good. I made the pink pig dance like a puppet in front of him. That didn't work either. I wished I knew words in Russian that would make him feel better.

Peter sat in a corner of the playhouse, his eyes straight ahead, his jaw clenched.

When morning came, we sneaked back to the camp. Some of our stuff was still there, but no Lydya. I noticed spots of red on the dried leaves along the trail she'd taken, but I didn't say anything about it. I didn't want Pasha to get upset again.

"We go make camp at different place," Peter said as he gathered up our blanket and the sheet.

"Lydya, Lydya." Pasha searched the bushes, looked behind trees, wandered in circles. "Lydya, Lydya."

Peter barked an order that sounded like *shut up*. He motioned for us to follow him.

"*Nyet Nyet*. Lydya, Lydya." Pasha wouldn't budge.

With a jerk of his shoulders, Peter turned and marched off down the path away from our camp. I followed him, every so often looking back to see if Pasha was coming.

I stopped. "He's not coming, Peter. I'm going back."

"*Nyet*." Peter put out his arm. "No Pasha come, is stupid boy." He spit out the word. "No need stupid boy."

I couldn't believe what Peter was saying.

My voice squeaked. "But he's just a little boy."

Peter put his face up close to mine. The hard look in his eyes scared me. "No is America, Katerina. No is good life. Is Ruseeya." He jerked his arm for me to follow. "Come."

I stepped back. "No way. I'm not leaving Pasha."

Peter stuck out his chin. "Okay, you want be stupid Americanka." He turned and left. His ragged Levis flopped against his legs as he headed off through the woods. The path curved, a tree branch snapped back into place, and he was out of sight.

My heart felt like someone had tied a bag of stones to it. Peter wasn't big, but he was protection. Without him there was no bebop act, no money. How would we make it, just Pasha and me and his tiny accordion?

I took off running after Peter. Maybe I could persuade him to go back with me for Pasha. After a few steps, I changed my mind and stopped. I needed to go back and get Pasha now. He was only six. He might get lost. We might not be able to find him. I turned and went back the way I'd come.

Finally, I just plain stopped. I didn't know what to do. The sun slid behind a cloud turning everything from green to gray. A breeze made the pine needles whisper. I listened.

Footsteps sounded, boots scuffing the ground. Pasha appeared, his face stained with tears. Seconds later from the other direction twigs snapped, bushes rustled, and there came Peter.

He gave me an angry look and dropped to the ground. "Stupid *Americanka*. Stupid Lydya. Stupid Pasha." He folded his arms and put his head down, hiding his face. His shoulders shook.

I turned away. He wouldn't have wanted me to see him cry.

* * *

About a week later the three of us happened to be standing at the crosswalk leading out of the park when Pasha began jumping up and down shrieking, "Lydya. Lydya."

I followed his gaze. Across the street about a block and a half down a man and a dog walked up the sidewalk. Thick brown dreadlocks swung from the dog's side, and it limped so badly that one of its hind legs barely touched the ground.

"It's Lydya." I shouted.

Peter squinted and frowned. "*Nyet*, Lydya."

I noticed a flash of white on the upper flank of the dog's hind leg. "*Da, da*, Peter. Look. It's got a bandage."

Pasha darted forward, and I had to grab him by his jacket to keep him from dashing in front of a bunch of oncoming cars. The light turned green for us to cross, but before we could reach the other side, a bus stopped, and the man and the dog got on board.

"Lydyaaaa," Pasha's voice faded away as the bus disappeared around a corner.

"Explain to him, Peter. Explain that Lydya's daddy came to save her. That Lydya's alive and safe and we should be happy."

Peter wrinkled his brow. "Lydya have man for papa? Crazy *Americanka*!"

I noticed he was grinning though.

That night we had a party to celebrate that Lydya hadn't died—half a can of sardines we found in the trash, some grapes Peter snitched from the back of a lady's stroller and, best of all, Hostess Cupcakes, fresh new ones right out of the package. We bought them with the extra money Peter had saved up. I had to tickle him and make him laugh to get him to do it.

* * *

The days were getting shorter. Darkness came at nine. Without Lydya, we had to snuggle close together just to keep warm. Sometimes we had the Northern Lights. Other times it was only the rain. Nights were the worst. That's when I thought about Mom and home and everything I missed. I tried not to cry, and when I did, I was careful not to make a sound. I needed to be strong and brave like my dad. Crybabies would never make it in Russia.

The icy air crackled. You could see your own breath. It had been so cold last night I'd hardly slept. Beneath the blanket my feet felt numb. They'd turned white, the big toe blue. I could barely stand to touch them.

Peter took one look at my feet and made the announcement, "We go Moskovsky Station."

I looked at the date on my watch. September 8th.

School would have started today. Without me. I remembered other first days of school, the smell of the erasers on new pencils, the crisp feel of Levis that hadn't been washed yet, shoes stiff and just out of the box. It didn't do any good to think about things like that. I had a new life to worry about now and a new home called Moskovsky Station. I needed to focus on that. I needed to be ready.

CHAPTER EIGHTEEN

On a cold gray morning we gathered up all our stuff and headed for Moskovsky Station. In Russian it's pronounced *Moskovsky Vokzal*, which means the Moscow Station because that's where the rail line goes. Our load was too heavy to jump the turnstiles in the metro so we had to walk the whole way.

Pasha stomped right in the middle of a big puddle, spraying muddy water all over the back of Peter's pants. Peter turned and gave him a dirty look.

I skipped to catch up with Peter. "What's the station like?"

He took a giant step to avoid another giant puddle. "Are many trains."

I could have figured that out.

The sidewalk narrowed. I slipped behind him and in front of Pasha so that we could go single file. "But where will we sleep? What will we eat?"

Peter shook his head. "Is too many questions." Head down, he marched onward, limping slightly. The day before the rubber tread came entirely off the bottom of his shoe.

"Fine. I'll just find out for myself."

A drizzly sky hung behind the train station as we approached it from Uprising Square. Big block letters ran along the length of the roof spelling out the name, "Моско́вский Вокза́л." In between the two words on the roof stood a huge clock tower with the Russian flag waving on top. The building had lots of fancy arches and columns and windows with decorations over them. It didn't look bad at all.

As we climbed the steps, icy raindrops slid down my neck and inside my jacket. We went through revolving doors into a large entrance hall. The first thing I noticed was the mosaic on the ceiling, people waving an Olympic flag on a bright blue background. It felt strange looking at that sunny blue mosaic sky when it was so cold and gray outside.

From the hall we moved into a giant room with glittery crystal chandeliers that hung in a row down the center. Everything was made of stone and marble with swirly carved out patterns along the walls. A train station? It looked more like a palace to me.

The huge empty space above us echoed with the sounds of people going places, suitcase wheels rolling, the tap-tap of shoes on marble floors. Over a loudspeaker a deep Russian voice made an announcement. We pushed past a group of grownups in wool coats and dodged a circle of older kids who'd plopped down on their duffel bags right in the middle of everything.

Through an archway held up by two naked statues we came into a long hall. On one side was a railing where you could see down to the train tracks. On the other side there were shops, restaurants, even an internet café. The food smells made my head whirl: a whiff of fried onions, Starbucks coffee, cookies baking. A bookstore had Harry Potter in the window. Next door a shop sold souvenir T-Shirts, baseball caps, backpacks. It felt like I was back in San Diego walking through the mall.

From somewhere down below us came the shrill sound of train wheels scraping against metal.

A group of older kids wearing college sweatshirts stopped and took chairs at a tiny round table in front of a food counter. I didn't understand what they were saying, only that it wasn't Russian. They looked so happy, jabbering away, punching each other, laughing at each other's jokes. I'll bet they were foreign exchange students having fun traveling through Russia.

I had twenty rubles I'd been saving for the internet café. It was only worth about seventy-five cents, but it wouldn't hurt to at least look at the menu. I pulled out a chair with a curved metal back and sat down. Peter watched me, frowning. Pasha walked across to the railing and stood with his head resting against it, staring down at the trains.

A waitress came by with a tray of food and some menus, which she handed to the college kids. Then she saw me. Instead of giving me a menu, she swatted me over the head with it. *"Provalivai, provalivai,"* she yelled.

I swallowed hard to keep the tears down. For just a minute I'd felt like I was back in my old life. The shops, the smell of the food, the kids—it had felt so good.

In the glass panel of a food display I caught sight of a poor street girl, stringy, greasy hair hanging down from underneath a baseball cap, cheekbones sticking out like she was anorexic, a dirty face. Her eyes looking back at me were so sad. *I'll never get to looking like that,* I promised myself.

Then I realized. The cap on her head had the big letters S D on the front, S D for San Diego Padres.

The waitress began unloading her tray of food onto the little table where the college kids sat. The onion rings smelled so good, and I couldn't have any. Before I even realized what I was doing, my hand shot out, and I snatched a bag off her tray.

Her mouth dropped open. She took a step back. When I realized what I'd done, I felt almost as surprised as she looked. Should I put the bag back? I almost did, but I saw Peter motioning for me frantically to get out of there, and then I noticed a policeman coming down the hall.

Peter streaked off in the other direction, dragging our heavy trash bag, his boom box under one arm. I sped after him. We found a hiding place behind a statue of a group of soldiers. A few seconds later, Pasha caught up, clump-clumping along in his poor old boots. We crouched there behind a bronze man holding a gun and grinned at each other as we munched onion rings. They were better than McDonald's, thinner, crispier, crunchier, the best I'd ever tasted. I'd never stolen a thing in my whole life. But I didn't worry about that or what Dad would say or what Gracie would say or what anyone would say. The only part I worried about was the policeman. If I was going to steal, I needed to be smarter next time.

* * *

As we approached the escalators from above we could see down to the train tracks, rows and rows of them, with long strips like sidewalks in between where people stood waiting. When we started down, my heart began to sink. Homeless people were everywhere, lining the walls, leaning against the columns, hunched over, hands held out. Some sat with their heads buried in their arms. Others lay on the floor curled into tight little balls. Even from a distance I could see that most of them were kids like me.

I didn't want to go down and be with all those people. I didn't belong there.

"Can't we please stay upstairs?" I asked Peter.

He pressed his lips together. "*Nyet. Meeleetsia* come. Make go away."

We stepped off the escalator into a long open area that ran in front of the tracks. There were columns and designs on the ceiling like we'd seen upstairs, but the floors weren't so clean, and the walls were smudged and tagged by gangs here and there. The whole place smelled of trains and oil and dirty steam.

Peter's eyes roamed. Pasha hovered close.

I moved past two stray dogs over to the tracks where I could see back up to the place we'd come from—the room with the glittery chandeliers, the shops, the snack bars, the nice smells. I wanted so badly to stay up there, but I knew better than to complain.

Pasha and I followed Peter as he looked for a spot for us to camp, past a kiosk selling Cokes, past another escalator, past a machine that sold newspapers, past a big poster advertising cell phones.

A kid lay asleep on the floor. In his outstretched hand he held his baseball cap with a picture of the Virgin Mary propped up inside. A passenger walking past almost stepped on his hand. Next to him sat a girl, resting her forehead on her knees, her hand held out to beg. Her arm was covered with pink scabby sores. She raised her head as we passed by. "*Pazhalsta?*"

I was afraid she was going to touch me and I'd get her disease.

As we continued down the hall, I kept seeing her eyes, flat, glazed over, almost as if she were blind.

"How about there?" I pointed at an empty space over by the wall. Peter shook his head. Something silver flashed. The kid sitting nearby had a knife.

We ended up way down at the end of the hall near platform eleven. I could see why no one else wanted to sit there. It smelled like vomit, and every so often I got a whiff of pee. Right in the middle of the passageway a girl about my age lay on the ground. She didn't move. I wondered if she was dead.

We dropped our trash bag and all our stuff and sat down.

I pulled up my legs and rested my head on my knees.

I'd wondered what Moskovsky Station was like. Now I knew.

* * *

10:00 p.m. We'd been sitting here for at least two hours. My bottom hurt, and I itched all over from not having had a bath in so long. I daydreamed of a hot shower followed by a steak dinner. My stomach was so empty it felt like it was eating itself from the inside out. Pasha slumped over against our trash bag, fast asleep. Peter read his comic books. I stared at the trains. Every so often my eyes drifted to the girl lying on the floor. I felt like I should do something.

A train whistle sounded. Light shone from one of the tunnels, getting brighter and brighter, closer and closer. A train came into view, silver and red with lots of windows and passengers looking out. Through one a little girl waved to an old lady standing on the platform. Lucky little girl. I'll bet it was her grandmother waiting.

Just as I was about to drift off to sleep, another train came. First the far-off whistle. Then came the rumble that grew louder and louder until you could feel its vibration in the floor. The brakes screeched as it pulled into the station. With a big whoosh it stopped, and I uncovered my ears.

11 p.m. My head snapped up. Another train coming. More noise. More passengers. The same thing all over again.

A stray dog wandered over and sniffed at the girl lying in the aisle. She still hadn't moved an inch. Not even a finger fluttered. Her baseball cap covered her face, so I couldn't tell if she was dead or alive. Passengers from the train that had just come in flooded toward her. Right at the last minute they parted, veering left, veering right, to avoid stepping on her. No one looked down. It was as if she wasn't even there.

I elbowed Peter and pointed. "Do you think she's dead?"

He shrugged and went back to reading his comic book.

A guard in a uniform stood further down, his arms folded, gazing out over the trains. He wasn't a policeman. I decided to risk it. I got to my feet and walked over to him.

I pointed at the girl.

He took a step forward and looked, shrugged, and stepped back.

"But—" If only I could make him understand. "*Dyevachka*," I said, which means *girl*. Again I pointed.

He flicked the back of his hand at me and turned around.

I gave up and returned to my seat by the wall.

Pasha woke up and began fiddling with his accordion.

I stared at the girl. What if it were me? If I were sick, would anyone care? The answer left me cold inside.

A little while later three men in orange jumpsuits appeared and huddled down over the girl. My hopes rose until I realized what they were doing. They stuffed her in a big plastic bag, carried her off, and that was that.

Beside me Pasha stared up at the ceiling and squeezed out the tune to It's A Small World, note by note. He should have been home safe in bed, with his mom and dad nearby. Instead this.

Oh, God. I buried my face in my hands.

* * *

Midnight. The trains finally stopped. The vendors closed the shutters on their kiosks. All the passengers went away. That left just us kids and the bums and the strays.

The lights in the station stayed on, but somehow it felt darker. A chilly draft snuck down the hall toward us. I shivered and pulled my jacket tighter. Beside me Peter slouched against the wall, hugging his boom box, half-asleep. Every so often his eyes would snap open when a group of kids walked too near. Pasha lay curled up beside me with his head in my lap. I wiggled my rear, trying to shift into some new position where my butt wouldn't hurt so bad without waking him up. I was so tired, and I wanted to sleep, but how could anyone sleep on this hard floor? All I could think about was a warm house and a cozy bed filled with soft feathery comforters. Even our tent in the woods had been better than this place.

1 a.m. A drunk swung down the hall toward us, crashed up against the wall, and vomited all over the floor.

I didn't have to convince Peter. We moved.

Our new spot didn't smell so bad. We sat across from a billboard advertising trips to the Caribbean. Something about the turquoise water, the palm trees, the beautiful white sandy beach made me relax. This was a better place. Much, much better.

I dreamed about surfing. It was a nice dream until a giant wave crashed over me. I awoke to find a fight going on. A skinhead pushed a guy with spiked purple hair hard, sending him careening across the platform. The purple-haired guy recovered just in time to keep from falling over the edge into the train pit. He rose to a crouch, his eyes narrowed. He sprang at the skinhead. A blade flashed and a line of red appeared down the skinhead's face. He stumbled backwards, put a hand to his face, turned, and ran screaming toward the escalators. The purple-haired guy slunk off in the other direction.

I wondered if I'd ever be able to go back to sleep after that.

Something bumped my foot. My eyes flew open. A kid with a narrow face and a long thin nose stood over me, half a cigarette dangling from his lips. Behind him stood two other guys with greasy hair and a girl wearing a buzz-cut. The four gazed down at me, paralyzing me with their stares. The kid with the wolf face kicked my foot again, then Peter's. Before Peter's eyes were even open, he was on his feet. Pasha sat up straight, his eyes wide.

The narrow-faced kid growled something at us in Russian.

Peter muttered to me under his breath. "He say is his place."

We didn't argue. We didn't say a thing. We just left.

3 a.m. A shrill, high-pitched scream jolted me awake. Stiff with fear, I sat there, not moving. Another scream. It came from down the long dark hallway that led to the metro lines.

Peter came awake just as a third scream faded off over the trains. Pasha opened his round dark eyes and stared up at me. Then came the scream again. It was a girl's voice. I couldn't tell how old. Was she being raped? Was she being murdered? I pulled Pasha closer.

We sat there frozen, listening, but nothing happened. Finally Peter closed his eyes. Pasha's heavy lashes drifted downward. I couldn't go back to sleep. Not for the rest of the night, period.

7 a.m. A whistle sounded. I never thought I'd be so glad to hear the sound. Night was over. Morning had finally come.

* * *

The second night was even scarier than the first.

"Mama. Mama." A little boy cried out in his sleep. All night long they wailed, all up and down the wall, worse than the first night, little kids, big kids, all crying out for their moms.

"Mama. Mama." It melted into the far-off sound of a train whistle.

Pasha lay with his head on my lap watching as I made the little pink pig scamper up and down his arm.

"Mama. Mama." It was the Goth kid with all the piercings, the same kid who'd challenged Peter for our spot earlier.

Peter winced and stared at the ceiling.

The boy cried out again.

Peter closed his eyes. A tear spilled out and crawled down his cheek. I wished there was something I could say to make him feel better.

Pasha stuck his thumb in his mouth and pretended to be asleep. His cheeks moved in and out as he sucked his thumb. I pulled it out, and it made a sound like a popping cork. He stuck it back in. I pulled it out again. Pop! I smiled. He giggled.

A drunk with a gray pony tail staggered toward us clutching a brown paper sack. His eyes were so red it looked like someone had poured chlorine in them.

A group of kids came up behind him. They began laughing and taunting him, pulling his hair, kicking him. He spun in clumsy circles and batted at them with his arms. Nothing was working. The kids wouldn't stop. One ran at him and butted him in the rear. The guy staggered, heading straight for us. I leaned over Pasha's body to protect him. Barely in time the guy recovered his balance.

Peter and Pasha and I scooted back as close against the wall as we could possibly get, hugging our legs, trying to keep our feet out of the way.

All of a sudden the drunk guy was on the ground and the kids were all over him.

Pasha pulled the hood of his jacket down over his face. I didn't want to watch either, but I had to in case the kids might come at us.

They pulled off his shiny blue baseball jacket, then his gray sweater, then his white shirt underneath that. He struggled but it did no good. Out of the corner of my eye I saw a guard headed our way. When he saw what was happening, he turned and went back the other way.

Finally the kids were done. They got up, and the drunk lurched to his feet. All he had on was a saggy pair of washer-worn underpants. He hugged himself and moaned, his face, hollow, hopeless. I realized I was shaking. What if it had been Peter? There's no way we could have held off a gang like that.

We moved twice more that night and ended up in front of platform nine near a silver trash cylinder that smelled like old cigarettes and pee—our new home.

CHAPTER NINETEEN

Winter was coming. There were fewer travelers, less money. Even the stray dogs were looking bony.

I tried to hide away as many rubles as I could for emails, but when I finally had enough for the minimum, a half an hour, there was a policeman standing guard at the internet café in the station so I didn't dare go in. I guess they'd had some trouble at this one. I would have gone to the other internet café way across town, but Peter didn't like it when I left for that long because someone always had to guard our stuff. It seemed like something was always keeping me from getting back online.

While Peter went off to search the trashcans upstairs, Pasha and I stayed to watch our stuff. A college girl in a heavy wool sweater and tight jeans strolled down the hall and stopped right in front of us to watch the trains. She pulled a small yellow package from her bag. I recognized the wrapping, a Double Big Mac with cheese. She unwrapped the burger, and I got a whiff of pickle relish that made my taste buds zing. She took a big bite. I could taste the cheese, all melted and gooey, the meat and its juices, the sauce, the relish, the onions, the bun.

Pasha licked his lips.

One of the stray dogs watched the girl too, strings of drool dangling from its jaws. Quietly, it sneaked up behind her, let out a deep growl, and nipped at her leg.

The girl's hands flew into the air, sending the hamburger sailing. It landed on the floor just inches from Pasha's feet. Pasha leaned forward and reached for it, but before he could pick it up, the dog pounced. Pasha was lucky it didn't bite his hand off. The dog devoured the burger in two gulps and slunk off down the hall after another victim. We'd already seen four dogs do the same trick. I wondered if they learned it from each other.

The girl fumed for a minute and shook her head, then walked off.

The dog trotted back our way. Pasha's glaring eyes followed it. A train pulled into the station. Passengers flowed past ignoring our outstretched hands. Pasha played his accordion. Still no rubles. Departing travelers approached from the opposite direction. A lady wearing a long black fur coat stood near the edge of the platform gazing out over the trains. She pulled out a sandwich wrapped in paper. It was a foot long, and the woman was teeny. I wondered if she'd be able to eat it all.

Pasha watched the lady take her first bite and licked his lips. He leaned forward onto his hands and knees and crawled toward her. The woman was too busy eating and watching the trains to notice him coming. I thought about stopping him, but by then it was too late. He crawled up behind her, let out a deep growl and snapped at the back of her coat. Sure enough, she dropped her sandwich.

A stray dog zoomed in and was about to snatch the food, but Pasha beat him to it. He kicked the dog away, grabbed the sandwich, and raced off down the hall. The dog chased him, but gave up when he got on the escalator. The lady started to go after Pasha, stopped, shrugged, and walked away. As she passed by, she gave me a dirty look. I just smiled.

Pasha returned ten minutes later with grease on his face, wearing a proud smile. He handed me the remains of the sandwich. I couldn't believe it. This little bitty kid had eaten practically the whole thing.

* * *

When you don't eat for a long time, something weird happens to you. You get to thinking funny things and your mind wanders all over the place. Pasha and Peter had gone upstairs to search the trashcans by the restaurants. I leaned against the wall and stared at the poster of the Caribbean. We'd moved back here last night when some gang kids stole our old spot. I liked this place better anyway. I stared at the turquoise water and tried to imagine myself a million miles away, on some warm sandy beach, riding the waves with Dad.

A man with blond hair wearing nice slacks and a long black coat walked by, smiled and winked. He looked exactly like my dad—same smile, same wink, same everything.

I had to smile back.

He stopped and backed up, doing this funny kind of walk like comedians do. "Hi."

I couldn't believe it. He said it in English. It was so spacey. Even his voice sounded like Dad's.

"Hi." I gave him a shy wave back.

"You're American?" he asked.

I nodded.

He cocked his head and smiled. "So, what's an American girl doing here in Moskovsky Station?"

"We lost our passports. Actually they were stolen. It's kind of a long story." I was so excited I was out of breath. I couldn't believe it. A real, live American.

He squatted to eye level. "I like long stories. Why don't you tell me?"

I wanted to tell him he looked just like Dad. Instead I told him about our passports being stolen and not being able to reach Gracie. He seemed so nice and safe that I almost mentioned the Vlad part, but at the last moment, I chickened out.

He balanced himself on the floor with his fingertips. "If you'd like, I could help you get in touch with your grandmother."

"But she's in the hospital and—" I couldn't bring myself to add that she might be dead.

"I'll bet I could find her." He winked. "I have connections in San Diego."

"Wow! Really?"

"Yes, really." He rose to his feet and took my hand to pull me up.

"My name's John."

"John." I dusted the back of my pants off. "My dad's name was Ian. That's Irish for John."

He grinned. "Maybe we're related. What's your name?"

"Carly, actually Katerina in Russian."

"Katerina." He rolled his eyes. "A pretty name for a pretty girl."

I blushed and looked away.

He studied me. "Are you hungry?"

Was he kidding?

He rubbed his stomach. "I'm famished. Let's go have dinner. You can tell me all about your grandmother, okay?" He took my hand, and we started off toward the escalator.

A hand grabbed my arm and yanked me backwards. "What you do, Katerina?"

It was Peter, his face furious.

John let go of my hand and stepped back, his eyes darting nervously about.

Peter took a step toward him and fired off a bunch of angry sounding words in Russian.

John raised his palms. "Okay. Okay." He backed up, turned, and walked off.

"But he was an American," I screeched at Peter, "and he was going to help me call my grandmother." Angry tears pricked the back of my eyes.

Peter took my arms and gave me a sharp shake. "Katerina, you have no brain?"

"But he was just like my dad," I wailed.

He spit on the ground. "They *all* just like Dad."

"He was going to buy me dinner."

Peter leaned in to where his face was just inches from mine. "He fuck you."

"Oh, God!" I turned and watched the man named John melt into the crowd. He had his arm around another girl just about my age, a station girl, just like me.

CHAPTER TWENTY

I dreamed at night about doing laundry, mountains and mountains of it. How I'd love a whiff of that nice, fresh-smelling detergent Mom used to buy. How good it would feel to sink my hands into clean clothes, soft and warm, just out of the dryer. I'd fold them all neat and tidy and put them in stacks, whites, pinks, blues, yellows.

Everything I had on was filthy. My hair was so oily I could barely stand to touch it. My scalp itched. Everything itched. Finally I just couldn't stand it.

From midnight until seven a.m. was the most dangerous time in the station. Peter said to never go upstairs then, that it was just too dangerous. I was going anyway.

Quietly I rose to my feet and headed for the escalator.

At two a.m. the women's restroom was empty. The stalls all stood open, their white metal doors gleaming under the bright fluorescent lights. Used paper towels spilled out of the trash bin onto the floor. Water spots spattered the mirrors and the countertops. Long strands of hair lay coiled in one of the sinks.

First I soaked a big wad of paper towels with water. Next I slipped into a stall, closed the door, and took off all my clothes. Shivering, cramped so I could barely move, I tried desperately to clean myself. The paper towels were useless. They shredded, leaving behind tiny bits of paper that stuck to my skin. Still damp, I changed into the last clean outfit I had, a pair of shorts and a pink sleeveless T-shirt. I put my dirty clothes back on over that. If I didn't, I'd freeze.

As I was washing my face in the sink I noticed in the mirror how bad my hair had gotten—flat, clinging to my scalp. I stuck my head under the faucet. Water splashed everywhere, all over the mirror, all over the floor, all over me. Next I pumped out a ton of green soap from the dispenser and began massaging it into my scalp. It smelled strong and mediciney.

Behind me the restroom door opened. I jerked my head up straight, sending water and green soap suds everywhere.

"Provalivai, provalivai," a woman's voice cried out.

In the mirror I saw the janitor lady rushing toward me. She swatted at my legs with her broom.

I grabbed my backpack and headed for the door, leaving behind a trail of sudsy water. The janitor lady watched me go, shaking her broom, scowling at the puddle on the floor.

The rest of the night I spent sitting next to the wall with wet hair, shivering and waiting for morning to come. I could still feel the tiny bits of paper towels clinging to my skin inside my clothes. My hair was so slimy from the soap I wondered if it would ever dry. When it finally did, I put on my Padres baseball cap and vowed never to take it off again. Not ever.

* * *

I'd just stepped off the escalator and was returning to our spot when something brushed the top of my head. Above me a kid perched like a monkey in the carved out place between two columns in the wall. He wore a mean grin and my Padres cap on his head. Just as I was about to make a grab for it, he jumped down from the wall and joined a group of other kids. One stopped, held a plastic bag to his face, and took a deep breath. I'd seen other kids in the station doing the same thing. Peter said it was *klay*, the same as sniffing glue. The group staggered off, giggling hysterically, howling like wolves. Their sound echoed in an eerie cloud over the empty space above the trains. The hair on my arms prickled. I was too afraid to go after them.

I returned to our place by the wall, pulled up my knees, and buried my face in my hands. My favorite Padres cap gone. Dad had bought it for me right before he left for Iraq, a summer night in San Diego, just the two of us at the game. We were playing the Giants. I'll never forget the smell of the peanuts, the taste of the hot dogs, the mustard, the relish, and the fireworks, red, white and blue flags, huge bursts of crystal stars. They'd been the best ever.

A few days after my cap got stolen, police trolled the lower passageway of the station, giving all of us along the wall the evil eye. With my hat gone I was scared they'd recognize me. I had no way to hide my hair. I'd lost my disguise.

A drugged out kid, stumbled toward us, tripped over someone's leg and fell flat. As he got up, his blue wool ski cap snagged on a screw sticking out from the edge of the trashcan. He didn't notice and staggered off. I checked to make sure no one was looking then reached over and snatched the cap.

It was still warm and smelled like dirty hair, but to me it was a gift from heaven. I tucked my hair up inside, and pulled it down low.

No one would know me now.

* * *

The cap made my head itch. I couldn't stop scratching.

A lady wearing black boots and a long gray coat wandered down the platform, pausing to talk to each group of kids along the way. My heart lurched, then sped up. Was she looking for me? I stopped scratching my scalp and hurried to put my cap back on. Clop, clop—the sound of her boots echoed off the hard marble floors as she came closer. I pulled my cap down low and hunched over, resting my forehead on my folded arms.

The boots stopped right in front of me. Through the slit between my knees I could see their black rounded tips pointed straight at my feet. I didn't look up. The woman spoke to Peter in Russian, something about baths and clothes. Maybe she wasn't looking for me after all. Suddenly my head began to itch so bad that I couldn't bear it. It felt like tiny pinpricks all over my scalp. I sat up, dug my fingernails underneath my wool cap, and scratched hard. Too hard. The cap slipped off.

The lady in the gray coat bent over and inspected my hair. She didn't touch me, just tilted her head from side to side and said, "Uh-hmm. Uh-hmm"

I held my breath and counted the tiny nubs of black on the hem of her coat. Was she checking to see if she recognized me?

She babbled something about *vshi* that I didn't understand, but I nodded anyway and pretended I did. She thought I was Russian. That was good. I'd fooled her.

"What's *vshi*?" I asked Peter after she left.

He pretended to hold something teensy-tiny between the tips of his fingers. "*Vshi* is very little animal. Not know word in English."

I leaped to my feet. "Lice." I must have gotten them from the cap. I tore it off and threw it as far as I could. Suddenly my whole head itched worse than ever. I could feel the lice crawling all over my scalp.

I leaned over and asked Peter and Pasha, "Can you see them?"

They examined my head. Neither would get very close.

Peter straightened. "I see *vshi*." He pinched his fingers together. "Is little white bugs."

Pasha wrinkled his nose.

I screamed and jumped up and down, scratching my head, trying to shake out the lice. Only bums, creeps, and street people get lice, people who aren't clean, people who never bathe.

Peter watched me. "Lady say come to place on street Sadovaya. Wash clothes. Have bath. Get clean."

I stopped. A bath? Clean clothes? Was I hearing things?

Peter went on. "Is new place for help street kids."

"Can you and Pasha come too? Can we sleep there?"

"No is place for sleep. Jus' for get clean, get medicine, get clothes."

"Clothes? You mean I could get a warm jacket or a coat?"

Peter smiled and nodded. "Is good, *da?*"

"Will they get rid of my lice?"

He bobbed his head up and down. "*Da, Da.* Fix *vshi*."

Would they recognize me? The lady hadn't. She thought I was Russian.

The next day we loaded all our stuff in the trash sack and headed for Sadovaya Street. When we arrived, we found a line that snaked down the sidewalk and around the block. There were no windows in the three-story building, just one metal door, with a sign over it.

After an hour of waiting, finally the door opened. The lady with the black boots from the day before sat at a computer just inside checking people in.

"I'm going to pretend I'm Russian," I whispered to Peter. Lying was getting easier and easier these days.

When it came to our turn, I went first.

"Name?" the lady asked me in Russian.

Panicked, I stared at her. Should I give my name? I didn't dare. "Uh. Uhm. Katerina Rushev." *Rushev* was my cousin Natalia's last name.

The lady asked me another question. I understood a lot of Russian by now, but I didn't understand what she'd said. I stared. I didn't know what to say. She stared back, waiting.

"Tell letters," Peter whispered.

I looked at him. "Huh?"

He turned to the lady and babbled something to her in Russian. She shook her head, her eyes sad. Very slowly he said some words to her that sounded like he might be spelling out the letters of my name. As he spoke, she typed them in. When he was through, she motioned for me to move on.

Peter went next, then Pasha.

I whispered to Peter, "What'd you tell her?"

He looked cross-eyed and stuck out his tongue. "I tell her you no think so good."

Pasha giggled. Peter grinned and shrugged.

I laughed. "Thanks a lot."

The room inside was huge and painted white with very bright lights hanging down from the ceiling on brown cords. On one side a man wearing a stethoscope and latex gloves examined a little boy's ears. Four kids lined up waiting, one with a cough that sounded like a dog barking. On the other side of the room washing machines chunked loudly. Dryers hummed. The clean smell of laundry detergent filled the air.

They stuck our clothes in bags with our names on them. Peter explained to me that we could come back later and pick them up. I couldn't believe it. Free and everything. After that they separated us into two lines, one for girls, one for boys. Everyone looked so skinny, their faces sunken in, like pictures of the starving people in Africa. When I got to the front of the line, they handed me some soap and a mediciney-smelling brown shampoo and pointed for me to go in the next room. I couldn't understand much of the Russian, so I just followed along, hoping I was doing it right. If I made a mistake, I figured they'd think it was because I wasn't very smart.

Two other girls about my age filed into the next room with me. Everything was very white, the walls, the ceilings, the benches with shiny tile floors that looked like they'd just been scrubbed. Three shower heads stuck out from one of the walls. Everything was steamy and smelled of chlorine like a swimming pool. We had to take off our clothes and wrap-up in teeny towels that barely fit around. A lady wearing a faded blue apron and latex gloves looked me up and down, made notes on a clipboard, and took my clothes. All the people there wore those same clear white gloves.

Next it was time for the showers. It was embarrassing being naked in front of the two other girls. I tried to keep my eyes pointed straight ahead, but I couldn't help noticing that one of them had boobs showing. It was the only part of her body that had any meat on it. The rest of her was just skin and bones. I didn't have any boobs yet. Neither did any of my friends. I wondered if I ever would.

You had to push a button to get the showers to go on, and they were on timers so you had to hurry. The water was only lukewarm, but it felt so good I didn't care. First I lathered all over with the soap, lots of suds, tons and tons of it. Then I stood under the shower and felt the slippery softness of the water wash over me as the timer ticked away. I never realized how wonderful it could feel. A puddle of dirty brown foam swirled at my feet and disappeared down the drain. Then everything was white again. The lady in the apron let me push the timer once more so I could do my hair. I used the strong-smelling shampoo and scrubbed and scrubbed until I didn't see how it was possible for there to be any lice left on my head. When I was done, my hair squeaked, it was so clean.

I used the tiny towel to dry off. Then the lady in the apron appeared and handed me a stack of clothes. She said I could keep them. The underpants had holes in them and pictures of Cinderella, something a five-year-old would wear. Nothing fit right. But I didn't care. They were clean. I was clean. Everything smelled good, even me.

After the showers they lined everybody up behind a sink, handed out free toothbrushes and toothpaste, and made us brush our teeth. Getting that awful slimy feeling out of my mouth felt almost as good as the bath had. Next we got to pick out another new outfit from a pile of used clothes in the corner. A big crowd of girls got there ahead of me and grabbed all the good stuff. All I could find was a red wool sweater with splotches of bleach down the front and a pair of saggy beige sweatpants. It didn't matter. They were clean. I was happy.

The woman in the white apron made me sit down after I dried my hair so she could have another look at my head.

"*Vshi*," she muttered. She tried using a comb with very fine teeth, but she couldn't get it through the snarls in my hair.

Finally she turned to the woman next to her and fired off a bunch of Russian, something about the lice. I didn't like the sound of it or the worried look on her face. The other woman stepped over and examined my scalp. Before I knew what was happening, she'd turned on a set of electric clippers and was running them up the side of my head. It was the same kind they use to groom dogs.

"Stop!" I screamed, grabbing my head.

The second lady clamped her hands down on my shoulders. "Is necessary," she said in Russian. The first lady began with the clippers again. The sound was like a power lawn mower.

Big wads of my blonde hair dropped to the floor.

They didn't have a mirror. They didn't need to. I could tell by the cool, breezy feel on my scalp that she was shaving me bald. Fat tears slid down my face and dripped off my chin onto the pile of hair on my lap.

When the lady was done with the clippers, I ran my hand over my scalp. It felt like bare skin, not even a prickle of hair left.

* * *

They gave everyone a brown paper sack with one apple inside, another new toothbrush, and a small tube of toothpaste. They gave me a wooly cap to cover up my head. It was ugly and brown and rough and scratchy on my bare scalp, but I wore it anyway. I sure wasn't going to walk around bald.

When I met up with Pasha and Peter, their faces were shiny and pink, their hair still damp and plastered to their scalps. They both wore something new from the used clothes pile.

Peter had exchanged his bad shoes for some thicker heavier ones and wore a cool camouflage jacket splattered with yellow paint. He smiled proudly as he opened it to show me the fleece lining and the inside pockets. "You like?"

I reached up and felt for my woolly hat. "Yeah, I guess."

Pasha tugged on my sleeve to get me to look at his shiny red baseball jacket. It was at least two sizes too big and the logo was been ripped off, but Pasha didn't care. I could see that from the giant grin on his face.

No one said anything about my woolly cap. I had it pulled down so low that I don't think they could tell about my hair.

When we got back to the station, I decided to go ahead and show Peter and Pasha what had happened. I watched their faces as I pulled off the cap. Their mouths fell open. Their eyes grew huge. Quick as a flash, I put it back on.

Peter patted my head and smiled. "Is okay, Katerina. Look good."

What a lie. I slumped down against the wall and stared at the train tracks trying to hold back the tears.

Something soft and fuzzy brushed my cheek. It was Miss Pig, the pink beanie-baby I'd given Pasha. "Is okay, Katerina," he said with a bright smile. He pointed at my head, then at his and said, "*malcheek.*"

Great! Now I looked like a boy.

CHAPTER TWENTY ONE

The internet café in the train station was crowded, almost every computer taken. Quickly I made my way between the neon orange and green panels looking for an empty cubby. As I went past, I felt people look at me. Had any of them seen my passport photo? Did they recognize me? I didn't worry so much about that downstairs. Passengers walking by never gave the station kids a second look.

I found an empty cubby over in a corner and a wobbly chair with a loose seat. The keyboard was so smudged you could barely read the letters. It had been over two months since I'd been able to get online. There was bound to be tons of spam.

I clicked on the round blue globe icon, and waited for the website to come up. The computer screen had pings in it that showed up as bright green sparks on the display.

Please, please, let there be something from Marisa. I was hoping she'd have read my last email and would get her parents to tell me what to do.

I typed in my user name and password and clicked *LogIn*. It took less than a second for this message to pop up:

MAIL ACCOUNT NO LONGER ACTIVE.

I tried logging in again.

MAIL ACCOUNT NO LONGER ACTIVE.

Over and over again I tried it. Same thing. I pounded the arms of my chair.

The guy in the next cubby leaned across and looked at my screen.

"Do you know what it means?" I asked him in English.

He nodded and spoke in English with a heavy Russian accent. "Mean account no longer active."

"I know, but what does *that* mean?"

He frowned. "How long time ven last you did email?"

I thought for a minute. "Gee, almost two months. Did they cancel me?"

He nodded. "*Da*, I think so."

My voice rose. My heart sped up. "But what can I do? I have to get my emails."

He scratched his head. "Not know. Is... How you say?" He made a big X in the air. "Kaput."

"You mean it's gone?"

"*Da*. Email is gone. Sorry." He straightened and went back to what he was doing.

My heart pulsed in my ears. This couldn't be happening. No more emails. I was completely cut off.

I jumped from my chair and raced out of the internet café. I'd paid for a half an hour—a whole twenty-five rubles. I should have tried to get a refund, but I was too shaken to care. Peter and Pasha stood just outside the entrance to the café and watched me as I sped past.   ·

Two women standing at the sink looked up from washing their hands and stared at me in the mirror as I careened across the restroom. I locked myself in one of the stalls, sat down on the lid of the toilet, and sobbed.

Something touched my shoes. I opened my eyes. Under the stall door a brown head appeared, two big brown eyes, a red jacket.

Pasha rose to his feet and put a hand on my knee. "Is okay, Katerina?"

I stared into his worried face and couldn't help but smile. "Sure, Pasha." I patted his head. "It's okay. Everything's going to be all right." It's what Gracie used to say after Dad died.

If only I believed it now.

CHAPTER TWENTY TWO

High above through the windows near the ceiling a single star shone inside the curve of a silver moon. I lifted off my cap and ran the palm of my hand over the top of my head. It felt like the bristles of the soft brush Mom used to use to put her makeup on.

A girl who looked a little younger than me came along and sat down near us. She wore nice clothes, a navy wool coat, white tights, and black patent flats. Her hair was the shiniest brown I'd ever seen, like a TV ad. There were a couple of holes in her tights and smudges on her face. Still, she didn't look like one of us. I couldn't figure out where she came from or what she was doing here in the station all by herself so late at night.

I slid my eyes her way and found her looking at me. Quickly, I pulled my cap down hoping she wouldn't notice my shaved head.

I darted another look and caught her watching me again. Real fast she looked away.

Finally I asked her name. "*Kak vas zavoot?*" I wasn't sure I'd said it right.

She nodded like she understood. "*Meenya zavoot* Anna." She said it in a timid voice like she might be about to cry.

"*Meenya zavoot* Carly," I said. "Katerina."

"Katerina?" She sounded surprised. "Katerina is a girl's name."

I stared at my feet and said in Russian. "I *am* a girl."

Her voice softened. "Oh, sorry. Is—" She pointed at my head.

I let out a disgusted puff of air. "I know. It's the hair. They—" I made a motion like clippers running up the side of my head. "*Vshi.*"

"Ahhhh, *vshi.*" She looked like she was thinking for a minute. "*Americanka?*" I guess she recognized my accent.

It turned out she spoke some English, so with that and my little bit of Russian plus some sign language we were able to talk for a while. She was ten, almost eleven. She'd just run away from an orphanage. When her parents died in a car crash, she went to live with an aunt, but then the aunt changed her mind and decided to put Anna in the orphanage. She said they made her mop the floors and clean the toilets with a toothbrush and that the woman in charge was real mean. It was so horrible that after a week Anna ran away.

As she told her story, she rubbed her eyes with the back of her hand. I felt really sorry for her.

I told her about Dad getting killed in Iraq. Her eyes grew soft as she listened.

She said she didn't have any money and hadn't eaten in three days. The most I'd gone was two. She was so nice, and she seemed so scared, so starved. If we'd met back at home, I'd have wanted her for my friend.

Peter and Pasha were still asleep so I checked our food bag. All that was left were a few crackers. I was just about to offer her one when Peter woke up.

His face turned fierce. "What you do?" He grabbed my arm and made me put the cracker back.

I gave Anna a sad smile. I hoped she'd understand.

During the next few days I taught her all the things that Peter'd taught me, like how to beg, where the best trash cans for food were, and about the homeless shelter. Peter didn't like it that she had become my friend. He was afraid I'd give her food. He was afraid I'd invite her to be part of our group.

As for Anna, she really tried hard, but nothing seemed to work for her, especially the begging. She stayed positive, though, and kept repeating what her mother had taught her, "No matter where you are or what you're doing, God is with you."

I used to think that too.

* * *

I ran my hand over the short fuzz on my head and checked my reflection in the silver trash can.

Anna flashed me a smile. "Is looking good," she said.

She was lying. I looked just like a boy.

In the two weeks since she'd been here, she'd gotten so thin that the bones stuck out of her wrists. Her cheeks caved in. She'd finally started eating garbage like the rest of us.

A man wearing a shiny, new business suit passed our way, stopped, turned, and began speaking to Anna in Russian. His suit was black with no wrinkles, his shirt crisp and white, nice, neat comb stripes through his hair. His red, white and blue tie made me think of our flag. Great smile. Friendly eyes. He reminded me of that guy John who'd offered to buy me dinner. By now I knew you couldn't trust guys like this.

Before I could warn Anna, she stood up. All smiles, she pointed at the man and informed me, "We go for eat." She waved at me over her shoulder as she left.

I got up, ran after her, and grabbed her arm. "No, no, Anna, don't go."

The man smiled at me and said something in Russian. He was asking if I wanted to come too.

"*Nyet, nyet.*" I tugged at Anna's arm.

"Is okay, Katerina." She smiled. "I come back soon."

"But—" It was no use. She was determined to go.

I returned to our place. Peter was asleep and hadn't seen what just happened. In the distance I could see Anna and the man riding up the escalator. He had a hand on her shoulder and was talking to her. She looked happy as could be. Maybe Peter'd been wrong. Maybe not all these guys were bad. Maybe this one was all right. What difference did it make anyway? Anna was going out to a restaurant. She was going to get something to eat, and I wasn't.

My stomach grumbled. I wondered where the man was taking her. I should have just gone with them.

I looked at my watch. It was ten o'clock. My stomach grumbled again. All I'd had to eat today was crackers. I imagined the restaurant where Anna and the man were enjoying their dinner, all the wonderful smells. If it were me, I'd order a jumbo hamburger with fries even though I knew I'd never finish it, and maybe a Caesar salad with chicken on top, and macaroni and cheese and a side of beans and salsa. Maybe not. This was Russia. For dessert, mud pie. Oh God, mud pie! But I might rather have blueberry waffles piled high with fluffy whipped butter, drowning in syrup. Or maybe some fried chicken or pizza or maybe….

I must have fallen asleep because when I looked at my watch again, it was two a.m. Off down by platform eleven I caught sight of Anna returning, head down, walking slowly. Her barrette had slipped down the side of her head. She took her place against the wall where she always sat and didn't say a word, didn't even look at me. I knew something was wrong. I could tell by the wet marks on her cheeks.

Then I noticed her hands balled into tight little fists. One clutched a wad of rubles. Tears slipped from her eyes, but she didn't make a sound, not one sob.

It made me sick to think what must have happened. I knew it was sex, and the scary part was that it could have happened to me too if I'd gone with them. I almost did. The man had looked so important in that business suit, like a big news guy on TV, and he'd acted so nice, and when you haven't eaten....

I asked Anna if she'd like to hold Miss Pig for a little while, but she said *no*.

I couldn't stop thinking about it. I kept imagining it happening to me. It made me feel like worms crawling inside of me.

The same man came back for Anna the next night. I thought for sure she'd say *no*.

She didn't. I couldn't believe it. Hadn't she learned her lesson? When she returned this time, there were no more tears. In fact she came back loaded with candy bars to share and bragging about all the rubles she'd made. The flat look in her eyes told me it was all a fake.

As the days passed her face filled out. Her bones stopped showing. Lucky thing. She was eating while the rest of us starved. She brought back stuff for us once in a while, mostly candy though, no real food.

For the rest of us the days were the same. We begged, but there wasn't much money. We ate garbage, and sometimes we got sick. Pasha's cheeks grew hollow. Peter's eyes sunk in his head. Finally one night I got up and followed Anna as she left with her man. Why not? I could do what she was doing too. It wouldn't be so bad.

Peter stopped me just as I was about to get on the escalator.

"*Nyet*, Katerina."

I looked up to where Anna and her man were about to get off on the floor above. "But I could bring back food for you and Pasha. We'd have money. Everything'd be better."

Peter tugged my arm. "*Nyet*, the men they hurt you."

"But look at Anna. She's doing okay."

Peter's voice was firm. "No is good. No is go."

I could see from his eyes. It was no use arguing.

* * *

When I woke up, I found Anna looking down at me, just back from going out with a different man. She wore a long fur coat and a big smile. Draped over her arm was her old dark blue one.

I hugged myself and shivered.

Anna handed me her old coat. "You want?" Her hair wasn't shiny and neat any more. The barrette was missing. She wore makeup, mascara that had smudged underneath her eyes and bright red lipstick, smeared around the edges. She didn't look ten any more. She looked eighteen.

I stroked the soft sleeve of her old coat. "How much?"

"Is nothing," she said. "Is for free."

My mouth dropped open. Free? Nobody gives anything for free, not when you live in the station. "Wow! That's really nice of you." I got to my feet and put on the navy blue coat. It felt soft as Mom's cashmere sweater. I pulled it tight around me and tilted my head so that my cheek brushed the collar. I smiled at Anna. "It's warm."

She smiled back. "We friends, *da*?"

I hugged her. "We friends."

* * *

At four in the morning there was no one in the ladies' restroom except Anna and me. She'd just returned from going out with another new man and had brought back a bag full of cosmetics. She unzipped the shiny new, zebra-striped case and walked her fingers through its contents. Her smile grew wide as she drew out a cylinder of raspberry pink lip gloss. She tore off the seal and pulled out the wand. In the mirror she said, "Make mouth." She opened hers slightly and stretched her upper lips down over her teeth to show me how. I copied her.

She began applying gloss to my upper lip. If it had been me, I would have saved my money for more important things. Still, it was awful nice of her to share with me. And it was fun putting on makeup, kind of like being at home, like the stuff Marisa and I used to do.

Anna picked up a mascara wand. "Make eyes go—" She pointed up.

"Did you go to a nice restaurant tonight?" I asked her.

"Was okay." She began darkening the upper lashes on my right eye.

"What's it like when you go out with these guys?" I asked.

She drew back and looked away.

Right away I felt bad. "I'm sorry, Anna. I shouldn't have asked. It's none of my business, anyway." There was a bruise below her left eye. I wondered if the man did it.

As she continued putting makeup on me, the subject changed to talk about Mom. By now I'd told Anna the whole story, about Vlad and the police and everything.

"Are you sure they took your mama to jail?" She asked me in Russian. She studied her palette of eye shadow colors. "Maybe they take place for sick people." She was trying to speak English again.

"You mean a hospital?"

She nodded. "*Da, da*. Hospital."

I held real still as she dabbed lavender shadow on my upper lid. "I've wondered about that too," I said.

She frowned. "I know where perhaps they take her. You want, I take you there."

I jerked backwards, causing her to dab shadow on my nose. "Oh, Anna, that would be awesome. Would you?" I wondered if it was the hospital where her parents died.

She licked the tip of her finger and rubbed the lavender dust off my nose. "Sure. No is problem." She smiled as she dusted my cheek bones with peach blush then stepped back and looked at the results of her work. "You like?"

I looked at my face in the mirror. "Wow!"

I looked like I'd stepped right out of one of the teen magazines. That is, if you ignored the ugly wool cap. I ripped it off and let out a shriek. It had been a month since they shaved my head, but only a half an inch of hair had grown back. I hated that it was taking so long. I hated that I looked like a boy.

I stuck my tongue out at myself in the mirror.

Anna giggled and stuck her tongue out too. Then we laughed out loud. It felt so weird to laugh. I never thought I'd be able to again. It was fun having Anna for a friend, and she was going to help me find Mom. It would happen. I was sure of it now. I took her hands and danced her around the restroom.

* * *

When Pasha saw me all made up, he giggled and covered his face.

Peter folded his arms and scowled. "Why waste rubles."

"I didn't." I gestured toward Anna. "It was her makeup, not mine."

Anna smiled.

Peter made a spitting sound and stared at the ground. "Look stupid."

A man walked by and winked at me.

I smiled back.

Peter pointed his finger in my face. "Go wash."

I ignored him and sat down. Pasha gave me a sideways look and scooted away. I inched up to him and pouched out my raspberry lips. He shrieked and jerked back. The two of us collapsed into a fit of giggles.

I didn't care what Peter said. He couldn't ruin my mood. I was going to find Mom. Anna was going to help me. We'd do it. He'd see.

* * *

After being up most of the night, Anna slept practically the whole next day. I was itching to have her take me to the hospital, but I didn't want to disturb her when she was so tired. A different man came for her that night. He had a lot of tattoos and wasn't dressed as nice as the other guys. At first she shook her head and wouldn't go with him, but then he pulled a bunch of rubles from his pocket, and she changed her mind.

It scared me that she went with him.

Morning came, and still she wasn't back. A day passed. No Anna. Then two, then three. She'd never been gone this long.

"Should we tell the police?" I asked Peter.

"*Meeleetsia*?" He made a spitting sound. "*Meeleetsia* no care."

One week passed, then two. Finally I realized. Anna wasn't coming back.

CHAPTER TWENTY THREE

Anna had only been with us a month, but it seemed like it had been much longer. I didn't like to think about what might have happened to her, too scary, too ugly. She'd been like a sister to me. Things had been happier, more normal, more like at home when she was around. Now she was gone, and I missed Mom more than ever. More than ever I was determined to find her.

On the morning I was going to go out and look for Mom, I woke up to find my wool cap missing. That ugly brown thing! Someone must have stolen it while I was sleeping.

"I need some rubles," I told Peter.

He made a sour face. "What need for rubles?"

"To buy a hat." I was planning to go to the hospital that Anna'd mentioned. I didn't have the address, but I had the name.

Peter wrinkled his brow and pretended not to understand.

I pointed at my head. "I can't go around looking like this."

He stared at me. "Shelter open in three days. Get hat then."

"They've run out of clothes." I held out my hand. "C'mon, just a few rubles. It's cold outside." The second-hand store down the street sold scarves real cheap.

Peter shook his head. "No need scarf."

I stamped my foot. "Yes, I do."

Pasha's eyes traveled back and forth between Peter's face and mine. He always looked worried when we disagreed.

Peter folded his arms and set his lips in a straight line. "Need rubles for buy batteries." He'd just bought batteries for his boom box yesterday. They couldn't be used up already.

I shook my open palm at him. "C'mon. Just a few. I'm going to look for my mom."

"Mom?" Peter let out a disgusted puff of air. "No is mom."

"What're you talking about?"

He batted the air and laughed.

I kicked his foot, hard. Our dance act had brought in two hundred and fifty rubles yesterday. That's almost ten dollars. Five of it should have been mine.

"Why are you acting like such a dickhead?" I asked him.

"Dickhead?" Peter frowned. "What is dickhead?"

Dickhead. Pasha's little mouth tried to make the word.

"Never mind," I said to Peter, "just give me some rubles."

"Dickhead? Dickhead?" Peter shook his head. "What mean dickhead?"

"Shhh." I could feel myself turning red. "It means jerk."

Jerk. Pasha mouthed the word.

I stuck my chin out at Peter. "Just give me some rubles."

"Okey-dokey, dickhead, jerk, *Americanka.*" He handed me five rubles.

Like that wouldn't buy a glass of water. I threw the money back in his face and plopped down on the other side of the trash can where I wouldn't have to look at him.

I'd show him. I was going to find Mom. I was going back to America. Then we'd see how smart he was.

Something soft tickled the side of my face, then again. Pasha had snuck up beside me and was brushing the little pink pig against my cheek.

"Miss Pig love, Katerina." He pronounced the words very slowly in English.

"Wow!" I leaned forward so I could see around the trash can. "Peter, did you hear that?"

He was busy watching a group of new kids that were settling down against the wall.

I peered into Pasha's face. "You wanna learn English?"

His chocolate brown eyes got very bright. "*Eengleesh*? *Americanka?*"

"*Da, da,*" I said. "*Americanka, *" It amazed me what a smart little kid he was.

I touched my chest. "How about *I* teach *you* English?" I pointed at him. "And *you* teach *me Rooskey.*"

His dark eyebrows came together in a frown.

I tried it again.

This time his head bobbed up and down. "Okey dokey, dickhead, jerkhead, *Americanka.*"

* * *

Warm air surrounded me as I stepped from the entrance hall into the lobby of Mariskaya Hospital. An old woman dressed in black mopped the floor with a strong yellow liquid that smelled like the kind they use in the restrooms at school. People crowded the walls, standing, sitting on the floor, sitting on couches, arms folded, some asleep.

One by one they noticed me. The woman mopping stopped and stared at my buzzed head. Nurses pushing patients in wheelchairs whispered to each other behind their hands. Others made sad faces and looked away. I wonder if they thought I had cancer or something.

Head down, I marched over to the reception desk.

"Umm, Is here Lara McOwen?" I said it in Russian, but I'm not sure I said it right.

The lady behind the desk glanced up. Her eyes softened when she saw my shaved head. "*Eezveeneetye?*"

I ran my hand nervously over the top of my head, feeling the prickly tops of each hair. "Lara McOwen? Is she here?" I asked in Russian.

The receptionist leaned into her computer screen and began scrolling down with her mouse. "Lara McOwen. Lara McOwen…"

I put my hand on her desk then pulled it away before she could notice my grimy fingernails.

She leaned back and gave me a bright smile. "Yes. She was here."

I gasped. "Really? She was?" I was so excited I blurted it out in English.

The softness that had been in the receptionist's eyes turned to something different.

I leaned closer wishing I could see her screen. I gave up trying to speak Russian. "So do you know where she is?"

She shook her head and shuffled through some papers on her desk. Her eyes returned to mine.

"Is something wrong?" I asked.

She frowned. "Are you the daughter?" she asked in Russian

"*Da.*" I couldn't stand it any longer. "She's okay, isn't she?"

No answer. Her eyes kept darting from the stack of papers on her desk to my face then back to her screen again.

Tears stung my eyes. "She didn't die, did she?"

She leaned toward me and squinted hard at my face. "*Nyet.* Not die."

I let out a huge sigh. "Do you know where she is?"

"Is gone away." Eyes back on her computer screen, she picked up her phone.

I stood on my tiptoes and craned my neck. Just an upside-down glimpse was all I got, barely enough to be sure that the picture on the sheet of paper she'd been eyeing was a photocopy of my passport photo.

She looked up. "Caterin McOwen?"

In a flash I was gone.

Three blocks later I slowed to a walk to catch my breath. Mom was alive. I felt like dancing. I felt like singing. I felt like kissing everyone I passed on the street. Now all I had to do was find her. My nightmare would soon be over. I couldn't wait to tell Peter and Pasha.

I got off the metro and ran all the way back to the train station. The usual bustle of people crowded the lobby. I wormed my way through them and hurried toward the escalator.

Just as I was passing by the internet café, I noticed a kid step out of the phone booth. I took a second glance and realized it was Peter. He'd never used the phone before. I wondered who he was calling. He looked so sad I almost didn't recognize him—the way he hung his head, the way his mouth that always turned up, turned down.

He hadn't seen me, so I waited for him to take the escalator first.

When I got down to our spot against the wall, the first thing he asked was, "You find mama?"

"*Da*." I told him what had happened. "Can you believe it? She's alive. She was there. Isn't it great?" I couldn't keep from jumping up and down.

Peter stabbed the floor with his finger. "Sure. But where is mama now?"

I stopped bouncing and looked at him more carefully. "She's somewhere. I just don't know where."

He rolled his eyes and sighed.

"Don't you believe me?"

He rolled his eyes again.

Jerk! He was spoiling everything.

"You'll see," I shouted. "I'll find my mom. No. She'll find me. We'll go back to America. You just wait. It'll happen."

He laughed. "Mom no come back. She find man. Go make home with him." He wiggled his fingers at me. "Then is bye-bye, Katerina."

Why was he acting so mean? He wasn't right, was he? There'd been that thing between Mom and Vlad, but she'd never make that mistake again, not after what had happened. She just wouldn't.

Would she?

I narrowed my eyes at Peter and screamed, "I hate you."

Pasha gasped and leaned away.

Peter smiled and shook his head. "No is mom."

I couldn't stand it. In a blur of tears I raced back upstairs and hid in the women's restroom.

She's not like that. I know she's not. I sobbed into my hands, trying not to make a sound. Someone had spray-painted a four-letter word in big Cyrillic letters across the back of the stall door. I stared at it and thought how much I hated Peter, hated everyone, hated life.

* * *

Three hours later I slunk back downstairs and collapsed into my space on the floor by the silver trash can. Pasha smiled when he saw me. Peter just stared off into space, looking grumpy.

A mom and daughter came toward us and stood waiting for the train on platform nine. The little girl clutched a pink blanket with one hand, dragging a corner of it on the floor. She looked a little old to have a blankey, seven, maybe eight.

She and her mom were both skinny and dressed in dark shabby clothes like street people. The little girl kept looking up at her mom, but her mom wouldn't look back. She just stood there staring straight ahead at the empty space where the train would come. Over the loudspeaker came the announcement of the arrival of the train from Moskow. Lights appeared in the train tunnel. The little girl began hopping from one foot to the other, pulling on her mom's coat sleeve, jabbering at her in Russian. The mom stared straight ahead, her face as worn out as an old dish rag.

The whistle blew, the train doors opened, and the passengers got off.

I could feel the little girl's worry all the way from here.

The mom knelt down, took her daughter by the shoulders, and began speaking in a real serious voice.

"*Nyet,* Mama. *Nyet.*" The little girl began to cry.

"What's the mama saying?" I asked Peter.

His voice was flat. "She say girl no can come."

I jerked away from him. "What? Her mother said that?"

Peter nodded. "Mama say she come back in few days." He shook his head and wrinkled his nose. "She no come back."

"But, but," I sputtered. "That can't be right. I mean, that's awful."

Peter shook his head. "What you no understand, Katerina, is mama of little girl—she no can help what she do. Little girl need be brave. Need understand."

I folded my arms and stuck out my chin. "Well, that's the stupidest thing I ever heard in my whole life!"

The mother stood, handed her daughter a big brown paper sack and stuck a small wad of rubles in the little girl's pocket.

The train doors began sliding shut. The mother stepped on board.

No! No! Someone stop her.

"*Nyet. Nyet,*" The little girl clung to her mother's coat.

I wanted to rush over and do something. Boost the little girl onto the train. Pull her mother off.

With a yank the mother pulled her coattail inside the car just as the doors would have closed on it.

"Mama, Mama," screamed the little girl. A few passengers in the area noticed, but no one did anything. As the train pulled away, I caught a glimpse of the mother's face in the window. Tears streamed down her cheeks.

I didn't feel sorry for her at all. Stupid, bad mother! I wished I could jump on board that train and tell her off.

The little girl raced down the platform after the train. "Mama. Mama." The train kept going. With a last blast of its whistle it disappeared into the tunnel. "Mama. Mama." The little girl's screams echoed off the walls of the empty tunnel where the train had just been.

I couldn't stand it. I covered my ears.

Inside my head Peter's words tortured me. *No is Mom. No is Mom. No is Mom.*

CHAPTER TWENTY FOUR

Beside me Peter didn't flinch, not an inch. He just sat there staring straight ahead, the muscles in his jaw twitching.

Pasha pulled his baseball jacket up over his head like a hood. When I glanced over at him, he pulled it further around his face. *It's a small world after all.* I could just barely make out the tune he hummed.

The little girl came down the platform toward us, turned and drifted off down the hall, dragging her pink blanket behind her. She wasn't crying any more. She looked lost and scared.

My eyes followed her down the hall. What would happen to her? Where would she spend the night? How would she stay safe?

I started to get up.

Peter put a hand on my arm. "*Nyet. Nyet,* Katerina. No is go." He pointed at our sack. "No is food. No is rubles."

I jerked my arm away and jumped to my feet. "I don't care. *Some*one's gotta do *some*thing."

He shook his head and muttered, "Crazy *Americanka*!"

Just past the Coke kiosk, I caught sight of the little girl. A priest in a long black robe held her hand and stooped down, talking to her. He pulled out a white handkerchief and wiped her eyes, then the two got on the escalator. The last I saw of the little girl was her pink blanket, dragging behind her as she rose to the floor above.

I stood over Peter. "Where will the priest take her?" I asked him.

He drew an invisible picture with his finger on the floor. "Take place where is many kids."

"You mean an orphanage?"

"*Da*, orphanage." He shook his head. "Is bad place, orphanage. Kids no stay. Kids come back to Moskovsky Station. Is better place for live."

"But maybe her mom'll come back."

He looked up at me. "I tell you, Katerina. Moms no come back."

I stamped my foot. "You don't *know* that."

He rolled his eyes. "Stupid, *Americanka*."

"Dickhead! Jerk!" I sunk down as far away as I could get from him without knocking over the silver trash can. He wiggled the other way.

Inside his jacket hideout Pasha hummed his little song. I wondered if he was thinking about the time when his mom left him.

A train came in, but no one moved an inch. The passengers came and went, and we didn't even hold out our hands. Finally Peter broke the silence. "Is mine birthday." He glanced real quickly at me then away.

"Your birthday?" I watched his face.

"*Da.*" He poked the trash sack with his toe.

I stared at my hands. "Oh, well, happy birthday, I guess."

He cleared his throat. "I call Mama today."

"Your mom? I thought you said your parents were dead."

"Father die. Mama marry new guy."

I took a deep breath. "Wow! So how come you're not living with them?"

Peter stared straight ahead. "New guy say I bad kid. Say I go." His voice was flat.

"But, what about your mom? Didn't she stick up for you?"

He frowned. "Stickup? What mean stickup?"

"Say you should stay? I mean, how could she let this guy send you away like that?"

He shook his head. "She no have money. She do what new guy say."

I pounded my fist on the floor. "Well, I think that's just awful." I looked at him. "So when you called her today, what'd you talk about?"

He shrugged his shoulders. "Nothing."

A janitor's shoes made a clip-clop sound as he walked by. I rubbed my finger along the place on my sleeve where the fabric had worn thin. Pasha squeezed his little accordion, in real slowly, then out real slowly, not making a sound. A train sighed and let off a whoof of steam.

Peter squirmed around on his butt. "I no talk," he mumbled.

I took in a deep breath. "You didn't talk? But why?"

"I jus' listen."

"What?"

He threw me an embarrassed smile then looked away. "I jus' like hear Mama's voice."

"Oh." I stared at my sandals. I didn't know what to say. All I knew was I couldn't be mad at him any more.

* * *

Midnight, and the trains had stopped running. Beside me Peter and Pasha sat staring into the empty space over the train tracks. Usually by now Pasha'd be fast asleep. He was worried about what happened to that poor little girl whose mother left her. Peter was too. I could tell.

I put my arm around Pasha's shoulders and squeezed. "How 'bout if I tell you a bedtime story, huh?"

Pasha looked up at me. "Story?" The bottom of his shiny red baseball jacket went all the way down to his knees.

Dad used to tell me stories every night. Some of them I think he made up. Those were always the funniest. I can still remember how warm and cozy his chest felt as I leaned against him, the nice lemony smell of his aftershave, the deep sound of his voice.

I pulled Pasha closer and rested my chin on the silky top of his head. He wouldn't be able to understand many of the words, but maybe he'd like it anyway. "Once upon a time," I whispered, "there was this teeny baby bird named Pasha…"

Pasha's eyes lit up. Peter leaned closer.

"…and Pasha's mommy was trying to teach him and his sisters to fly, but Pasha wasn't doing so well. His sisters caught on and flew off. Finally the mommy bird just flew off too and that left poor Pasha all alone in the tree. Poor little Pasha! He got so scared that he fell right out of that tree and landed on his head on top of a big fat pig. Snort went the pig." I snorted into Pasha's neck.

He squealed and giggled.

Peter let out a grunt and rolled his eyes.

I ignored him. "'So,' said the pig, 'Snort. Snort. Slobber. Slobber. I don't like little birds landing on my back.' 'Will you be my mommy?' Pasha asked the pig. 'Don't be silly,' said the pig. 'I'm a pig.'"

A drunk staggered past, leaned over the pit where the train tracks are and threw up. Peter pulled his camouflage jacket tighter around his chest.

I took a deep breath and continued. "So Pasha left the pig and got on a boat for Africa—"

Pasha's dark lashes kept falling.

"There he met a hippopotamus and—"

Somewhere down by platform three a shrill scream rang out.

"'Will you be my mommy?' Pasha asked the hippopotamus. 'Don't be silly,' said the hippopotamus."

Pasha's eyes were closed now, his breathing, slow and rhythmic. I yawned and closed my eyes too.

"So what is happen to this bird Pasha?" Peter's voice startled me. He sat with his arms folded, a worried frown over his eyes.

I hadn't even realized he was listening.

"Well, Pasha finally found a lady elephant and she agreed to be his mommy. She fed him peanuts and taught him how to fly by flapping her ears." I looked at Peter. "That's it. The end."

"Stupid story." He leaned back against the trash can and closed his eyes. Slowly a smile crept across his face.

* * *

Nothing was left of the trees along the canal except gray branches. The benches where people had rested to enjoy the sunshine during the summer were all bare. No more tourist boats chug-chugged under the bridges. Only a working boat with a crane on top plowed through the thick layers of black water.

I pulled my new scarf up over my head. Inside a wool sweater from the homeless shelter and Anna's coat I still shivered.

After fifteen minutes of walking, I turned onto my grandparents' narrow street. There were a few parked cars and a dumpster standing near a heap of black snow. I stood across the street in the long shadows of a building and watched the windows of my grandparents' apartment. Nothing but blank reflections stared back at me.

A car whizzed silently by and honked, making me jump. Finally, I got up my nerve and crossed the street. It was a big chance. Someone might recognize me and call the police. Still, I had to do it. I'd tried everything else, searched the whole city. This was all I had left.

Quickly I climbed the steps to the building entrance. Slowly I pulled the door open and looked around. There was no one in the lobby. The rubber soles of my shoes squeaked on the tile floor as I crossed the large room. On the other side the caged elevator sat empty.

When I reached the third floor, there was no one there either. So quiet—not even the sound of televisions blaring, even in the middle of the afternoon. I dug my key out of my backpack, then stood outside the door to my grandparents' apartment, afraid to go in. I held my breath and turned the key in the lock, slowly, quietly, hoping no one would hear. I pushed the door open a few inches and listened.

Nothing.

I pushed the door a little further. The bottom of it shushed against the carpet. I set one foot inside, then the other. The hallway that had always been dark in the daytime seemed even darker now. Then I realized why. The green night light that had stayed on day and night wasn't on any more. I noticed other changes. The mirror was missing and so was the table by the door where I used to drop my backpack.

I tiptoed into the kitchen, stopped and took a deep breath. A square brown stain outlined the spot on the floor where the refrigerator had been. Across the way the living room was nothing but a wide open space of dirty beige carpet. I rushed down the hall, opening the door to each bedroom. Nothing. Everything, everyone gone.

It was scarier than anything I would have expected, like one of those weird movies where the life you think you had turns out not to be real at all.

I stood in front of Mom's and my bedroom, shaking, afraid to open the door. I made myself do it. Something of Mom's might be in there, some clue.

At first it was the colors that came back. Red. Blood. Lots of it, and white, the color of Vlad's face. I remembered the surprised look in his eyes as he fell backwards, the way his hands clawed the air, the sound of the crack as his head hit the table. On the wood floor there was still a big patch of brown stain where the blood had been.

My heart quickened. My breath came in short fast bursts. I'd killed someone right in this very room.

I wanted so bad to get out of there, but I forced myself to search the room first. It was a waste of time. No clues. Nothing. I returned to the kitchen, my heart still pounding. Out of the corner of my eye something moved in the next room. I jumped and almost let out a scream.

The yellow cat, skinnier than ever, zipped across the living room carpet and stood at the bottom of the stairs, its tail twitching, staring up at me. A second cat appeared, gray and much smaller than the yellow cat. This one climbed the stairs into the kitchen and stood meowing up at me with all its might. Its shoulder blades poked up on its back. Every rib showed.

Suddenly I remembered—the tiny kitten that Grandpa Ogi'd thrown in the trash. How wonderful! It lived.

I sank to my knees and held out my hand. "Here kitty, kitty, kitty." Just as I reached out to pet it, it hissed at me and streaked away.

I couldn't stand to be in that place one more second. I turned and let myself out the front door.

As I stepped out into the hall, I almost ran into an old man carrying a sack full of trash. He had a shiny bald head with droopy cheeks, and his sweater was buttoned all wrong. I remembered him from before when I was staying at my grandparents' apartment. Behind him down the faded red carpet a door stood open. Violin music came from inside, something low and scratchy-sounding like an animal growling.

He dropped the trash sack and took me by the arm. He looked into the empty apartment behind me, then at me. "What are you doing here?" he asked in Russian, his voice low and gruff.

I stepped halfway back into the apartment. "I, uh, I was just—" My heart stuck in my throat. Did he know about Vlad and what happened? Did he know about me?

He pointed at the inside of my grandparents' apartment. "Nobody lives there now. Why are you here?"

I decided to play innocent. "I was looking for my Grandfather Ogi. Do you know him?" I asked in Russian.

"Ogi Kuznetsov?" He made a sour face and let go of my arm. "*Da*. I know him."

"Do you know where he went?"

He looked at the ceiling and scratched the gray hairs on his chest. "I'm not sure. I think maybe he went to live in Moscow. A rest home or something like that. It was two weeks ago."

"Do you know where my mother is? Lara McOwen?"

"Lara McOwen?" His eyes widened a fraction, but then he shook his head. "*Nyet. Nyet.* I don't know." He picked up his sack and took off down the hall toward the trash shoot.

CHAPTER TWENTY FIVE

The thick metal cords holding the elevator clanked, dropping me slowly down the long dark shaft. The old man knew something. I felt sure of it. Would he call the police? I listened for sirens.

Three blocks away from my grandparents' apartment I slowed to a walk to catch my breath. Dead leaves swirled down the sidewalk and crunched under my feet. Ahead of me an old lady wrapped in a lavender striped shawl trudged up the path to the blue and white church. She moved slowly like it hurt, every so often using her cane to keep her balance. A burst of icy wind made the bare tree branches sway. She put a hand to her head to keep her scarf on.

She climbed the steps to the church. As she opened the door to go in, I caught a twinkle of light, a glitter of gold. Gracie used to say that no matter how big the problem, you could always take it to God and he'd make it smaller. I followed the old lady inside.

The church was big and empty except for a few people wandering about. Clusters of tiny candles flickered out of dark corners. I smelled hot wax and something moldy. Surrounding me on the walls there were pictures painted in bright colors. Bible stories—I recognized a few, like St. George and the dragon, Jonah and the whale.

Three women knelt on a small bench in front of a golden altar. On the other side of the room two men with long beards stood talking in low voices. I wondered if Mom used to go to a church like this when she was a little girl.

I caught sight of the old lady's lavender shawl as she disappeared around a pillar. I followed her into a hidden alcove hung all over with framed boxes covered with glass doors.

Icons. Gracie told me a little about them before we came to Russia. You pray to them for something special, like for a safe trip, or a healthy baby, or even for good grades. Your prayer goes in through the glass door, out through the back, and up to God. Or something like that. Gracie called them windows to the soul, which I didn't really understand, but it sounded good.

Candlelight reflected off the icons like a million winking stars.

The old lady hobbled up to one, brought the tips of her fingers to her lips, then stretched her arm up as far as it would reach until her fingertips just barely brushed the glass. She mumbled something, bowed her head, turned, and left.

I wondered what she'd prayed for. Was it for someone who was lost or to keep her hopes up or maybe just to be brave? If you were old and living in Russia in the wintertime you'd need to be brave for sure.

Slowly I walked around the pillars and in and out of the little side rooms. I studied the icons. Maybe if I prayed to just the right one, God would help me figure out how to get Mom and me back together.

It was hard to decide which one might work. One was of a bald-headed man holding an open book with his fingers crossed as if he might be making some kind of secret signal. Next to that was a collage of saints made out of thin pieces of shiny metal whose faces were painted onto the wood in back. Finally I came to one of Mary and Jesus. The baby Jesus was kind of weird, like a miniature grown man, but there was something in Mary's face that made me think of Mom, maybe the sad eyes, the lines of worry across the forehead, the turned-down mouth.

Mary and Jesus. Mother and child. Mom and me. Maybe it would work.

I whispered my prayer, "Please, dear God, bless Mom and me, and help us get back to San Diego."

Was it the right thing to say? Would it make it through the window to God? I kissed the tips of my fingers, stood on my very tiptoes, and touched them to the glass.

"*Dobriy dyen,*" said a deep voice from behind me.

I nearly jumped out of my shoes. When I turned, there was Father Alexander, the priest I'd met at the internet café back in July, the same man who'd saved me from those kids. It seemed so long ago, way back in my other life. I remembered he'd said this was his church.

He gazed down on me, candlelight twinkling in his eyes. I'd forgotten how tall he was. He wore a black gown that hung all the way to the floor and a black hat with a veil in back that looked like the kind nuns wear. A fancy golden cross hung from a gold chain around his neck. I remembered it from before.

I fluttered my fingers. "Oh, hi. I mean, *preevyet*

His bushy eyebrows came together. "You are American?"

I nodded.

His face lit up. "I study in America, Boston University. You know of it?"

"Yeah, well sort of. I guess." He'd told me all this before.

He leaned down closer and studied me, my face, my scarf, my clothes. All of a sudden he stepped back and clutched his cross. "Katerina? From internet café?"

Had I really changed that much?

He dropped the surprised look and gave me a big smile. "So, then—" He swept his arm "—welcome, to my church, Katerina."

Did he know I was wanted by the police? I didn't think so.

He pointed at the icon. "You pray to Our Lady of Kazan?"

I nodded and blushed.

"Is very famous Russian icon." He reached deep in the side pocket of his robe, pulled out a stack of little folded pamphlets, and fumbled through them.

"Aha!" He licked his thumb and slipped one from the stack.

The paper was thin and gray like newspaper and on the front was a picture of the icon, Our Lady of Kazan, and below some writing in Cyrillic.

"*Spaseeba* ," I said.

His golden brown eyes searched mine. "If you will forgive me, Katerina, I will ask you this question. Why do you stay in Russia and not go back to the United States?

Why do you come to my church all by yourself?" He looked around. "Where is your mama? Where is your papa?"

I stared at my feet, at the ugly boy's shoes the shelter had given me, at the flower patterns on the tile floor swirling around them. Should I ask for help? Priests are supposed to help people. I raised my eyes and searched his, looking for something I could trust.

He put his hands on my shoulders. "You know what a priest's job is?"

I shook my head.

"A priest's job is to help people who have problems." He tilted his head to the left and the right as he examined my face. "I think there is a problem. *Da*?"

"*Da*," I whispered.

He patted my shoulders. "Come." He motioned for me to follow him.

He led me through a side door into a cozy little room where there was a desk, a bookshelf, a tiny sofa and lots of icons all over the walls.

After flipping on the switch of an electric heater, he gestured toward the sofa for me to have a seat. "Please." He waited for me to sit down then settled himself into the chair behind the desk.

"So?" He put his fingers together and sat there waiting for me to say something. Off somewhere in another part of the church I heard men's voices singing, just one long note, deep and low.

"Well—" I rubbed the stain on my knee "—me and my mom. We lost our passports."

He nodded his head. "Ahh, *da*. I remember that now. Stolen passports. This is a problem we have in Russia." He leaned forward and I caught a whiff of something spicy that smelled like the tiny sandalwood guest soaps Gracie keeps in a jar. "So, if you will forgive another question, Katerina. Where is your mama now?"

"Well—" I ran my St. Christopher medal up and down on its chain. "—we kinda got separated, and then when I went back to where we were staying, no one was there any more."

He frowned. I couldn't tell if he believed me or not.

"Please, Katerina." He passed me a notepad and a pen. "Write your name and the name of your mother."

I wrote on the pad, *Catherine McOwen, Lara McOwen* and handed it back to him.

He studied it as he stroked his long dark beard. "I think first we shall try the American embassy."

I jumped to my feet. "Oh, no!"

His eyes opened wide and he leaned back.

I lowered my voice. "I mean. No." I sat back down again. "It's just that I've already tried them."

He put out his hand. "It's okay, Katerina. Relax. We will find your mama. Do not worry." He opened a desk drawer and riffled through a stack of papers, then picked up his phone. It was all too much like the guard at the embassy had done and the lady at the hospital.

I jumped to my feet again.

Father Alexander patted something invisible in the air. "It's okay, Katerina." He reached in the drawer, pulled out a little wrapped package, and handed it to me.

Through the cellophane I could see it was some kind of a bun.

Food. I hadn't had a thing to eat since last night. I plopped back down onto the sofa and tore through the plastic with my teeth. The smell of cinnamon blasted from the package. The bun was one of those kinds with the brown swirls in it, coated with a sugary white glaze. I took a big bite, almost more that I could chew. The taste was even better than I'd expected, buttery, sugary, full of cinnamon. I took another bite feeling the stickiness cling to the roof of my mouth, feeling the warm fullness as it dropped into my stomach. In two seconds the bun was gone. I licked my lips, then my fingers, very carefully, one at a time, not wasting anything.

While I was doing all this, Father Alexander was speaking to someone in Russian over the phone. He was talking so fast I couldn't understand half of what he was saying, but I did hear Mom's and my names mentioned a few times.

All of a sudden his face changed. His eyes widened. His words slowed. "It's the same girl?" He glanced at me and quickly glanced away. I tried not to show anything on my face that would let him know I understood his Russian.

Was he talking to the police? I couldn't tell, but one thing was for sure. The person on the other end had told him about Vlad.

Inside my stomach the cinnamon bun turned into a heavy wad of dough. I felt like I might throw up. My eyes flitted back and forth between Father Alexander's worried face and the door. Maybe if I told him the whole story about Vlad and trying to protect Mom, he'd understand that it wasn't my fault. Should I risk it? Should I stay and try to explain?

He nodded his head. "Yes. Yes. I will keep her here."

I will keep her here? That did it. He wasn't on my side at all, not if he said that. Before he could blink I was on my feet, across the room, and out the door.

"Katerina, stop," he called after me. "There is something I need to tell you."

CHAPTER TWENTY SIX

Mom's face filled my thoughts. Every night when no one was looking, I slipped the pamphlet on Our Lady of Kazan from my pocket and prayed to it. *Please, God. Please, dear lady of Kazan. Please, help me find my mom.*

Once in a while I wandered back to my grandparents' neighborhood. Peter never liked it when I'd leave like that, but at least he'd stopped giving me a hard time about looking for my mom. Maybe she'd moved in somewhere nearby. She had to be looking for me. Maybe she'd see me. *Never give up hope.* That's what Dad always said.

One day I found a bouquet of wilted flowers that someone had dropped on the sidewalk outside a church. They were light yellow tied up with white ribbon and still kind of pretty even if they were a little droopy. I tried to sell them, but no one seemed interested. The cemetery where Grandma Olga was buried wasn't far, so I decided to take them and put them on her grave.

The curlicue metal gate creaked as I pushed it open. I trudged up the gravel path that led through the middle of the cemetery. All the trees stood bare. The sky above me lay out flat like an old sheet. Piles of dirty snow lined the pathway, and most of the graves were bare, but on a few there were vases of faded plastic flowers, and on some, small framed icons.

My feet crunched on the crusty snow as I left the path and crossed over to a tree with bare gray branches where I thought Grandma Olga was buried. It turned out to be the wrong tree. Without their leaves they all looked the same. I remembered her grave was near a stone bench, but there were lots of those too. I was looking for a gravestone with "Казнэтсов" on it, Cyrillic for "Kuznetsov," Grandpa Ogi's family name. I found one, but the stone was shaped different with roses carved down the side. Grandma Olga's tombstone had been plain.

I found another Казнэтсов, but it wasn't right either. It seemed like there were Казнэтсов's everywhere. Then I remembered Mom saying that *Kuznetsov* was like *Johnson* in the United States.

I looked around. All of a sudden I remembered—near the wall. I walked along slowly, reading the engraving on each of the tombs. *Виноградов, Петров, Белов...* Someone had stuck red plastic roses in the snow near one. A gold picture of Jesus and Mary glittered beside another. In the distance horns honked, brakes shrieked, faraway sounds.

Казнэтсов. I'd found it. A plain rectangle of stone with chunks worn out of the sides. It looked just like I remembered it. Aunt Zoya had stood over there, Mom here, Grandpa Ogi and the priest over under the tree near the big pile of dirt.

I squatted down and began reading through the names.

Григорь Казнэтсов
1880–1951
Катрин Борисов Казнэтсов
1890–1940
Серге Казнэтсов
1901–1901
Наталья Соколов Казнэтсов
1915–1994
Борис Казнэтсов
1912–1997
Ольга Смирнов Казнэтсов
1930–2006

Ольга Смирнов Казнэтсов 1930-2006. It was Grandma Olga. Underneath her another name had been added. It was so low to the ground that the snow almost covered it.

I sunk to my knees and began tracing the letters with my finger.

Лара Казнэтсо McOwen 1970 - 2006

Lara Kuznetsov McOwen.

The world spun above me. Far off down the street a kid shouted. A baby cried.

"No, no, it can't be!" I jumped to my feet and threw the bouquet of wilted flowers at the gravestone.

* * *

I didn't take the metro back. I ran all the way. Peter was busy patching some places on his boom box with some silver tape he'd stolen from one of the janitor carts. Pasha sat in his baseball jacket humming a song to Miss Pig. I sunk down into my place against the wall and sat there panting. Everywhere I looked things seemed out of focus, fuzzy, sounds muffled. It was like being under water. For a minute I didn't say anything and concentrated on getting my breath.

Finally, I turned to Peter. "I took some flowers to put on my grandma's grave." If only I could stop panting. It was making me feel dizzy.

"Flowers?" He sat up straight and gave me a sharp look. "Where you get flowers?"

"Don't worry," I puffed. "I didn't buy them." Why wouldn't my heart slow down?

Peter ran his finger over a crack on the corner of the boom box. Pasha made the pig dance, trying to get my attention.

I looked down at the palms of my hands and swallowed a big gulp of air. "I don't think I found the right grave."

Peter nodded like he was listening, but he didn't look up.

"I couldn't remember exactly where it was. Everything looks so different in the winter." Peter nodded as if he was listening, but his forehead was wrinkled like he was concentrating on his work too.

I stared at my hands. "The scariest thing happened." My breath came faster and faster. Peter looked up. Pasha stopped playing. I needed to blow in a paper bag or I was going to pass out.

"I found this gravestone that said Kuznetsov on it." I gulped for air. "And there was an Olga Kuznetsov—that's my grandma—and underneath that there was a Lara Kuznetsov. Lara Kuznetsov *McOwen*." My voice cracked on the *McOwen*.

Peter's boom box slipped off his lap and landed with a clatter on to the floor. "Your mama?"

"No, no, don't worry, it wasn't her. It couldn't have been." I needed to stop talking so loud. I was almost screaming.

Peter tilted his head. "Yes, but if is name of mother on family grave—"

The words raced from my mouth. "No, no, Peter. It wasn't Mom." I stopped to catch my breath.

He frowned. "But—"

"The lady at the hospital said she was alive. Remember? And, anyway, couldn't there be another Lara Kuznetsov?" I stared at Peter and Pasha waiting for them to nod, say something, do anything to show they agreed.

"I mean, Kuznetsov is like *Johnson* and Lara's a common name too." I wished I could stop my voice from squeaking. "And McOwen. Hey, there're tons of McOwens in Ireland. They're all over the place."

Peter and Pasha nodded.

I choked back a sob. "She's not dead. She couldn't be."

They didn't move. They didn't speak. They just stared at me.

I leaped to my feet and screamed at them, "she's *not* dead." The screech of a train echoed through the empty air above us. Without another word, I turned and raced upstairs to my hiding place in the women's restroom.

* * *

That night I hardly slept except for the nightmares. There was one dream I kept having. It was about that afternoon after I shoved Vlad when I was hiding in the closet. In the dream the police tortured Mom right in front of me. They were trying to get her to tell them where I was hiding. When she wouldn't, they finally killed her. I knew I could have saved her, but I didn't because I was too scared. All night long I kept having that same dream over and over again and kept waking up feeling guiltier and guiltier. Near morning a different dream came. Mom stood over me. Behind her there was this pretty golden light. She looked so real that I felt sure if I reached out, I'd be able to touch her.

"I love you, Carly," she whispered.

"I love you, Mom," I whispered back. Just as she was about to hug me, I woke up.

* * *

The next morning I grabbed my backpack and left without telling Peter or Pasha where I was going.

In the light just before sunrise, the whole cemetery was silvery gray. Every tree branch, every tombstone, every blade of grass glistened with frost. Far off in a corner a man pounded the ground with an ax making an icy, *chink-chink* sound.

Slowly I made my way up the gravel path and across the snow toward my Russian family's grave.

Please, God, I prayed, *let there be a mistake.*

When I got closer, I noticed the bouquet of yellow flowers still lying there where I'd tossed it the day before. The sun climbed up a few inches and shone on the gravestone. I closed my eyes, afraid to look. When I opened them, Mom's name was still there.

"But, Mom," I cried, "I didn't get to tell you good-bye."

I sunk to my knees. "Oh, God, Mom. If only I could have protected you." I reached out and tried to hug the gravestone, but it was too big, too square, too hard, too cold.

She hated the cold. How was she going to stay warm now? And what about nighttime? She'd be so scared, lying out there in the dark, all by herself. Would Grandma Olga protect her? It seemed like she'd never been able to before.

I patted the gravestone. "Don't worry, Mom, I'll never leave you."

I don't know how long I stayed there like that, hugging myself, swaying back and forth, trying to say things that would make her feel better.

A hand tapped me lightly on the shoulder. I turned and looked up. There was Pasha, standing over me, shivering, wearing nothing on top but a thin cotton T shirt. It was ripped around the neck so that part of his pale, bony shoulder showed through.

"Pasha." I wiped my eyes with the back of my coat sleeve. "What are you doing here? Where's your jacket? What happened to your shirt?"

"I follow you." He stamped his feet like a pony trying to keep warm. There was something dark under his nose that looked like dirt.

"You followed me?"

He nodded.

"You came all the way here, all by yourself?"

He pointed at the grave. "Is mama?"

I sat back on my heels and let out a sigh. "*Da.* Is mama."

I took a closer look at the dark stuff on his face. "*Krov*?" I asked. "Blood?"

He rubbed a finger under his nose and nodded. He'd begun to shake all over.

"Where's your jacket?"

His lip quivered. "Kids take it."

I leaned away. "They took your favorite baseball jacket?"

He sniffled. "*Da.*"

I punched the air with my fist. "Jerkheads! Dickheads! Bastards! Don't worry, Pasha, we'll find them. I swear we'll find them, and I'll beat them up. I'll kill them."

"You come back Moskovsky Station?" His teeth chattered so bad he could barely get the words out.

He took my hand. "Please, Katerina. Please to come home."

CHAPTER TWENTY SEVEN

There were fewer people traveling these days and those who did seemed to be less willing to stop and watch our dance act. It seemed like we were always running out of money. With Mom dead I hardly cared. It felt like someone else was walking around inside my body. A train would come in. Passengers would begin flowing down the platform. Peter'd start up the music. I'd paste a smile on my face and take his hand. *Dance, Carly, dance.* I was a windup toy, not a real person.

At night Mom kept coming to me in my dreams, as real as if she were standing right there beside me. I'd feel her arms around me, hear her soft voice. Then a train whistle would blow and wake me up, taking me far away from her and back to the real world, back to Moskovsky Station.

It made me crazy that I didn't know what happened to her. Did she die from when Vlad beat her up, or did the police put her in jail for murder and hang her?

"Shit on them. Fuck on them all. I'll kill them."

* * *

"Story, Katerina?" Pasha looked up at me from beneath his thick dark lashes.

"Not tonight, Pasha." I felt bad, but I just couldn't get myself in a story mood. "Sorry." I turned away from him and swallowed back a tear.

He tapped my shoulder. "Is good story, Katerina."

I turned back to him. "You mean *you're* going to tell *me* a story?"

He nodded, his face very serious.

"Well, okay. Go ahead then." I folded my arms and gave him my full attention.

"Once 'pon time was small Americanka dog—" He frowned and looked at the ceiling. "—name Katerina."

I elbowed Peter and grinned.

"Was preety dog Katerina…"

My smile grew bigger.

"Like dance." Pasha raised his fingers and swayed back and forth. "And sing." He barked a scale of notes.

Peter rolled his eyes.

"And," Pasha continued, "was big man dog name Peter."

Peter groaned and shook his head.

"Peter dog like Katerina dog." Pasha's eyes twinkled. "Peter dog say, 'I can sing.'" Pasha woofed some notes. "Peter dog say, 'I can dance.'" He raised his fingers and hummed a tune. "Peter dog say to Katerina dog, 'Please Katerina dog. Please to dance with me.'"

Pasha's eyes grew big "And know what Katerina dog say?"

I smiled, "No, what?"

"Say, 'No way dickhead Rooskey dog."

* * *

Peter ran his fingers through a hunk of his blond hair and pushed it out of his face. He seemed taller these days and thinner, the bones in his face bigger. We stood leaning against the stone railing, pretending to watch the trains, but what we were really doing was casing out the restaurant across the way.

Peter glanced over his shoulder at a couple sitting at a little round table eating their lunch. "Is simple," he said in a low voice. "Jus take rubles and run."

I'd seen him do it, and it did look easy, but, still, what if the police came? Just a week ago we saw them beat up a kid for stealing a pack of chips. A stupid bag of Fritos, and they nearly killed the kid.

The two at the table stood to leave. The man counted out three bills.

"Now," Peter hissed.

I took a tiny step forward and stopped.

"Quick." Peter gave me a shove. "Go."

Too late. The red-haired waitress stepped over to the table and picked up the money.

Peter stamped his foot. "Three times now you miss, *Americanka*. Why you be so slow?"

I didn't know what to say. I knew we needed the money. We were all out, and the batteries for the boom box just went dead. No batteries meant no music. No music meant no money. We hadn't eaten for a whole day—not even trash. The janitors had picked it all up. And we'd left Pasha downstairs guarding our stuff. We couldn't just hang around here forever.

"Can't *you* do it?" I muttered.

Peter let out an impatient sigh. "I already tell it to you, Katerina. I no can do." He pointed at his face, the dark eyebrows, the pale skin, the wide gray-green eyes. "They know me."

He was right. Practically all the waitresses in all the cafés in the train station knew his face by now. He'd stolen from all of them.

A group of three sat down at the little table the others had just left. The waiter brought them something that smelled like beef and garlic and made me weak with hunger. Fifteen minutes later they rose to leave.

Peter glanced over his shoulder. "Now." he commanded in a loud whisper.

Lightening fast I shot across the walkway and snatched the rubles from the table. The waitress with the red hair was practically on top of me before I got there.

I took off, and she took off after me.

"Stop you little ..." She yelled a word I'd heard Peter say before. Her high-heeled shoes clattered against the marble floor as she raced down the walkway after me, past the Starbucks and the magazine stand, past the kiosk selling beer and the souvenir shop.

"Whumpf." I ran head first into the back of a fat lady wearing a wool coat. She smelled like the chest where Gracie keeps her antique clothes. I veered around her. Up ahead were the escalators. I took the up escalator and ran down, dodging angry-faced people who flattened themselves to the right and the left to get out of my way. I could hear the waitress behind me yelling *stop*. From the sound of it she was pretty far back. I leaped over the last two stairs and landed with a thump on all fours. I sprang to my feet and raced toward the hall that goes to the metro lines, sprinted down to the end, and slipped behind the city map.

I must have stood there for at least fifteen minutes, sweating, panting, waiting for the panic juices to drain away. When I finally got the nerve to peek out, the coast was clear. Still clutching the money, I started down the hall back toward the trains. I was almost at the end when around the corner came Peter. He saw me, and his face turned into one big grin.

"High five, *Americanka*." He raised his hand, then, instead, leaned over and kissed me on the lips. I was so surprised I nearly fell over backwards. My first kiss. In a train station. In Russia. After stealing money off a table in a restaurant. How weird. I laughed, and Peter laughed too, and then we did the high five anyway.

A little while later I stared at myself in the mirror in the women's restroom. My hair had grown back, about three inches, the same length all over. It didn't look that bad, but my face was so thin. Marisa always said I looked like Mom. I touched my lips. Did Peter think I was pretty? I stood there mesmerized in front of the mirror until an old lady nudged me so she could get at the sink.

* * *

Out of rubles. Forced to steal again.

I stood on guard in the doorway to the little gift shop holding Peter's boom box while he went inside. We'd done it before. Never a problem. Pasha stood outside in the hallway with all our stuff. If he saw anything, he was supposed to let me know, and I'd warn Peter.

Peter wandered from display to display pretending that he was actually going to buy something. Suddenly I realized that the storekeeper was on to him. Peter had his back to the guy so he didn't know he was being watched. If only Peter would look my way so I could signal him.

Just as Peter's hand reached out to take the batteries, Pasha waved to get my attention. He pointed down the hall to where two policemen were headed our way. It was too late. Peter was already stuffing the batteries inside his jacket. He headed out of the store, saw the two policemen coming, and took off.

"Stop," the shopkeeper shouted after him.

If it hadn't been for the woman who wheeled her suitcase into Peter's path, I think he might have gotten away. Instead he tripped and fell, and that's when the policemen caught him.

Peter jerked the batteries out of his jacket and sent them skidding across the floor. One of the policemen grabbed Peter by the back of his jacket and threw him against the cement railing. Peter crumpled to the ground. The second policeman kicked Peter in the stomach. Peter grunted and pulled his legs up, hugging himself, trying to roll out of the way. Jaws clenched, lips pulled back, the guy kicked Peter, over and over again. It looked like he was having fun. I felt like I was going to throw up.

"Stop." I charged forward and pounded the guy on the back. I didn't care if he was a policeman. I didn't care if he recognized me. I didn't care about anything except getting him to stop what he was doing to Peter. He turned and looked at me, his eyes round with surprise.

"Stop," I shouted again.

He responded with a blow to my chest that sent me sailing. I landed against the wall and hit my head. By the time I'd recovered, it was all over. The policemen simply walked away. Most of the crowd that had formed lost interest and walked away too. They all just left, leaving Peter lying there on the ground, moaning.

"Peter! Peter!" I fell to my knees beside him. There was a big lump over his left eye and blood running from his nose. He couldn't even talk. I looked around at the few stragglers remaining. Wasn't anyone a doctor? Would no one help? One by one they walked away.

Then I saw Pasha. He stood alone over by the wall with our trash sack, sucking his thumb. He'd seen the whole thing. Poor kid.

It took a week for the swelling on Peter's face to go down. He pretended like nothing had happened, but I noticed him wincing when he moved. There was something different about him, a new way he clenched his jaw and a hard glint in his eye when he thought no one was looking. There was something else too. His mouth didn't turn up at the edges anymore.

CHAPTER TWENTY EIGHT

On my way back downstairs, I happened to pass a newspaper stand when something caught my eye. Just a glance, I wouldn't have even been looking if a kid zipping by hadn't knocked me into the stand and one of the newspapers hadn't fallen to the ground. There on the front page was a picture of me, the same one I'd seen before, my passport photo. There was a headline in Cyrillic. I didn't know what it said, but I could imagine:

Wanted for Murder. 11-year-old American Carly McOwen

I glanced around to see if anyone else was looking. The man behind the counter watched me. His eyes narrowed. Casually, I put the newspaper back on the stack and strolled off. Forcing myself to slow down, to breathe, I headed for the escalator.

By now I'd thought people would have given up looking for me. I pulled my scarf down lower over my face. I'd need to start being more careful again.

Three days passed, and then the police came. It started with a big commotion down by platform one. Four policemen hovered over someone in a wheelchair, an old lady wrapped in a bright pink shawl. By the way people were acting, I figured she must be having a heart attack, but then everybody backed off, and I saw one of the policemen talking to the kids along the wall.

Slowly the wheelchair and the policemen moved down the passageway toward us, past platform two, past platform three, talking to the street people as they came. Kids began looking around, whispering to each other, acting nervous. The kid next to the Coke kiosk said something to the kid next to him, who told it to the next kid and on down the line. A red-haired boy crawled over to Pasha and whispered something in his ear.

Pasha told Peter.

"Is trouble," Peter informed me. "Police look for American girl."

My eyes darted to where the group was just moving past platform five. I could see more policemen now and someone tall dressed in black. The beard, the flat shape of the back of his head—it was Father Alexander. I'd told him I lived in the station, and he'd told the police. I'd trusted him, and now he was helping them. I felt like I'd been slammed in the chest.

I jumped to my feet and grabbed my backpack. "I've gotta get out of here."

Peter and Pasha had already started to gather up our stuff. The police were getting closer. Pretty soon they'd be by the escalator. I needed to get there before them.

I shifted from foot to foot. "I gotta go, Peter. Now."

"Okay," he said. "We meet outside."

I was afraid to run because then people would notice me. Careful not to push, I slipped past passengers, staying as close to the wall as I could. The street kids watched me go, whispering to each other behind their hands. I made it to the escalator just in time.

All of a sudden a lot of people began yelling, "ona tam," *there she is*. The kids probably figured they'd get some money for ratting on me. I sprinted up the escalator two stairs at a time, bumping into people, practically climbing over them as I scrambled to the top. I could hear the policemen's voices shouting from down below as I raced down the hall by the restaurants.

When I reached the lobby, I buried myself in the crowds, worming my way toward the exit as fast as I could go. No one seemed to notice me. People were too busy searching for train tickets, fiddling with luggage, trying to keep track of their own kids.

The revolving door swept me out into a world of icy blue snow that made my lungs ache. After all the crowds and noise of the station, it seemed so quiet. I hurried down the steps to the sidewalk, waited for the light to change, and crossed the six lanes of Nevsky Prospekt to the other side.

I stopped near a dark doorway to catch my breath and stood watching the train station from across the street. All lit up, it glowed green against the dark blue sky. The clock on top of the station said four in the afternoon, already night time in Russia in December.

There weren't very many people on the sidewalk, just a few bundled up in long fur coats and hats. The cold seeped right through Anna's coat. I stomped my feet to keep warm. If Peter and Pasha didn't come soon, I'd freeze to death.

On the other side of the street five empty police cars sat lined up against the curb. I wondered if they were still looking for me inside. A van zoomed up and skidded to a stop behind the police cars. CNN was printed in big letters along its side and on top was a satellite dish. A man in a bright red parka jumped out and ran up the steps toward the station. Another guy, also wearing a red jacket, carried a TV camera on his shoulder and followed the first guy. A third man strung a bunch of black cord from the van to a search light and aimed it at the station. All of a sudden the whole front wall was lit up bright as day.

From where I stood it was like watching a play on stage. Policemen came pouring out of the train station along with some men wearing long wool coats. A CNN guy grabbed one of them and stuck a microphone in his face. The cameraman caught it all. I wished I could hear what they were saying, probably something like, "Search continues for American girl…"

The policemen raced down the steps, jumped in their cars, and took off.

Father Alexander came out of the station wearing his thick black coat and furry hat. They interviewed him too. People on the sidewalk near me stopped and watched. If only I could hear what the reporter was saying. A crowd had formed on the other side of the street. If I crossed back over, I could blend in without anyone noticing me. Maybe I could find out what was going on.

The symbol on the crosswalk light had a red slash through it, but I went ahead anyway. I reached the other side just as the line of trucks and cars started toward me. Careful, trying not to nudge anyone, I worked my way through the circle of people until I was right in front. It was pretty dark where we stood. No one would notice me. The lights and all the attention was focused on the reporter up on the steps.

His red jacket had the letters CNN printed in white on the front.

The CNN cameraman moved in and pointed his camera at a piece of paper in the reporter's hand. I didn't need to guess. It was a copy of my passport photo. Another searchlight came on and swept over the crowd. The cameraman turned and began shooting the audience. Panicked, I took a step back. The surrounding people blocked me from going further.

All of a sudden the search light stopped on me. I froze. I could felt its heat. It was so bright I had to close my eyes. When I opened them, the TV camera was aimed straight at me. I should have turned around or buried my face in my coat, but I was too stunned. It had all happened so fast. The cameraman lowered his camera and stepped over to look at the piece of paper in the reporter's hand. A quick glance and his camera was back on me.

The surrounding crowd pressed against me from all sides.

The cameraman pointed and shouted, "It's her. It's Katerina McOwen."

Mumbling rose from the crowd around me. I felt a finger tap the top of my head, then someone grab my arm. The cameraman, his camera still on his shoulder, ran down the steps and grabbed my other arm. He leaned down and peered into my face. "Katerina McOwen?"

"*Nyet. Nyet.*" I said, trying to tug away.

The reporter joined the cameraman, and they both stared down at me.

"*Da.* Is Katerina," said the cameraman.

My heart fluttered like a moth caught in a lampshade. Would the police beat me like they did Peter or would they just throw me in jail? A Russian jail—it had to be the worst place in the whole world.

The reporter pulled out his cell phone and punched in some numbers. He spoke in rapid Russian for a few seconds, then said, "We keep her here."

He snapped closed his phone and took my other hand. The two dragged me through the crowd over to their van. The cameraman opened one of the doors, and the reporter shoved me into the back seat.

I went crazy then, kicking, biting, anything to get away. The reporter's legs felt like pieces of steel against the toes of my shoes. My teeth wouldn't go through his gloves. My arms weren't strong enough to break his grip. He cussed but he still wouldn't let me go.

"*Nyet Katerina McOwen.*" I kept telling them. They wouldn't listen.

The reporter jumped in beside me and slid the van door closed with a bang. There was barely room for the two of us on the seat with all the piles of papers and books, equipment and things. I would have tried to escape, but he held my arm too tight.

People crowded around. Faces pressed against the windows. Back in the United States when someone killed a policeman, the whole city got in an uproar. Is that how these people would be? I couldn't look at them. It was too scary.

The reporter pulled out a tape recorder and began questioning me in broken English. "You speak Rooskey?" he asked.

I didn't know what to do so I played dumb. After a little he gave up, and the two of us just sat there, staring straight ahead, our breath making clouds of frost that fogged up the windows.

In the distance sirens sounded. It was all over. Soon I'd be in jail. At least maybe it'd be warmer than on the streets.

An icy draft hit the back of my neck as the cameraman opened the rear doors of the van. I could hear him loading in his equipment. More and more people crowded around us. All of a sudden the reporter beside me let out a shout. There out the window on the sidewalk was Peter holding one of the T.V. cameras. How had he gotten hold of it? Where had he come from? I hadn't seen him in the crowd.

I focused my gaze on him and pleaded with my eyes.

The cameraman in the back was still loading stuff into the van. I don't think he realized Peter had taken his camera. Peter held it close to the window pretending to shoot pictures. He swayed back and forth and did a little dance, grinning, teasing. Beside me the reporter went ballistic, shouting and waving his hands for Peter to stop.

Peter held the camera out in front of him by the tips of his fingers, looking like he was about to drop it on the sidewalk. The reporter'd seen enough. He let go of my arm, slid the door open, and made a lunge for Peter. As he did, the door on my side slid open too. I couldn't figure out how until I looked down. There was Pasha standing in the street staring up at me. He motioned furiously with his hand. I leaped over the piles of books, equipment and papers and fell head first down into the street. Cars screeched. Taxis honked. It didn't matter. I was free.

* * *

A cheerful yellow glow spread from the windows at McDonald's lighting up the snow on the sidewalk outside. Inside, the room was filled with warm, steamy air, the smell of French fries cooking, the noise of people talking, the clatter of trays. A small bag of fries sat on the table in front of us, a special treat. Peter had stolen the reporter guy's wallet when he gave him back his camera.

Pasha sucked red liquid from a straw. Tomato juice. You make it by mixing ketchup with water and adding sugar.

Peter grinned. "You famous *Americanka* now. Be on TV." His face looked so cool when he smiled like that, the wide forehead, the dark eyebrows, the pretty gray-green eyes. Beside him on the seat was all our stuff, the big heavy trash sack, the boom box, Pasha's stool and accordion. They'd had to leave it behind a dumpster, hoping no one would steal anything while they came to my rescue.

It made me nervous even being in McDonalds. I faced the wall and pulled my cap down so low I could barely see out. I couldn't go back to Moskovsky Station again. That was for sure. Everyone was looking for me there.

Peter must have read the worry in my eyes because he smiled. "Is okay, Katerina." He pointed at his chest and smiled. "I know place where is safe."

* * *

Outside the train windows the light at a railroad crossing glistened on a snow bank. Then the windows went black again. Pasha's sleeping body slumped against mine. On the other side of me Peter sat silent, staring straight ahead. The train rounded a curve, and he swayed, his shoulder pressing mine. He'd not really explained where we were going, except that we had to take the metro to a different train station, Baltiisky Vokzal, and from there catch the train that would take us out of town. He used the reporter's credit card to pay for the tickets.

The train stopped, and we were the only ones to get off. I couldn't tell where we were. The only thing lit up was an empty bench and the cement shelter around it, its walls covered with advertisements, most of them peeling off.

Peter led us down the edge of a narrow, bumpy road made of cracked pavement. After a while my eyes got used to the darkness, and I began seeing the bare branches of rows of trees, a few houses, fences, everything fuzzy through the falling snow. No one was around, not even a car on the road.

We trudged along in silence hugging ourselves, trying to keep warm. Snow flakes burned as they landed on my face. The cold made my bones ache. Peter turned down a narrow dirt road beside some pine trees and stopped in front of a wooden fence that surrounded a little house. It was so small I would have guessed it was a garage or a tool shed except there was a front porch and smoke coming from the chimney. Two windows were lit up. In the yard a bright orange and yellow plastic slide and a red plastic wagon gathered snow.

Peter told Pasha and me to wait by the gate. We watched as he crossed the yard, climbed the steps, and knocked. A woman opened the door. With the light from behind her, I couldn't see her face. She raised her hands to her chest and took a step back.

Peter said something to her. She didn't move, didn't speak. Peter turned halfway round and swept his arm toward us. I heard him say, *Americanka* . The rest I didn't understand.

The woman shaded her eyes and peered out into the darkness. A man came up from behind her and began talking in a loud voice. Peter said something back, his voice getting louder too. Clouds of icy breath rose in the air. The woman slipped back inside, and then it was just Peter and the man. He waved his fist at Peter. Peter shouted back. Finally the man stepped back inside and slammed the door. Hard.

Peter turned and trudged back to us. I couldn't see his face. I didn't need to.

"Who was that?" I asked as we passed out of the yard.

"Why you ask so much questions, *Americanka*?" He flung the gate closed so hard it practically flew off its hinges.

CHAPTER TWENTY NINE

On the way back Peter didn't say a word. He just sat there staring straight ahead, the little muscles around his jaw twitching. I'd guessed by now that the man and woman in the little house were his stepdad and his mom. When we got off the train, he led us onto a dark, quiet street across from the Baltiisky station. He left Pasha and me shivering on the sidewalk while he walked into the middle of the street. I listened for cars, scared at any moment one would come speeding around the corner and smash Peter. He squatted to look at something in the road, felt around on the black ice with his fingers, then stood, moved a little further on, and did the same thing again. He walked over to a dumpster on the side of the street, tugged and pulled on the metal rod that goes through the handle until it broke loose from its icy crust. He slid it out and walked back into the middle of the road. Stooping, grunting, straining, he used the rod to pry up the lid on a manhole. All of a sudden I understood where he was taking us.

Rats crawling in filth, flesh eating diseases. Only criminals and weirdos lived under the streets.

He went down the ladder first. Then we handed him the trash sack, the boom box, Pasha's accordion, and his stool. Pasha climbed down next.

I stood over the hole looking down at them. "I'm scared."

Peter motioned with his hand for me to come. "Is warm. You like."

"Isn't there some place better we can go?" I asked.

He gave me a look that made me wish I hadn't said anything. After all he and Pasha had left Moskovsky Station just for me. Peter had tried to get his parents to take us in just for me. We were a team. No complaining.

I put a foot on the first rung of the ladder. Slowly, step by step, I lowered myself down. A creepy, damp kind of warm wrapped itself around me, along with the smell of dirt and mold so strong it made my eyes water. The stink of sewer lay over everything, faint but there.

As my foot hit ground, I found myself in total darkness. I flailed with my hands. "I can't see. I can't see." Everything sounded hollow. My hand hit Pasha's head. He reached up and gripped it tight. I reached out with my other hand and felt something warm and solid with a slimy coating that came off on my fingers. I wiped my hand on my pants.

Peter struck a match. In the flickering light all I could see was a rounded, bumpy cement surface just inches from his left shoulder, the slimy thing I'd just touched. He took a step forward. Pasha and I followed, single file. I dragged the trash bag scratching along the ground behind us.

Near my left ear came a high squeaky noise and the sound of something scratching cement. I jumped a mile. "What was that?"

Peter stopped and lit another match. The sound went away.

A car rumbled overhead. The ground shook. I hoped the ceiling wouldn't cave in.

Lights appeared in the distance. Finally my eyes adjusted to the darkness. Pipes as tall as Pasha ran along beside us disappearing into a maze of smaller ones that snaked off into the distance. I heard noises, voices. As we moved closer, I realized it was the sound of children—laughing, screaming, screeching children, a whole playground full of them. A little girl's smudged face peered at us over the top of a pipe. She giggled and disappeared. The pipe was warmer and drier than the one I'd touched before. Peter hefted our sack on top of it and climbed over. I went next and pulled Pasha up behind me.

From the top of the pipe I could see down the valley between it and the next pipe over. It looked like a party going on, kids jumping from pipe to pipe, doing somersaults, pushing, shoving, laughing, shouting. A little boy held up a pink heart-shaped pillow with the words, "I love you," embroidered in English across the front. A little girl pulled a Barbie out of a store sack and stuck it in Pasha's face. It looked brand new. Four little boys raced tiny toy cars along one of the sewer pipes, crashing them into each other. The cars looked new too. I wondered where they stole all this stuff.

Flickering candlelight reflected off the cement ceilings, off the gray pipes, off the kids' faces. Candles were everywhere, melted down and stuck along the tops of pipes, on wooden boxes, in bottles. A lot of these kids didn't look old enough to be handling fire. A bunch of them even smoked. I'd seen kids at the station smoking, but mostly teenagers. These were little kids.

Some boys about Peter's age appeared out of the dusty darkness. One waved a flashlight. Another with a round face took a swig from a giant vodka bottle and passed it to his friends. The tallest of the three had to stoop to keep from bumping his head on the low ceiling.

"Where you come from?" one of them asked us in Russian. A line of stitches just above his left eyebrow distorted the shape of his eye.

Peter explained that we'd been living in Moskovsky Station. He introduced himself and Pasha and me, as *the Americanka*.

"*Americanka?*" The boy looked at Peter. "She your girl?"

"Da." Peter put his arm around my shoulder and pulled me close.

I was glad he did. I didn't like the looks of these boys.

The kid named Boris took another swig of vodka, put his flashlight under his chin, and leered at us. He had ears that stuck out straight and a face like a monkey's. Dimitri, the kid with the stitches, grabbed the flashlight, and shined it under his chin. He bared his teeth at Pasha and growled. Pasha jumped behind my back. The tall kid named Ivan leaned toward me and stuck out his tongue. It was almost long enough to touch his nose. The three hooted and howled and laughed the way drunks do. It scared me. Everything about them scared me.

From somewhere off down one of the tunnels, came the sound of a man's voice mumbling. A bum wearing a coat that was way too big staggered out of the darkness. The three boys ran at him screaming and waving their arms. The tall kid Ivan pushed him and told him to go away. Boris chased him, and beat him on the head. The kid with the stitches kicked him in the rear. When it was all over and the man was gone, the boys returned and stood in front of Peter, smiling proudly. Peter smiled back. I wouldn't have.

The kid named Ivan shoved the vodka bottle in Peter's face. A frown formed across Pasha's brow. Peter stared at the bottle for a second or two, long enough that I thought he was going to refuse, but then his arm shot out and he took it. Pasha's chin dropped, and he stared at the ground. My heart went cold. A picture of Mom taking that first drink flashed inside my mind— her trembling hand, Vlad watching her, smiling.

I put a hand on Peter's arm. "*Nyet*," I whispered.

It was too late. He already had the bottle to his lips, his head tilted back. It felt like my whole world had turned upside down. Peter was our only protection. There was no way Pasha and I could make it without him.

Peter choked, wiped his mouth on his sleeve, and passed the bottle on to the kid named Dimitri. Dimitri took a big swallow and waved the bottle at me. His weird left eye wouldn't stop twitching.

I put out my palms. "*Nyet. Nyet.*"

Dimitri waved the bottle at Pasha. A confused frown crossed Pasha's brow. He started to reach for the bottle, but I grabbed his hand away.

Even the little kids took sips of vodka. Their playing grew wilder and crazier. One tried to do a flip off the top of a pipe and landed on his head. He lay there for a minute, not moving, but nobody did anything. Another knocked a candle over. It missed a little girl's blond head by less than a quarter of an inch. A girl with fly-away red hair wiped the scum off the side of one of the pipes and rubbed it on her face pretending to be putting on makeup. She looked up and gave us a green smile.

When the bottle came back around to Peter, he raised it high like a salute. *"Na zdarovye!."* He swallowed and wiped his mouth. In the candlelight his eyes glowed bright. "What wrong, Katerina?" The sloppy grin on his face made me cringe.

"I don't like it here," I said to him. "Can't we go someplace else?"

"No is someplace else." He gestured with the bottle. "Is good place here." He took another swig and held it out to me. "Have vodka. Make everything better. You see."

* * *

"I am a bum. I live in the sewer.
All I do is play.
No need Mama. No need Papa
When is vodka and klay."

Dimitri leaned against one of the sewer pipes, his bad eye half-closed, a stupid smile on his face. One of his fingers was still looped through the handle of the empty vodka bottle. He kept singing the same dumb song, over and over again. It sounded like he'd made it up except that it was in English. The other kids had stopped playing and were all sound asleep, some sprawled over pipes, others lying on little hills of blankets they'd built in the valleys between the pipes. I spread our blanket on the ground next to one of the fat warm pipes, and Peter, Pasha, and I sat down.

"I am a bum. I live in the sewer..." Would he never stop?

Pasha frowned. "Vodka bad."

I put my arm around him and pulled him close. "You're right, Pasha. Vodka *is* bad, and don't ever forget it."

He looked up at me, his eyes serious. "No story tonight."

I shook my head. "No story tonight."

A car rumbled overhead. Peter slumped against my shoulder, sound asleep, his mouth slack. Pasha's chest rose and fell in a soft rhythm. I was too worried to sleep.

The candles all burned down until only one flickered in the darkness. My chin rested on Pasha's silky head. In his sleep he rubbed his nose. Beside me Peter grunted and tipped over onto the ground.

I am a bum. I live in the sewer...

CHAPTER THIRTY

Jelly beans and Twinkies for breakfast—that's what the sewer kids ate.

The girl with the fly-away red hair pulled a package of Hostess miniatures from a paper sack and bit through the plastic wrapping. The sweet smell of powdered sugar drifted my way. How long had it been since I'd had a real doughnut? I imagined biting into one, the feel of the cakey texture turning soft and wet in my mouth, the powdery sugar sticking to my tongue.

Pasha played peek-a-boo with Miss Pig while a little girl just a year or two older watched. Each time the pig jumped out from behind Pasha's leg, the little girl would crack up. Then she'd pretend to feed the pig a jellybean which of course would end up in Pasha's mouth.

I licked my lips as I watched the red-headed girl take a bite of a doughnut.

"Where'd you get those?" I asked her in Russian.

"At Pushkin Supermart," she replied in English.

"You bought them?"

She nodded.

"Where'd you get the money?"

She popped the last bite of doughnut in her mouth and brushed the sugar from her hands. I would have licked it off. "We get rubles for be in movies," she said.

"Movies? What kind?"

She lowered her eyes. "Is bad kind."

"Bad kind?"

She still wouldn't look at me. "Make for remove clothes."

"Ohhhhh." I didn't know what to say.

Her eyes brightened. "Is okay. When get rubles, we buy big house." She stretched her arms wide and smiled. "Place for *all* street kids can live."

* * *

A week went by. We hardly ever climbed above ground. When we did, we stepped into a world that had frozen solid. The days were dark. Even at noon the sun barely rose above the buildings, and the sky over the city never got much brighter than a faded out blue. It always felt like night was coming even in the middle of the day.

The places where we begged weren't as good as the train station. We had to get most of our food from the trash, frozen stuff that turned to mush when it thawed. Sometimes we even stole from the other kids. I always felt bad about that.

Down in the sewer everything I touched was filthy, even my own clothes, my hair, my skin. Anna's beautiful coat now had green slime stains down the side. I would have died to go to the homeless shelter for a shower and clean clothes, but it was way across town, and we'd heard that it was hardly ever open anymore. Sometimes it seemed that the sewer smells had soaked right into my skin. I wondered how many germs we were being exposed to.

Night before last I woke up and found a rat crawling over my leg. More of them crawled over people's backpacks. Beady eyes. Scaly tails. I screamed and sat up straight. The whole pack took off, squeaking and scratching their claws over the cement pipes as they scuttled off down the tunnel into the darkness. I closed my eyes for just a second, and when I opened them, they were back. Rats everywhere. A few of the other kids woke up, yawned and went right back to sleep. I guess they'd been here so long they were used to rats.

* * *

It must have been close to noon, but not even a speck of daylight reached us down in the sewer. Candles flickered in the darkness. Pasha ran Miss Pig up and down his leg and hummed a sing-song tune. Peter and I sat next to each other against a pipe, silent, staring at nothing. Further away an argument had broken out among some of the kids—lots of angry voices, shrieks, and shoving. No one was happy today.

Dimitri signaled Peter aside and said something to him that I couldn't hear. Peter reached inside his jacket and handed Dimitri some of our rubles. Dimitri and his other two buddies disappeared off down the tunnel.

"Is he going to get us food?" I asked.

Peter stared at the ceiling. "Is okay, Katerina. No is worry."

I looked into his face. "Are you sure?"

He exploded. "What wrong, *Americanka*?" He pointed at his chest. "Now you not believe, Peter?"

I shook my head and walked away. He was right, I didn't believe him. He was crazy to trust those boys with our money.

Two hours later, and the three boys were back. They staggered down the tunnel toward us, the beams of their flashlights bouncing on the dirt as they walked. Every so often a cone of light glanced off the plastic bag in Ivan's hand. When they reached us, they stopped. Ivan leaned against one of the pipes and put the bag to his mouth. He blew out filling it with air then took a deep drag in, making it collapse. Glue, *klay*. It was the same thing I'd seen kids do in the train station. One time a policeman caught one of them and poured the glue over his head. The kid bawled for hours afterwards. It had been terrible watching him try to pick the thick, sticky strands off his face. It's lucky he didn't suffocate.

I glared at Peter, but he wouldn't look back. Our good money. Gone. Spent on drugs.

Ivan pulled the bag from his mouth, threw back his head and let out a long, low howl. Arms out straight, he began spinning, bumping into everything, twirling out of control. He knocked two lit candles off the top of one of the pipes. Luckily they landed on the ground instead of on top of someone's head. Eyes glazed and unfocused, he lurched forward and offered the bag to Peter.

Peter put out his hand. "*Nyet. Nyet.*"

Ivan lowered his face to Peter's. "What? You never do *klay*?"

Peter shook his head.

Ivan waved the bag. "*Klay* is good. *Klay* is heaven."

"Stop." I pushed his arm away.

His mouth stretched into a fat, ugly grin. He looked at his friends. "*Americanka* protect little *Rooskey* boy."

The three boys giggled and pointed at Peter. "Poor little *Rooskey* boy."

Without warning, Peter reached out and snatched the bag.

"No, Peter. Don't." I tried to pull his arm down.

"*Nyet, nyet.*" Pasha's high-pitched squeal came out of the darkness.

Too late. Peter already had the bag over his mouth. It filled with air as he blew in, then collapsed as he sucked the fumes out. His chest rose and fell twice more before he pulled the bag away and let out a deep sigh.

He held the bag out to me like a toast. "*Klay.* Is good, Katerina." I caught a whiff of something that smelled like Super Glue.

I batted his arm away. "You told me it was bad," I shouted. "You said you'd never do it." I took a step toward him and gave him a little shove. "You gave them our money, and now look what's happened. All wasted on drugs."

He laughed and wagged his head. "No be so serious, *Americanka.*"

"Jerk!" I went over and stood by Pasha.

Boris and Dimitri got into a loud argument over something. Within seconds Boris wrestled Dimitri to the ground and pounded him in the face. Dimitri squealed and tried to get away. When it was over, the stitches above his left eye had opened up and there was blood all over his face.

After the *klay*, they started drinking vodka, a new full bottle that they'd probably bought with our money. Ivan came and stood in front of me and began grinding his hips back and forth. Peter moved to my side and flopped his arm over my shoulder. "*Americanka* is *my* girl," he announced.

His words slurred. His eyes held a glazed look like oil on water.

I brushed his arm off my shoulder. "I'm *not* your girl. Not when you act like this."

Peter put his face close to mine. "What? Now you no like Peter?" His breath smelled like alcohol, the way Mom's had when she'd had too much to drink. She wasn't my mom when she acted that way. I didn't want Peter to become like her. He put his arms around me and kissed me on the lips. With all my strength I pushed him away. He grabbed my arms and pulled me toward him again. This time the kiss was harder, his teeth grinding against mine, forcing my mouth open. My lips burned from the vodka. I felt his tongue, slippery and hard as it entered my mouth.

I wrenched myself away. "Don't ever do that again," I screamed.

I settled down beside Pasha and closed my eyes. How had this happened to Peter? He'd always been the one I could count on. Now he was becoming just like the other sewer guys. Tears rolled down my cheeks and plopped onto Pasha's dark head. If only we hadn't had to leave Moskovsky Station. Now we were losing Peter, and it was all my fault.

* * *

The next morning Pasha began to cough. He shivered, and his face felt hot, and all he wanted to do was lie with his head in my lap. If only we had some medicine to give him.

With a grunt, Peter cleared his throat and sat up straight. I put my face in his. "So what's with the drugs and the vodka? You told me you didn't do stuff like that."

He smiled and rolled his eyes. "Is fun. Make feel good. You try."

"No way." I shook my head hard. "I hate how you guys act. It's dangerous. It's crazy."

"What crazy, Katerina?" He made a half circle with his arm. "See this place? Is not so bad if have vodka, have *klay*. If not vodka, what is life?"

"But Pasha's sick, and we need money, and if you're drunk, you can't help us." I'd seen him giving some more of our rubles to the boys, money we needed for food and for medicine for Pasha.

Peter slipped his arm out from under the blanket and put it around my shoulder. "Is okay, Katerina. I protect you." It might have made me feel better if he hadn't slurred his words.

* * *

A pyramid of Styrofoam cups—chicken noodle soup—sat on the display table right in front of me, but every time I got ready to reach for one, the woman behind the stand gave me the evil eye.

At the next stand over a woman in a dark green coat inspected turnips. Her bag didn't have a latch on top. I could see the tip of her wallet sticking up. Just as I was getting ready to move toward her, two boys came along. One of them bumped her, and when she looked, the other kid snatched her wallet. The lady didn't even realize what had happened.

Darn! Why didn't I move faster?

The two boys were just turning to walk off when a policeman appeared from behind the cereal display and grabbed the one with the wallet. He wrestled the kid to the ground. Then he kicked him in the ribs, in the stomach, in the head. It was just like what happened to Peter that day.

When it was all over, I realized I was shaking. It could have been me getting the beating instead of that boy.

I wandered along until I came in front of the meat display.

Beside me an old lady held her money purse in one hand while she inspected the three whole chickens lying just behind the glass. Her eyes were bright blue like Gracie's and her hair the same silvery white.

The man behind the meat counter came up and asked the old lady if she would like a chicken. She pointed at the one next to a pig's head and asked him to hold it up. As he did, she laid her little purse down on the countertop. She took the chicken in both hands, held it up by its legs, and felt its wings, its breasts, its stomach.

No one was looking. I snatched the little purse off the counter and slipped it inside my coat. Casually I turned and strolled off. I stopped on the other side of the vegetables. From there I could see when the lady realized her purse was gone. She put a hand over her heart and swayed a little. She looked so confused and worried it made me feel terrible. Slowly she turned and walked away leaving the chicken behind. Would this mean that she wouldn't have dinner tonight? There was a big hole in the back of her sweater I hadn't noticed before. I swallowed the lump in my throat and blinked back the tears. Maybe I should go give her back her purse. It would be so easy. I could just say I found it on the ground.

No, I couldn't. I needed to get the soup for Pasha. Lots of liquids. Lots of chicken soup. That's what Gracie would have said.

* * *

Peter was gone all day. He left with Ivan, Boris and Dimitri in the morning and didn't say where he was going or when he was coming back. I worried they were going to buy more drugs.

Pasha slept with his head on my lap. I worried about him too. I'd fed him the chicken and noodles, but it hadn't done much good. He'd coughed all night, and his face was flushed. He felt like he was burning up.

Carefully, I slipped out from underneath him and propped him over against the cushion of clothes inside our trash bag. Quietly, I got to my feet and tiptoed away.

All of a sudden from behind me a high-pitched voice shrieked, "Where you go, Katerina? Where you go?"

I turned and hurried back. He'd begun to cry.

"Pasha, Pasha." I cupped his face in my hands. "I'm just going to look for Peter. I'll be back as soon as I can." I made him lie down again. "You're sick. You need to stay here."

"But, Katerina." He sniffled. "I afraid you leave me."

I put my hands on his shoulders and looked him straight in the eye. "Now, you listen to me, Pasha. I'll never leave you. I promise. Never, ever, okay?"

"Okay, Katerina."

I didn't find Peter, and I didn't dare stay away from Pasha too long. When I returned, he was sitting up against the pipe his eyes huge with worry. I don't think he'd slept the whole time I was gone.

I dropped down beside him. "I've brought you a surprise, Pasha." I gave him a big smile hoping it would cheer him up. "Ta da!" I pulled a little bag of cherry cough drops from my backpack. I would have bought him some real medicine, but I didn't have enough money.

Just then Peter appeared.

"Where'd you go?" I asked him. "I was getting worried."

He sat down beside me and pulled a wad of rubles from his pocket. "You say I no get money?" He shook the rubles in my face. "What this?"

"Wow! Where'd you get all that?"

He scowled and shook his head. "Is too many questions, Katerina, okay? Just be happy for rubles." He slumped over and buried his face in his hands.

The red-headed girl signaled for me to come near her. She nodded at Peter and said in a low voice, "I know where go boyfriend."

I moved closer. "You do?"

She nodded. "He go for make movies." Her breath smelled like strawberry gum.

"What? Oh, no!" I glanced over at Peter and cringed. *Poor guy.* No wonder he didn't want to talk about it. I wanted to say something to him to make him feel better, but I couldn't think what to say.

The red-headed girl shrugged. "Why is bad? Is money."

* * *

"I can't see. I can't see." Dimitri stumbled backwards grabbing at the air, his eyes wild and weird. The other boys cheered him on, laughing, jeering.

Peter put his arm around my waist, grinned at Ivan, and pointed at me. "We go America." He looked down at me. "Is right, Katerina?" His eyes weren't focusing straight.

I jerked away. He wasn't the Peter I knew.

"You bad sport, *Americanka* " He grabbed the bag of *klay* from Ivan and took a deep drag. His chest rose as his lungs filled with fumes. The bag fell from his hand and he began to gasp. His body crumpled and hit the ground just inches from where Pasha lay sleeping. Pasha's eyes snapped open, and he sat up straight.

Peter lay sprawled on his back in the dirt between two giant pipes, thrashing with his arms, struggling to take a breath. I dropped to my knees beside him. I didn't know what to do. He was having trouble taking air into his lungs. In the flickering candlelight his face looked grayish green.

Everyone stopped what they were doing and gathered close, even Dimitri, Ivan and Boris. Some stood. Others hung over the pipes.

Peter had stopped moving. I put my hand on his chest. It was still.

"Peter! Peter!" I straightened and looked at the others. "Call 911," I screamed at them. Blank faces stared back. There probably wasn't 911 in Russia.

A sob rose in my chest, but I forced it back down again. *Stay calm. Don't panic.* That's what they taught us at Junior Lifeguards. I closed my eyes and tried to remember what I'd learned in C.P.R. *Make sure the airway is open.* I lifted Peter's neck and tilted his head back. I pinched his nose shut, put my mouth over his, and blew. When I came up for breath and looked around, no one had moved. Didn't they get what was happening? "Help!" I screamed at them.

I tore Peter's camouflage jacket open and pulled up his shirt. My hands were so clumsy I couldn't make them do anything right. His chest was white, almost shiny. I felt around for that bony place between the ribs where you're supposed to do compressions. His skin was barely warm and stretched tight. My fingers came to a stop right where the V of the bones come together. Was it the right place? Doing something was better than doing nothing. They'd taught us that too.

I placed the palm of one hand over the other and began pushing. Was it twelve compressions or fifteen? I did fifteen and prayed it was right. I breathed in his mouth again.

Nothing. His chest didn't move. I pressed my fingers to his neck. No pulse.

More compressions. Another breath. Again and again. Peter didn't react. Sweat pored off my forehead. I was getting dizzier and dizzier by the moment. I couldn't stop thinking, *this is all my fault.* If it hadn't been for me, we never would have had to leave the train station. This never would have happened.

I took Peter by the shoulders and shook him. "Come on, Peter, breathe. Come on, you can't die on me. You just can't."

More compressions. More air into his lungs. I didn't know how long I could keep this up, but I knew if I stopped, he'd die.

"You can't leave us, Peter. We need you." I was running out of breath, slowing down. It felt like his body was pushing back at me, like the air wouldn't go into his lungs.

"We're going to America, Peter. Remember?" My voice broke.

Finally, after I don't know how long, I sat back on my heels to rest. It was then I noticed his eyes. They'd flipped open and were staring straight ahead, not moving, not blinking, flat like there was no one inside.

I knew he was dead.

CHAPTER THIRTY ONE

I collapsed over Peter's body and pressed my face up against his. "Please, Peter. Please, wake up."

I knew he couldn't. He felt so cold, so stiff.

I straightened and looked around. Pasha knelt beside me. I hadn't even realized he was there. His face had turned as white as Peter's, his eyes huge, terrified. Dimitri, Boris and Ivan stood behind him. They narrowed their eyes and moved closer.

Fear made me stop crying. I had to think fast.

Money. Where had Peter put the rubles he made from the movies? I felt in the pockets of his jacket. Nothing but old packets of sugar and catsup. It took all the strength I had left to turn him over. There was a lump stuffed tight in the back pocket of his jeans—the rubles. I yanked them out, and they tumbled into a pile of folded bills onto the ground. As I reached to grab them, a foot came down on my hand. Boris squatted beside me and put his face up close to mine. The gravel on the bottom of his shoe pressed into my skin. The pressure pinched my fingers. From behind him the candlelight shown through his ears, turning them bright red. I screamed in pain and tried to pull my hand away. He smiled and lifted his foot slightly, just enough for me to slide my hand out from underneath. In a flash he grabbed the rubles and stood up.

The rest of the kids swarmed over Peter's body. They took everything, his army jacket, his T-shirt, even his pants. They screeched at each other like a pack of crazed rats. They fought over the stuff in his backpack. They tore his clothes. I couldn't watch.

* * *

No one saw us leave. They were too busy fighting over Peter's dead body. As fast as I could, I hefted our heavy trash sack up onto the street and crawled up the ladder after it. Pasha stood waiting for me. He wore his backpack with his accordion inside and held his stool.

At two in the morning the street was completely empty and dark except for the reflection of starlight on the snow. Frosty clouds of my breath rose in the air. I couldn't decide where to go. Moskovsky Station was too far to walk, and it was too late for the metros. We had to keep moving. Otherwise we'd freeze.

So cold. So tired. After what had just happened, all I really wanted to do was dig a hole some place and crawl in. But there was Pasha.

From behind us I heard the slap of something hitting the ground. I glanced over my shoulder and saw Peter's dead body lying there in the street. They'd left him in just his underpants, tossed there like a piece of meat. His skin shone transparent in the moonlight. I wanted so badly to go back and cover him up, but we didn't have enough time. We'd freeze.

I positioned myself directly behind Pasha to block his view and urged him on. I didn't want to let him see what I'd just seen.

Each step was work.

I stopped and hefted the trash sack to my other arm. The boom box weighed a ton. Pasha had slipped behind me. He scuffled along in his red cowboy boots, panting, coughing, trying to keep up.

One step. Two steps. Three steps. From behind me Pasha's weak little voice cried out, "Stop, Katerina. Stop." He'd unfolded his stool and was sitting on it in the middle of the sidewalk in the snow.

"I rest, Katerina." His round eyes peered out at me from underneath the layers of clothes I'd made him wear—his sweater, my sweater, his jacket, a wool scarf wrapped three times, a wooly cap.

One step. Two steps. Three steps. In ten minutes we'd only made it about half a block. I pulled Peter's boom box out of the trash sack and looked at it. Too heavy. I left it in the snow.

One step. I got rid of the extra batteries. Two steps, our bottles of water. Three steps, Pasha's stool.

A beggar huddled asleep in the dark corner where two buildings met, a blanket draped over him and his crutch propped against the wall. Beside him was a big cardboard box with a rope attached and all his things inside. When we reached the end of the block, I told Pasha to wait. I hurried back to the beggar, dumped his stuff in the snow, and took his box.

"Stop," he yelled after me.

When I got back to Pasha, I stuffed our trash sack into the box and our backpacks on top of that. The old beggar limped up the sidewalk toward us. He grabbed for his box.

.ch slid on the snow, and he went down. We kept

ι just wished I hadn't seen his face.

A breeze with knives in it cut through me as we got nearer the river. I'd been carrying Pasha piggyback for the last few blocks. I didn't think I could go a step further.

Across the street the long buildings of the Winter Palace lit up the snow. It made me think of warm rooms and heaters and hot things to drink. Out in the middle of the square stood the orange pole with the angel on top. Looking at her bare arms in that thin dress made me feel even colder.

Warm. We had to get warm.

Clouds of steam rose into the air from different spots along the square. I crossed the street and plowed through the snow toward them. Someone had made a tent over one of the steam vents using a stand like they use for roadwork signs with a blanket draped over.

I found another vent and left Pasha by it. A group of construction stands stood huddled together over by the sidewalk. It took forever to drag one back through the snow. I didn't think. I didn't feel. I just did it. With the last bit of energy in me I tossed our blanket over the stand and crawled inside beside Pasha.

All night gusts of wind blew the blanket off. All night Pasha shivered from the cold. Knives of pain stabbed my heart whenever I thought about Peter. Mostly I was too tired to think. I wondered what would happen if I decided to stay right here by this steam vent forever. Forget about food. Forget about water. Forget about everything. It would be giving up, and I almost could do it, but then I remembered what Dad used to say. "Never give up. You can't for the sake of your troops." He was right. I had to stay brave for Pasha.

Daylight finally came, nothing but a gray mist that rose halfway up the sky. Pasha needed to see a doctor. I just hoped he could make it all the way to the homeless shelter on Sadovaya Street.

This time there was no line of kids waiting outside on the sidewalk. As we entered, three sad-faced boys in worn-out clothes shuffled out. Each carried a piece of pink paper folded in half.

A single table sat in the middle of the big empty room. The lady with the black boots sat behind it, a stack of folded pink papers in front of her. She gave us a worn-out smile as we entered. The washing machines and driers sat, silent against the far wall. There were no doctors, no ladies wearing latex gloves handing out soap like the last time we were there.

I pointed at Pasha. "He's sick. He needs a doctor."

She tilted her head and studied me for a minute. I was too tired to worry about whether or not she recognized my American accent. She pointed at the sign above her head. "The shelter is closed."

"But—" I nodded at Pasha. "He's sick." My lip quivered. "He needs a doctor."

She handed me one of the folded pink papers and pointed at an address written at the bottom. "Go there. They will help. It's where we're sending the street kids."

"You mean an orphanage?"

"*Da. Da.* Orphanage."

"Ohhhhh." I hadn't eaten in a whole day. Peter was dead. There was no doctor for Pasha, and now she wanted to send us to an orphanage. One by one the bits of bad news sank into my brain. One by one the tears slid from my eyes and fell onto the spotless white floor, only it wasn't spotless any more. There were brown spots now from my tears.

Suddenly I couldn't stand it. "You're a homeless shelter," I shrieked in English. "You're supposed to help."

Her face sagged. "Am sorry," she answered in English. "No is money."

* * *

When I got back to the river with my groceries, the sun had sunk to where it hit me straight in the eyes. Bolts of golden light shot from the windows of the Winter Palace. The glare off the leaves on the columns was so bright it hurt my eyes. Pasha sat waiting for me, just his big brown eyes peeping out from underneath our blanket tent. He looked like such a small bump in the snow with that great, huge, wide palace behind him. As I got closer, he blinked back tears. "I so worried, Katerina. I think you no come back."

I set my bags down and dropped to my knees beside him. "What're you talking about?" Real lightly I cuffed his ear. "I always come back." I forced a bright smile. "I brought you more chicken soup. It'll make you well." Carefully I poured from the cup of hot water I'd gotten at McDonalds into the Styrofoam cup of noodles. I had to pay a whole twenty-five rubles for the hot water. I kept the teabags in case I could sell them.

Pasha would hardly eat the soup. He said he wasn't hungry, he just wanted to sleep.

With the clouds gone it was colder than ever. In the middle of the night he woke coughing again. I propped him up, leaning him back against my chest so he could breathe better. He stared at the starry sky through the opening in the tent. "Is up there Peter?" he asked.

"I guess." I didn't like thinking of Peter's pale body freezing in that cold dark sky. "Actually I think he's in America, now, making his debut on Dancing With The Stars."

Pasha looked up at me from beneath his thick, dark lashes and pointed at the sky. "Have America up there?"

"Sure, there's America." I rocked him back and forth. "And mommies and daddies and cheeseburgers and chocolate cake too. And beaches and surfing and..."

The next morning I tried to tell myself Pasha was better, but he wasn't. His face still felt hot. He wheezed and he could barely sit up.

A day later, and Pasha still wasn't better. His breathing scared me. All night long he'd wheezed. In his sleep I could feel his chest working hard, struggling to take the air in, struggling to push it out. In the morning I pulled the pink flier out of my pocket and stared at it. It was the third time I'd looked at it in the past two days. I sat with my face turned away from Pasha, so he couldn't see my tears.

I couldn't understand how mothers could leave their kids—like that lady at the train station who went off and left her little girl that day. I could never do that, not to Pasha.

I licked at the salty tears and studied the flier some more.

Beside me Pasha lay half asleep, his mouth open, his chest working hard. Even from here I could tell that he wasn't getting much air into his lungs. His lips had turned blue, the same color Peter's had been.

* * *

He wasn't heavy, but it was still awfully hard trudging with him through the snow. I carried him like you would a baby, up against my chest, his arms wrapped around my neck, his legs dangling down almost to my knees.

I left all our stuff behind, even the blanket and Pasha's accordion. I had to.

The address the lady had written on the pink flier turned out to be a short gray building squeezed in between two taller ones in the middle of the block. I knew the neighborhood. Father Alexander's cathedral was just down the street.

"He's sick," I said to the lady behind the desk in my very best Russian. "We want to go to an orphanage."

"Names?" She had grayish blonde hair, tugged back tight into a bun. She sat up straight and stiff. Her feet in heavy men's shoes and thick white socks stuck out from beneath her desk.

I didn't know Pasha's last name so I used *Rushev*, my cousin Natalia's last name. I told the lady I was Katerina Rushev, Pasha's big sister. She raised her eyebrows at that.

She asked our ages. Six and thirteen, I told her.

After she wrote it all down, she began thumbing through some papers.

Pasha was getting so heavy, I finally had to let him down. He stood leaning against me, holding my hand, sucking his thumb.

The lady got to the bottom of her stack of papers and looked up. "I don't have a place right now." There was nothing on her face to show she even cared.

"But the homeless shelter said you'd help." I nodded at Pasha. "He needs a doctor. He's very sick."

She frowned and looked me up and down. "You are not Russian. You are American."

I stopped breathing. I couldn't think what to say.

She leaned across her desk and studied my face. "Are you missing girl?" she asked in English.

Would she call the police? I didn't care. All that mattered was getting help for Pasha.

"Missing girl?" I said it real casual sounding in Russian, pretending I didn't understand.

She pursed her lips, shook her head, and began pouring through her papers again. Silently I let out a deep breath. Halfway through the stack, she pulled out a sheet as thin as tissue paper.

"Ah, here's a place. Maybe they will have room." She was back to speaking Russian. She got on the phone and punched in a number she read off the sheet. "*Dobraye dyen.*" She spoke to the person on the other end, her words coming so fast that I couldn't understand much. She hung up and smiled. "We have luck."

She stood and reached for Pasha's hand. He jerked away and hid behind my back. "Come now." She made another grab for his arm. He dodged away.

"Maybe if *I* take him," I said.

The lady's face turned sour. "You can't come."

My heart raced. "But, I'm his sister. We go together." Pasha's sharp little fingernails pricked my hand.

She shook her head. "We don't take Americans. Only *Rooskey.*" She made a little nod toward the door behind me. "It's best for the boy you go now."

"But—" I thought it would be Pasha and me together going to the orphanage.

She leaned toward me and looked me straight in the eye. "You know how many orphanages in St. Petersburg?" She spoke in English this time.

I shook my head.

She tapped her piece of paper with the back of her hand. "Only forty. Thousands of children need go. No is room." She pointed at Pasha. "Is big luck for the boy today." She looked at the ceiling and tilted her head. "Tomorrow? Who can say."

It felt like my heart would stop beating. I didn't know what to say.

She watched my face. When I didn't say anything, she said, "Okay, then." She got rid of the piece of paper she'd been holding and reached for Pasha with both hands. This time she managed to get a grip on his arm.

"*Nyet. Nyet.*" Pasha screamed, but barely any sound came out.

"Come." She pulled, and I felt his grip on my arm loosen.

She turned and started dragging him away.

"Katerina, Katerina," Pasha wheezed. By now he'd begun to cry. He kept looking back over his shoulder like he expected me to do something, come after him, take him away from the mean lady, save him. I didn't know what to do.

"*Nyet. Nyet.*" Pasha whimpered. With a burst of strength he pulled his arm right out of the sleeve of his two sweaters. With another tug the sweaters came off over his head. His backpack dropped to the floor. The orphan lady was left standing there, holding the sweaters with no boy inside. He raced back to me, clamped his arms around my waist, and began coughing his head off. One bony white shoulder stuck out through the neck hole of his T-shirt. Without all the sweaters, you could see he was just skin and bones.

The orphan lady marched back down the hall toward us.

Pasha buried his face against me, coughing and sobbing. It was too much. I couldn't do this. I looked at the lady and shook my head. "He's not going."

Pasha dropped to his knees, wheezing and gasping. I lowered myself to the floor beside him and pounded him on the back. Finally the coughing stopped. I got up and pulled him to his feet where he stood, his arms clamped around me, panting, trying to get his breath.

The woman handed me his backpack and two sweaters then leaned in close and drilled me with her eyes. She spoke in English. "This boy, Pasha—he remain with you, he die."

I hated her then, more than I've ever hated anyone in my whole life. I hated her mean face, her stupid white socks, her ugly black shoes, but most of all I hated her because I knew she was right.

Pasha looked up at me, pleading with his eyes. I pried his fingers off my arm and bent down so we could be face to face. "You have to go, Pasha."

"No." His thick dark lashes were soggy with tears.

I swallowed the lump in my throat and made myself smile. "I know, but you've got to. They'll take you where someone will give you medicine. Make you better." I had to keep talking so I wouldn't cry. "Here, let's put your sweaters back on so you won't get cold." I pulled them down over his head and helped him get his arms through the sleeves, then I put his backpack on, the whole time holding my breath to keep from crying. He looked up at me again, so small in all those big clothes. "You say never leave Pasha."

That did it. Tears flooded down my face. "I'll come visit you. I promise." It was a lie. I'd never see him again.

The lady picked him up.

As she carried him away, he kept looking back at me over her shoulder. "Katerina. Katerina."

I sobbed so hard I couldn't get my breath.

Pasha's whispery voice grew softer and softer, weaker and weaker, as she carried him further down the hall. He lowered his head like a sad dog. After that he didn't look back at me again, not even once.

The last glimpse I got of him was of his red cowboy boots, dangling, about to fall off. The two disappeared through a set of double doors leaving me alone in the long empty hall.

There was nothing left for me to do but go.

CHAPTER THIRTY TWO

$\mathbb{B}$y the time I reached the river, it had begun to snow so hard that everything looked fuzzy. The angel statue in her thin silk dress still stood on the pole in the middle of the square, but the bump where our tent had been was gone. Our blankets were gone. Our trash bag was gone, the cardboard box, our backpacks, the metal road stand. Everything. Gone.

It didn't matter. Nothing did. All I really wanted was Pasha's accordion. They'd taken that too.

* * *

I spent my nights sleeping by steam vents on Nevsky Prospekt. During the day I wandered the streets with nowhere to go. I couldn't tell how long it had been since I left Pasha at the orphanage.

A girl about my age huddled along the wall near a steam vent, begging, her chapped fingers poking out from her cutoff mittens. I stopped near her to warm up.

"*Provalivai!*" She shoved me, knocking me into the man who'd stopped beside us. He wore a beautiful black fur coat and a gold ring with a big blue stone on it. "You girls look hungry," he said in Russian, smiling.

The other girl nodded and smiled back.

He put a hand on my arm and raised his eyebrows, questioning.

He looked so rich. I hadn't had anything to eat for a whole day and a half. Maybe the other stuff wouldn't be so bad. Lots of girls did it. Why shouldn't I?

Something made me put out my hand. Something made me say, "*Nyet.*"

He walked off, his arm over the shoulder of the other girl. She looked back and threw me a smug smile.

Two blocks up and across the street was the cemetery where Mom and Grandma Olga were buried. I pushed open the rusty gate and plowed through the snow between the gravestones. Way on the other side by the wall I found it again. Just the Казнэтсов part showed above the snow. I sunk down and began digging down until I could see her name, "Lara Kuznetsov McOwen."

I knelt in front of the gravestone. "Mom, can you hear me?" Thinking that maybe she could made me cry. "I've lost everyone, you and Gracie, and now Peter and Pasha. If only I could come be with you and Dad."

It was late in the afternoon, growing darker, growing colder. Around me everything had turned an icy, silvery blue. I curled up into a tight ball in front of the gravestone. Maybe I'd just lie there for a while and go to sleep. Maybe when I woke up, Mom and Dad and Gracie would all be there beside me.

Church bells clanged four o'clock. It was dark now, and my bones ached. The feeling was gone from my hands and feet. Dad's St. Christopher pressed into my chest, hard and icy cold.

At first when I tried to get up, I couldn't. Nothing would bend, my arms or my legs. I used the tombstone to help me get to my feet. Once I was up, I began to shiver so badly I could barely stand. My teeth rattled. I wasn't sure I could walk.

I looked at the gravestone one last time. "I can't stay here any longer, Mom. I have to go now."

* * *

Squashed between two large buildings on the other side of the cemetery was a tall, narrow gray church—no fancy domes on this one, just plain cement with a bell tower on top. A line of families with children crowded up the walk to go in. Each time the door opened I caught a glimpse of golden light. It would be warm inside.

It felt like none of my body would work right. Every part of me shook. A babooshka wrapped in gray shawls gave me a worried glance as she passed me on the sidewalk.

Just a half a block. Could I make it?

At first the tall wooden door wouldn't budge. It felt like it was being sucked closed from the inside. Finally, when I leaned back and used all my weight, it opened.

A blast of heavy warm air that smelled of incense and hot wax hit me. The church was dark inside except for a bright circle of candles that made shimmery waves along the walls. As the door closed behind me, the warm began to seep in. It felt so good I could have stayed there in that one spot forever.

Up in front three priests in heavy golden robes stood before an altar. All had long dark beards. Two of them wore black hats. The third wore a fancy gold one, triangular shaped on top and covered all over with something that made it glisten.

I began to shiver again so I inched my way up the side of the church where it would be warmer, careful to stay in the shadows. It was a small church, and there weren't any pews. The people all stood, the candlelight bouncing off their faces—children in their parents' arms straining to see, grandmothers leaning on canes, teens holding hands. I imagined I was part of them, that I had a family too.

Up at the altar the middle priest held up a bald baby wearing a long white dress. I remembered my dreams of having a husband and a family and a baby some day. Now it would never happen. I squeezed my eyes closed and tried to concentrate on how good if felt just to be warm.

They were taking the baby's clothes off now. The middle priest dangled its naked little body over a bowl of water, chanting in Russian as he raised it high. I recognized some of the words.

"In the name of the father." He dunked the baby once. "In the name of the son." He dunked the baby again. "In the name of the holy ghost."

The baby made mewing sounds and batted its fists. Soft *ahhhh's* rose from the crowd.

I stepped out of the shadows and into the aisle so I could get a better view. No one would see me. Everyone's attention was focused on the baby at the altar.

Just then a toddler in its father's arms pulled the binky out of its mouth and threw it to the floor. It landed right at my feet. The father, still holding his child, reached down to get the binky. As he rose, he looked straight in my face.

His eyes widened. He stepped over to his wife, pointed at me, and said in a loud whisper, "It's her. It's the girl they're looking for." The word spread fast. Everyone turned and stared. Fingers pointed. People whispered. Their voices grew louder. The whole baptism was disrupted. I heard words like *Americanka* and *CNN*.

I backed up, one step then two. The wall stopped me. My eyes darted from left to right. All I could see was people staring at me, but no way out. The crowd moved in. Bullets of adrenaline shot up and down my spine.

One of the priests, the one with the tall golden hat, stepped away from the altar and hurried down the aisle toward me. He took fast, long strides that made the skirts of his gown rustle. The flats of my hands pressed against the wall. He a came closer and, suddenly I recognized him.

"Father Alexander."

"Katerina, is it you?" he asked in English.

I nodded, my eyes flitting from his face to the faces of everyone around us. If only I could get out of there. If only there was a way.

He gripped my shoulder. "There are many people looking for you."

I stared up at him in his golden robes and hat. "I didn't think *you'd* be here."

He pointed at his hat. "I am the bishop. Is my job." With his free hand he struggled to pull up the side of his robe and get at the cell phone in his pants pocket. Still holding my shoulder, he punched in some numbers and began to talk.

No one needed to tell me who he'd called. The police.

"Yes, I'm sure." He clapped shut his cell and returned his attention to me. His golden brown eyes probed mine. "So, Katerina, I wanted to help, but you ran away. Why do you do that?"

Help? How could he say that when he'd just called the police? I stared at my feet and remained silent. Sirens sounded in the distance, getting closer.

Father Alexander took my hand. "Come with me, Katerina." I had no choice.

The sirens were right outside now. Three men in uniform burst through the front door of the church. I clutched Father Alexander's hand, my heart pounding.

"Is this Katerina McOwen?" the first one asked in Russian.

"*Da*," Father Alexander replied.

It was all over. In a weird way I was almost glad. Maybe jail wouldn't be so bad. At least I'd be off the streets.

One of the policemen took my arm and started to lead me away.

"Wait," said Father Alexander. He took two of the policemen aside. The three huddled close, speaking in low voices. I couldn't hear what they were saying, but I could tell they were arguing about something. Father Alexander's eyes turned stormy. He gestured and pointed at me.

Around me the people were beginning to get restless. Some looked angry. A man even raised his fist. I stared at my feet and tried not to look. It was too scary. They hated me. I'd killed a policeman, a Russian, one of them.

Father Alexander threw up his hands. He and the two policemen rejoined us. I wondered what the three had talked about. Maybe Father Alexander had asked them to treat me nice. I knew he liked me even though he was turning me in. Whatever it was he'd asked for, from the grim set of his mouth, I could tell it hadn't worked.

All eyes watched us as we left the church. As we passed a pillar, I glimpsed the icon hanging there. It was Our Lady of Kazan, just like the one hanging in Father Alexander's church. A lot of help she'd been! I'd prayed to her for protection for Mom and me and look what happened. *I hate you. I hate you.* For a tiny second I worried that God might hear what I'd just thought. So what! I didn't believe in Him anymore, anyway.

Outside flakes the size of quarters floated in the light from the street lamps. Two police cars sat at the curb, the red lights on their roofs flashing circles in the snow. One of the guys put my wrists together and clamped on a pair of handcuffs. He made me get in the back seat of the first patrol car and slammed the door. There were no handles inside. Even if I hadn't been handcuffed, I couldn't have gotten out.

That's when it really hit me. A Russian jail. How would I keep from being raped? How would I keep from being murdered? My eyes raced over the seat of the car, then over the carpeted floor. I needed something sharp, something I could use for a weapon, a pocketknife, a safety-pin, anything. Nothing. The car was so clean it looked like it had just been vacuumed.

The first police car drove off, its tires making crunching sounds through the snow. The two remaining policemen jumped in the car I was in, and we followed.

Frantically I wiggled my wrists trying to pull them out of the handcuffs. Over the car radio a woman spoke Russian, her words coming fast like a machine gun, too fast for me to understand, except that every so often I heard her say *Americanka* and my name, Katerina McOwen. We stopped in front of a huge gray building shaped like a big cement block with tiny windows way up high. It looked like a place where they torture people.

The policemen got out, and one of them opened the back door. I considered jumping out and making a run for it, but I couldn't figure out what I'd do about the handcuffs, and, anyway, if they caught me, the punishment might be even worse.

Two policemen sat behind a desk in the lobby. One of them rose to his feet when he saw us and came running over. He had shiny pink skin just like Vlad's. He studied me for a second, then said to the other two guys, "She looks like a corpse. Are you sure it's her?"

"The priest says it is."

The guy with the pink cheeks pulled off my wooly cap and held a picture up next to my face—my passport photo. His eyes traveled back and forth between my face and the photo. He stood so close I could feel his breath on my face. It smelled like stale cigarettes mixed with breath mints and a hint of coffee. He slapped the paper with the back of his hand and turned to the other two guys. "The last girl looked more like Katerina than this one." He studied me some more. "What's your name?"

"Ka—" I stopped. They weren't sure it was me. Maybe I could make them believe they had the wrong person. "Natalia Rushev," I said.

"Stupid idiots!" the man spat at the other two guys. "You brought in the wrong girl again."

The guy who'd handcuffed me spoke up. "But the priest said she was Katerina McOwen. He was sure." He turned to me. "Say your name again."

I stared at my feet and muttered, "Natalia Rushev."

He smiled. "See. She is lying. She is American. I can hear it."

The other guy shook his head. "Okay, we'll hold her. But if it's the wrong girl again, you two are in big trouble." He took my arm and led me to the elevators. We rode to the third floor, my heart pounding the whole way. Would they beat me like I'd seen them beat Peter? When you're getting kicked, you need to put your arms up so they won't get you in the head.

We got off in a hall with lots of plain white doors with numbers on them. The policeman opened one with a key, pushed me in, and left me there all by myself. A single bright light hung from the ceiling in the middle of the room leaving the edges in the shadows. A plain white table with two metal chairs sat directly beneath it. I tried the door with my handcuffed hands, but I couldn't get it to open. There were no windows, nothing but plain white walls, plain white ceiling, plain white floors.

If I didn't get out of there, I was going to explode. My breath came in short quick pants. My head spun. I sank to the floor in a corner of the room and buried my face against the wall. I was too scared to cry.

The sound of voices outside in the hall made me jump. A click in the lock, the door opened, and three men walked in. Were they here to interrogate me? The bright light blinded me. The taller one stepped closer, and I saw that it was Father Alexander. The two policemen who'd picked me up were behind him.

"Katerina." Father Alexander rushed over. "Are you all right?" he asked me in English. Gently he pulled me to my feet. I felt his hands touch my wrists. He dropped them and spun to face the policemen. "It's no way to treat a little girl," he shouted in Russian. "What's wrong with you?"

The two stepped back. One of them replied with a squeaking voice, "but we were afraid she'd run away."

Father Alexander pointed at my hands. "Get those things off her right this minute," he roared.

The policeman with the key ring on his belt hurried to my side and unlocked my handcuffs.

I rubbed my wrists. It felt so good to have them free.

All of a sudden I noticed another shape in the doorway, someone in a wheelchair. The chair moved closer and stopped, still in the shadows. It was an old lady with real white hair. I still couldn't see her that well. Was she the old lady whose purse I'd snatched in the market that day? Was I in trouble for that too?

I lowered my eyes.

She strained forward to look at me.

Father Alexander watched the two of us, his eyes darting back and forth.

The old lady had a shocking pink shawl draped over her shoulders, the same color as the shawl on that lady in the wheelchair at Moskovsky Station that day. It didn't make sense. None of it did. I stared at her face, still in the shadows. There was something about her. I took a step toward her, and our eyes locked. It couldn't be, could it? She said something, and I recognized the voice.

"Carly, is it you?"

CHAPTER THIRTY THREE

Gracie, here in Russia? It didn't seem possible. All those emails I'd sent. All those times she never answered her phone. I thought she was dead like everyone else.

Father Alexander pointed and asked me, "Is this your grandmother?"

The lump in my throat was so big I could barely breathe. All I could do was nod.

He turned to Gracie. "Is this your granddaughter, Mrs. McOwen?"

Her mouth opened, but only a squeak came out before she began to sob.

I'd never seen her cry like this before, not even after Dad died. I knew I should hug her, but I was too numb. Finally I reached out and stroked her arm. "It's okay, Gracie. It's okay."

* * *

I was surprised that they were letting me leave with Gracie. Maybe they were waiting for the trial to happen before they arrested me. I was afraid to ask.

As we stepped out the front doors of the station, a bright light blinded us. It came from the top of a van parked down below at the curb. News people with cameras stood on the steps. When we appeared, they practically knocked each other over in their rush to pounce on us. People shouted questions, some in Russian, some in English. "How did you survive, Carly?" "Where did you sleep?"

Two policemen drove us back to where Gracie was staying. We got out in front of an old stone building with fancy carvings over the windows. One of the policemen rode with us up to the fourth floor and pushed Gracie's wheelchair down the hall. When we got to her apartment, he didn't come in, but he didn't turn to leave, either. Instead he leaned against the wall and folded his arms. I guess he was going to stay out there and keep guard in case I tried to escape.

A blast of warm air hit me as we entered Gracie's apartment. My eyes zoomed straight to a bowl of half-eaten soup and a basket of rolls that sat on a table across the room. It felt like every part of my body was being sucked toward that food.

Gracie saw what I was looking at. "You're hungry, aren't you darling?" She wheeled herself past me. "Have a seat. I'll heat up some more soup and get you a clean spoon." There wasn't time for that. I grabbed the bowl of soup, raised it to my face, and slurped down the thick, lukewarm liquid practically all in one gulp. There were lumps of vegetables and some meat, but I didn't slow down enough to figure out what they were. Gracie returned from the kitchen and watched. Halfway through the fourth roll I could feel my stomach stretching like a balloon about to pop. Quickly I slipped the fifth roll into my pocket.

My stomach began to lurch. I turned and scanned the room for the door to the nearest bathroom. Would I be able to make it in time? Too late. I threw up all over the carpet.

I was afraid to look at Gracie. The mess I'd made was disgusting. *I* was disgusting.

Gracie's wheelchair squeaked toward me. I felt her hand on my arm. "You couldn't help it, Carly. Now, don't you worry." Her voice was so soft and gentle it brought tears to my eyes.

She wheeled herself down the hall and returned with some damp towels and a bottle of something that smelled like vinegar. I rushed to help her. When we were finished cleaning up the rug, she gave me a cheerful smile. "Now what you need is a nice warm bath."

The bathroom was toasty warm with shiny white tiles on the walls and smaller white tiles on the floor. Everything looked so clean. Gracie rolled up her sleeves, leaned over, and turned on the tub faucets. Next she began helping me off with my clothes.

One by one my dirty, raggedy things dropped to the floor: Anna's coat all filthy in back from sitting on the train station floor, my favorite terry hoodie so dirty now you could barely recognize it, the ugly torn stuff the homeless shelter had given me to wear, my underwear all full of holes. Gracie barely touched any of it.

When she saw me naked, she gasped. I looked down at my body. Nothing but bones. It'd been such a long time since I'd seen myself naked. I hadn't realized I looked this bad. I tried to cover myself with my arms.

"Never mind, sweetheart," Gracie said. "We'll fatten you up in no time."

The bath water felt warm and silky. Gracie leaned over the tub and scrubbed my back with a soapy washrag. She rubbed and scrubbed till my skin felt raw and the bath water turned the color of tea. Next I felt shampoo, cool and thick, being poured over my head and Gracie's hands working it into my scalp. Mom used to do that when I was a little girl. Even the shampoo smelled the same. Huge tears dribbled off my cheeks and plopped into the dirty bath water. I turned to face the wall.

Gracie's voice was gentle. "It's all right, darling. You can cry now."

I swallowed hard and turned to look at her. "Mom's dead, Gracie." I could barely choke out the words. "I found her grave. I'd been looking and looking for her, and then when I finally found her, she was... she was..." I covered my face and sobbed.

Gracie swiped her hand across her forehead and shook her head. "Oh Carly!"

"And Peter died too." I gasped. "And Anna." I told her about Pasha and how he got so sick and I left him with the orphanage lady. "He was scared to death, Gracie, and I just left him there. I'd promised I'd never leave him, but then I did." I hugged myself and rocked back and forth, sobbing.

Gracie put her hand under my chin and looked me in the eye. "He would have died if you hadn't taken him to the orphanage, Carly." Her voice was so gentle. "It was a very brave thing you did." If only her words could make me feel better.

She had me stand up so she could drain out the muddy bath water. Then she refilled the tub and told me to sit and soak. Next she got a plastic trash sack from the kitchen and began filling it with my clothes. She held each piece at arm's length, only touching things with the tips of her thumb and fingers. As she lifted Anna's coat, I noticed something bulging from the pocket.

"No! No!" I jumped out of the bathtub dripping water all over the floor. "It's Miss Pig. I wanted Pasha to have her. Now he's there all alone by himself with nothing to hug at night." I grabbed for the coat. "It's in the pocket. Please, Gracie," I sobbed, "don't throw it away."

"Carly, listen to me." Gracie's voice was firm. "It wasn't your fault. None of it. You did what you had to do, and you survived. Your father would have been so proud of you."

I remembered something Dad always used to say: *"Marines never leave their buddies behind."*

* * *

It felt strange to be in a real bed again. A warm comforter, a soft pillow, fresh-smelling, clean white sheets—I didn't dare get to liking them too much because I knew it wouldn't last.

In the middle of the night I woke up to total darkness. I was back in Moskovsky Station, and all the lights had gone out. I smelled the oil from the trains and felt the cold, hard floor.

"Peter! Pasha!" I screamed.

Gracie's voice came out of the shadows beside my bed. "It's okay, Carly. I'm here."

Could I believe it? Was she real?

I drifted back into the dream, only it changed—Vlad, his face white as death, running after me, policemen chasing me through the snow.

"Nyet. nyet," I screamed.

A hand on my arm and Gracie's voice again. "Carly, Carly." Her wheelchair squeaked as she reached over to stroke my forehead. "It was just a bad dream, sweetheart. Go back to sleep."

"I killed someone, Gracie."

"No, no, sweetie. It wasn't your fault." She stroked my forehead, over and over.

"But I *did* kill someone, Gracie. Mom's boyfriend. He was a policeman."

The room fell silent. I wondered what she thought of me now. Her voice came out of the darkness, calm, strong, reassuring, the Gracie I could always count on. "Why don't you just tell me what happened," she said.

I took a deep breath. "Vlad was beating up Mom. It was terrible. Her face was all puffed up and bloody. I pushed him. Hard. And then his head hit the table and there was blood everywhere and I was sure he was dead. When do you think they'll come for me?"

"Come for you?"

"To put me in jail."

Gracie's voice rose. "Why, you were protecting your mother, Carly. Anyone in their right mind would be able to see that. If it'll make you feel better, we'll have Father Alexander check into it."

"Put you in jail?" she grumbled. "Over my dead body!"

It felt so good to have her here with me. It was like when I used to stay at her house after Dad died. If only I could believe her about Vlad, but he was a policeman. I'd seen what they did to street kids. I was an American. It'd probably be even worse for me. I strained to see Gracie's face in the darkness. "Everyone's gone now, Gracie—Dad, Mom, Peter. Are you going to die, too?"

Gracie swallowed hard. "No, honey, I'm not going to die." Her voice lightened. "The doctor said I'm going to be just fine."

"But Marisa said you were in the hospital. I thought your cancer'd come back?"

"Cancer?" Gracie took a deep breath. "No, no, no, honey, it wasn't cancer."

"But I left all those messages on your phone, and you never answered my emails. I—" My voice choked, and I could barely finish my sentence "—I thought you were dead."

Gracie squeezed my arm. "Now you listen to me, Carly. I'm not going to die, not for a long, long time. I'll be around to see you off to college. You just wait." She leaned over and put her arms around me. The nice fresh scent of the soap she always used made me relax. "Maybe I'll even be lucky enough to have great-grandkids one day." She sighed and sat back. "Here's what happened, honey. I fell and broke my hip. Bones are a little brittle from the cancer. It was right after you left that first message. Stupid me! I was running for the phone, thinking it might be you again. I had to have emergency surgery. They ended up replacing my hip. It didn't go well. I picked up a staph infection, and it got into my blood. I was in a coma for three weeks. When I woke up and remembered what had happened to you, I was nearly frantic. The minute I was able, I contacted the American Embassy here."

She patted my head. "There's more to the story, honey, but you need your sleep now."

* * *

Daylight streamed down from the frosty window high above my head. It must have been noon already. Miss Pig, dirty, an ear missing, peeked up at me from where I held her crushed against my chest.

My eyelids closed, and I began floating toward my dreams again.

I heard the front door of the apartment open and Gracie's voice say, "Father Alexander." I slipped out of bed and shuffled down the hall.

Father Alexander's face brightened when he saw me. "Katerina!" He crossed the room and took my hand. "Come. We sit." He led me over to the couch. The long flannel nightgown Gracie'd put me in caught under my feet, and I nearly tripped. He grabbed my arm and held on until I was safely seated next to him.

He twisted to face me. "This man, Vladimir Chazov?" He gestured toward Gracie. "This man you tell your grandmother you kill? He works for the police department of St. Petersburg."

I frowned. "You mean he's not dead?"

"Is not dead, but maybe he should—" He looked at Gracie "—I will not say it. He is member of the Russian mafiya. They deal in drugs, stolen passports, crime. They infiltrate police. It is bad problem for Russia."

Gracie put a hand over her heart. "Oh, my God, and to think that Carly and Lara were living right in the same apartment with this man."

I sat there for a minute staring at my hands. I didn't know what to think. "You mean I really didn't kill him? I'm not going to jail?"

Father Alexander smiled and shook his head. "No, you did not kill him. You will not go to jail."

"But what about all those people chasing me? And my picture was in the newspaper and on the wall at the embassy."

Gracie's face scrunched up as if she were in some kind of horrible pain. "Oh, you poor thing, what you must have been going through." She pounded her fist on her knee. "It just makes me so damn mad. You on the streets, scared, starving. Oh, my God!" She let out a deep breath. "They weren't chasing you to put you in jail, honey. They were trying to find you to send you home."

"You mean all that time...." I stared at the ceiling. It made me dizzy trying to think of what it meant. "But what about Mom? Where was she?"

"She was looking for you too."

"I thought she was in the hospital."

Gracie shook her head. "She was only there for about a week. Then she went back to your grandparents' apartment. I even spoke to her on the phone. She sounded a wreck. She and your Aunt Zoya had been searching for you for over a month."

"Wait a minute. If Mom was staying at the apartment. What about Vlad?"

Gracie and Father Alexander looked at each other. Silence.

I pounded the couch. "He killed her, didn't he?"

Father Alexander cleared his throat. "Is not exactly that way, Katerina."

Gracie wheeled her chair over in front of the couch where she could face me. She took both my hands in hers and spoke quietly. "No one killed your mom, Carly. It was alcohol and drugs."

I shook my head hard. "No. No. Vlad did it. He must have. You should have seen him beat her up."

"There was an autopsy, Carly. They found no sign of foul play, not even a bruise, just a lot of drugs and alcohol in her blood."

I continued shaking my head. "But why did Mom go back to Vlad? Why did she keep doing drugs?" I fought back the tears. "Did she give up looking for me?"

"No, no, Carly." Gracie opened her arms and pulled me close. "Your mother never gave up on you, darling. She loved you with her whole heart. Believe me, I know she did." Gracie sounded almost in tears herself.

She released me and sat back. "It's just that, well..." Her eyes roamed the ceiling as if she were searching for answers up there. She focused back on me. "For some people life becomes more than they can take and they..." She looked at Father Alexander.

I wanted to scream, *it's not true*, but then I remembered what the psychologist at our school once told me—*some people just can't handle it when bad things happen*, and I remembered those times I'd found Mom in bed in my grandparents' apartment, her face chalk white, her body so still. I remembered how she kept sneaking vodka after Grandma Olga died and doing drugs with Vlad.

Father Alexander took me by the shoulders and turned me to face him. "It is not like that for you, Katerina. You are strong." He waved his hand. "Just see how the world has given you so much trouble. And look what happens." He shook me gently as he said these words. "You survive!"

* * *

From: mar999@abcmail.net
Subject: *wuz up?*
like dude, ur famous!!! when ya comin home?

I closed the lid of the laptop Father Alexander had loaned me without finishing Marisa's email. Would she even know me now? Would I even know her?

It had really been nice of Father Alexander to loan the computer to me so I could get my emails, but once I started looking at them, I just wasn't interested.

We couldn't go back to the United States right away because of all the paperwork, and getting me checked by doctors to make sure I was fit to fly. Gracie suggested we go clothes shopping or to the movies, even to McDonald's. Where Peter and Pasha and I used to eat out of the trash? I didn't tell Gracie that part. There was a lot I didn't like to talk about. When Gracie heard the story about Anna, her face turned pale. "I really hate to have to ask you this, Carly, but did anything like that happen to you?" She wept when I assured her it didn't.

I felt bad that I couldn't get excited about all of the nice things she and Father Alexander were trying to do for me. It was like I was stuck between my old life on the streets and my new life back with her. I knew I should be happy that I'd been found, but I'd grown a layer of skin so thick that it wouldn't let *happy* seep in. All the bad things—Mom's name etched on the gravestone, Peter lying there on the ground, his face gone blue, and Pasha, the way the way his head sagged when he realized I was leaving him. I kept seeing his little face everywhere I turned.

The days passed, getting closer and closer to the time we'd be leaving Russia. I hardly thought about going home, seeing my friends, going back to school. All I thought about was Pasha.

CHAPTER THIRTY FOUR

It should have been the happiest moment of my life. At last we were going home. I'd been waiting for this day ever since I came to Russia.

Outside the airport window men with fur hats pulled down over their ears loaded luggage onto a British Airways jet. In the snowy distance the hillsides had turned light purple under the pale morning sky. A man with a British accent announced flight 8940 to London.

Gracie checked her watch. She wore the same bright pink shawl she'd worn that day in Moskovsky Station. She pointed at an area over by the window. "We might as well have a seat."

I sat down at the end of a row of metal-backed chairs. Gracie wheeled herself over beside me. She patted my hand. "You all right, sweetheart?"

I swallowed the lump in my throat and looked away. If only I could at least pretend to be happy. She'd come all this way to Russia with a broken hip just to save me, and now she was going to take me home and let me live with her. I ought to be grateful. I ought to be happy.

I unzipped my backpack and checked for the umpteenth time that Miss Pig was still there. She sat right where I'd left her on top of the stack of letters. Over the last two weeks they'd come in from all over the United States, grandmas, moms, school kids, even one from the president on White House stationery, all telling me how happy they were that I'd been found.

"Everything okay, honey?" Gracie asked again.

I nodded then quickly turned toward the window so she wouldn't be able to read my face.

The U.S. consulate man who'd been helping us walked over. "I got them to change the seat assignments so you could have three together."

I looked at the clock on the wall—nine thirty. Our plane would leave at ten. My heart sped up. I didn't want to go.

I glanced over at Gracie. Her mouth drooped, and the tired lines around her eyes were deeper than I remembered. The thought of disappointing her made me feel sick.

I stared out the window again. *Pasha. Pasha. Where are you?* Tears filled my eyes.

Slowly I turned back to Gracie. "I can't go."

Her eyes opened a fraction wider. "What do you mean, honey?"

I swallowed hard. "I can't leave Pasha. Couldn't we at least find him so I could say good-bye?"

Before Gracie could answer, Father Alexander appeared. "*Dobraye ootra.* Good morning," he said as he walked up. Today he wasn't wearing black robes, just a long coat and a dark brown fur hat that matched his beard.

He smiled at me, then frowned. "Such a sad face, Katerina."

I bit down hard on my lip to try and hold back the tears.

He tilted his head and asked, "You know what day is today?"

I shook my head.

"This is January six, eve of Epiphany. In Russia we celebrate." He looked past me over my shoulder and waved at someone across the room. "It is a tradition we give gifts."

A man wearing a heavy parka and baseball cap approached us, dodging people and suitcases as he came nearer. He stopped, and a little kid peeked out from behind his back. The wooly cap was pulled down so low, and the neck scarf pulled up so high that I barely would have known who it was if it hadn't been for the eyes.

Those big brown eyes.

I sat there frozen, afraid if I moved I'd break the spell.

The little boy took a few shy steps toward me, looked around, then streaked across the floor and buried his face in my lap. The man in the baseball cap turned and walked away.

"Pasha! Pasha!" I could feel him. I could hug him. He was real.

I looked at Gracie. She waved two passports. Had she known all along? I felt like I was about to explode. It was Christmas and New Years and the Fourth of July all at once. I looked at the passports in Gracie's hand. "You mean he's coming with us?"

She nodded. "We weren't sure. I didn't want to get your hopes up. But, yes." She winked at Pasha. "He's coming with us."

"Oh, Gracie!" I scrambled out of my chair and practically jumped in her lap.

Pasha backed up and stood watching us hug. His big round eyes moved from face to face. He was clean and not so thin as before, but he still wore stained, raggedy clothes from the homeless shelters.

"I can't believe you did this," I said to Gracie.

She looked up at Father Alexander. "He's the one you can thank."

Father Alexander was so tall I could barely reach his waist, but I gave him a hug anyway.

He stepped back and opened his eyes wide. "I almost forget, Katerina." He reached in his coat pocket and handed me a small package wrapped in thin yellow tissue paper. "There is one more gift for you."

Carefully I peeled away the paper. Inside was a small picture, covered in glass, framed in gold, a miniature exactly like the icon I'd seen in his church. Our Lady of Kazan.

He raised his eyebrows. "You remember you prayed to this?"

I frowned and nodded. "For God to help Mom and me get home to San Diego."

"And Our Lady—" Father Alexander tilted his head and gave me a sad smile. "—she did not answer your prayer. Am I right?"

I looked away. It was still hard to talk about.

Father Alexander put his hands on my shoulders so that I had to look him in the eye. "It is very difficult when a prayer is not answered, Katerina. But sometimes the way the answer comes is not the way we see." He made a broad sweep of his hand in the direction of Gracie and Pasha. "Never give up on prayer, Katerina. Just like your grandmother and I never gave up on you." He raised his finger. "And whenever you look at this icon, I want you to do one thing." He smiled and pointed at his chest. "Remember your friend in Russia. Will you do that?"

I smiled up at him. "I'll never forget you. I'll email."

A man in a British Airways uniform interrupted us. "It's time to go."

Father Alexander stepped back and watched as the man from the U.S. Embassy pushed Gracie toward the long hallway that would lead us to the gates.

Pasha looked up at me, excitement bursting like fireworks from his huge brown eyes. "We go America, now, Katerina?"

I took his hand and danced him down the hall.

"*Da*, Pasha," I sang out. "We go America now."

EPILOGUE

The trains stretch out below me. Long chains of gray metal cars. Long stripes of empty track. The familiar smell of steam and oil and dirt drifts up to me. As I move closer to the top of the escalator and look down, I see them, just like in my nightmares, lining the walls, leaning against the columns, hunched over, hands held out. In two years nothing has changed. I put my first foot onto the escalator then pull back. Suddenly I don't want to go down there any more. I don't want to look in their faces. I don't want to see what's in their eyes.

The far off rumble of a train grows louder. It turns into a roar and there's the whistling and the screeching of brakes. I cover my ears, but I can't cover up that sound. Finally, I take a deep breath and step onto the escalator. Down, down, down I go. The number for platform nine is coming into view. Our place by the wall is right over there near the poster ad for the Caribbean.

Father Alexander waits for me at the bottom of the escalator. He puts a hand on my shoulder and stoops slightly so he can look into my face. "Is okay, Katerina?"

The warmth from his golden brown eyes meets mine, and I relax.

I nod. "*Da*, is okay."

He straightens. "Then we begin."

I approach a girl who sits leaning against the wall hugging her knees. She looks about the same age I was when I lived at the station. She holds out a grimy hand. I ignore it.

Standing over her I say in Russian, "I can help you."

A glimmer of something like hope flashes in her eyes, but when I don't put anything in her hand, it disappears. I wonder how many times she's thought help might come, and it never did. Her greasy hair clings to her scalp almost as if it's wet. I remember when mine got that bad. I sink down to where I can talk to her face to face. Something about her smells like damp earth. Her dull stare, the way her eyes keep sinking—I have to force myself to keep from looking away.

"There's a place where you can go," I explain.

Her eyes lower.

"No, please, listen—"

She folds her arms over her knees and buries her face.

"A place where you can have medicine and food—"

Slowly she raises her head.

"—and clean clothes—"

Her eyes widen.

"—and a shower and—"

Suddenly she smiles.

It makes me so happy I almost laugh. I jump to my feet and beckon to her. "Come on," I say in Russian. "Come with me."

I find four other station kids to come with me. Marisa and two boys from our school back home pass out little green leaflets that explain everything in Russian. They manage to collect three more kids that way. Father Alexander finds a little boy no more than five or six and his older sister, only eight. They have pink sores all over their arms. We all meet outside the station and climb aboard the school bus that will take us to Father Alexander's new homeless shelter.

It's a place a lot like where Peter and Pasha and I used to go on Sadovaya Street, only this place has beds, twenty-five of them. They wanted more, but that's all they could afford. I got a bunch of kids at my school to help me raise money for it. We had car washes and bake sales and all kinds of events. Our cause got on the local news, and then some people back in New York called, and I went back there to be on T.V. Because of all the publicity, Gracie told me that people in the U.S. were beginning to adopt older Russian orphans. Before that they only wanted babies.

It feels so good helping. Gracie says Dad would be proud.

Marisa points out the bus window at the monster castle with the gold and bright colored onion domes on top. "Wow! What's that?"

I laugh. "That's what I said when I first saw it. It's the Church of the Spilt Blood."

"Awesome!" She pressed her nose to the window. "What's it like inside?"

"Totally cool," I answer.

A little ways further and McDonald's comes into view. I point. "We used to go there."

Marisa raises her eyebrows. "But I thought you didn't have any money."

"We didn't." I look away. "We ate from the garbage cans."

"Ohhhh," Marisa says in a hushed voice.

The tears that sting my eyes come unexpectedly. It happens every so often. Like some nothing thing will make me feel all emotional inside and I'll start sobbing.

When I first got back from Russia, I wasn't sure Marisa and I would be friends any more. She wanted to hear about everything that happened to me, and I didn't want to talk about it. But she caught on right away and stopped asking questions. She even stuck up for me at school when the other kids would get in my face. So now she and I are best buds again. We both have boyfriends, well, sort of. Her little brother and Pasha are going to surf camp together this summer. Pasha said he'd rather stay at home with Gracie and do that than come over here with me.

The bus stops at a red light, and through the window across the aisle I notice a little boy sitting on the curb playing an accordion. "Oh, my gosh!" I spring to my feet and point. "Look, Marisa. He looks just like Pasha." We've only been gone a few days, and I can't believe how much I miss him.

When we first got back to San Diego two years ago, he would never leave my side, slept curled up at the end of my bed, followed me everywhere like a stray pup. I didn't mind. He's my brother. Gradually he began noticing the other kids and branching out. We got him an accordion and music lessons, and now he's doing great in school. Smart little kid. I'm so proud of him.

The only problem we ever had with him was that at first he kept snitching people's wallets. It was kind of funny the way he'd bring them back to me with a big grin on his face, but the guards at Target didn't think it was so funny. Neither did Gracie. She said we'd better channel his talent for sleight of hand in a more positive direction so she got him a magic kit. "We don't want this little rascal growing up to be a pickpocket."

* * *

The coarse summer grass scratches my knees where I kneel over Mom's grave. The tulips were Father Alexander's idea. The color—yellow—was mine. It took me about ten minutes of digging with the small trowel to get down deep enough. Father Alexander said the hole should be at least eight inches deep. He didn't come with me. He said it would be better if I did this alone.

I place three bulbs in the bottom of the hole, pointy tops up, scoop the dark soil back in over top of them, and pat it down. From a tree nearby a bird chirps. Off in the distance children shout. I sit back on my heels and wipe the sweat off my forehead. "There. I hope you like them, Mom."

I crawl closer and rub the palm of my hand over the stone, feeling the grooves where her name is etched. "I'll always love you," I whisper. "You're my mom."

I rise to my feet and flutter a small wave. "I'm going back to the United States now, but I'll be back. I promise. Next year."

"There'll be more flowers."

Cathy Worthington is author of ***Watch Over Thy Child***, winner of the **2005 San Diego Book Awards** in the fiction category.

She lives in San Diego, California, is married to Barry Worthington, a child psychologist, and has one son, Nicholas Carter, a commercial real estate appraiser in the bay area.

Inspiration for ***Moskovsky Station*** came in 2006 when, just prior to a trip to Russia, Cathy happened upon the television airing of a documentary entitled ***The Children of Leningradsky***. The plight of the homeless children depicted in this Academy Award nominated film so moved her that she felt she just had to write their story. Though ***Moskovsky Station*** is a work of pure fiction, many of the details that make the story come alive were derived from the film. Cathy remains in contact with film director **Hanna Polak** and plans to support her drive to save children. Learn more at http://www.childrenofleningradsky.com/

My profound thanks to all who contributed to Moskovsky Station.

My fellow writers who refused to let me give up:
Carolyn Wheat, Matt Coyle, David Dooley, Murray Hagen,
Suzanne Lowrie, John Mullen, C. Lee Tocci,
Linda Shroeder

Rev. Richard Leif and the Very Rev. Jim Carroll
who explained the meaning of icons.

Jessica Webster who helped with the young teen lingo.
Sophie Stephens for the making the emails sound real.

JoDee Fulton, Suzy Spafford
and the Point Loma Book Club.

First readers: Nita van der Werff and Deana Golden.

The Wednesday Club of San Diego for allowing me to
present my paper, "Journey To Moskovsky Station."

Loyal supporter Nan Lutes.

A special thank you to Virginia Tate for her beautiful letter
describing her reaction to the book.

And special love and thanks to

*My husband Barry and my son Nicholas who were always
there to listen.*